Elena Chizhova

Little
ZINNOBERS

TRANSLATED BY CAROL ERMAKOVA

ИНСТИТУТ ПЕРЕВОДА

AD VERBUM

Published with the support
of the Institute for Literary Translation, Russia

GLAGOSLAV PUBLICATIONS

LITTLE ZINNOBERS

by Elena Chizhova

Translated from the Russian by Carol Ermakova

© 2018, Elena Chizhova

Introduction © 2018, Rosalind Marsh

Agreement by www.wiedling-litag.com

Published with the support
of the Institute for Literary Translation, Russia

Publishers Maxim Hodak & Max Mendor

© 2018, Glagoslav Publications B.V.

www.glagoslav.com

ISBN: 978-1-91141-439-1

Published: 18.12.2018

A catalogue record for this book is available from the British Library.

Elena Chizhova

Little
ZINNOBERS

GLAGOSLAV PUBLICATIONS

London

Contents

Translator's Note

Elena Chizhova's *Little Zinnobers* is not an easy read, and translating it has been no easy task either. Chizhova's style and content are both kaleidoscopic. She delves deep, exploring themes such as ageing and loss of innocence, the individual versus society, and, of course, how learning another language alters our perception of the world, providing us with another filter, another formula we can apply as we evaluate the events of our seemingly ordinary everyday lives.

Yet Chizhova never labours her point; her message is conveyed subtly, almost by-the-by, in throwaway remarks and sidelong glances, veiled references and allusions. As translator, it has been my task to pick up on these hints and gently weave the thematic threads into the narrative's tapestry as it unfolds. Some allusions to political events or literary figures would, I felt, be lost on an English-speaking reader, so I have added footnotes here and there to clarify some points while honouring the understated nature of Chizhova's prose.

One stylistic device Chizhova is particularly fond of is the extended metaphor. Perhaps the clearest example of this surfaces in the chapter entitled 'Incomplete Circle Dance.' The image of the incomplete circle recurs throughout this chapter – where it takes on a very graphic form as the children literally circle through the hall – but the image echoes throughout the story as a whole, too, reflecting the cyclical nature of life. As a teacher, F. is well aware of this; she sees an unending stream of pupils waltzing through her classroom doors, then out into the big wide world where they 'age,' completing the incomplete circle. For a translator, extended metaphors pose a challenge as the image must light up in the reader's consciousness creating a pattern of connections without dazzling or becoming ponderous.

Sometimes Chizhova turns to more simple repetition as a stylistic device to reinforce her motifs and metaphors, encouraging the reader to recognise the image and what it stands for each time it crops up. Take the colour red, for instance, so readily associated with Communism. It is present in the school, in the flag, in Maman's dress, in Marina's lipstick, and – perhaps – even in the title, since Hoffman's hero is called Zinnober, which literally means 'cinnabar', a red pigment. In translating, I felt it important to keep this repetition of exact words or phrases – which sometimes occur close together, or sometimes resurface after several chapters – so they run through the novel as a recognisable beat alerting the reader to the motif they represent.

Surprisingly, one of the trickiest translation challenges was rendering the title into English, especially bearing in mind that, as one of the Glagoslav team put it: "It's pretty straightforward in Russian." Chizhova's original title is *Kroshki Zaches*, which literally means 'Tiny Zacheses' and is itself an allusion to ETA Hoffman's nineteenth century tale *Klein Zaches genannt Zinnober,* translated into Russian as *Kroshka Zaches, po prozvaniyu Zinnober* and into English (by Michael Haldane) as *Little Zaches, Great Zinnober*. Russian readers are far more familiar with Hoffman's tale than their English-speaking counterparts; indeed, one TV programme specialising in political satire even based a 10-minute sketch on the tale, poking fun at Vladimir Putin and the other politicians. As Rosalind Marsh has since picked up on this in her paper, I shall not develop the point here.

Chizhova sees both the Soviet Union and F.'s pupils as 'Zacheses' in that they are lauded as something they are not. The name Zaches jars on the English ear so it was decided to use Zinnober instead, which left the problem of 'tiny ones.' By extension, 'kroshki' can also refer to small children, so 'poppets' seemed the obvious choice, especially bearing in mind the historical usage of this word: 'a small figure of a human-being used in sorcery and witchcraft,' a nuance that sits well with the rather dark undertones of Hoffman's tale. But Nicholas Kotar, the American editor who worked on this translation, pointed out that even educated American readers would assume 'poppet' was a misspelling of 'puppet' and so this idea was dropped, to be replaced by the more neutral 'little.' And this nicely brings us back to Haldane's title. Many references will be lost to those unfamiliar with *Little Zaches, Great Zinnober*, and it is beyond the scope of this brief note to elucidate them here. Suffice to say, parallels can be drawn between F. with her golden locks and the Fairy Rosabelverde with her golden comb, and perhaps also between B.G. and Hoffman's wandering magician Prosper Alpanus. Interestingly, there is a clear link to Shakespeare in Hoffman's tale, too; Oberon and Titania in *A Midsummer Night's Dream* resonate with Rosabelverde and Prosper Alpanus, who in turn suggests Prospero in *The Tempest*.

In Chizhova's *Little Zinnobers*, F. uses Shakespeare to create an inner world of truth where there is no place for falsehood or the banal, a world underpinned by honesty, loyalty and inner freedom for both the teacher and her pupils, where the children, if not innocent, are at least protected from 'ageing.' The language of this unfettered microcosm is English, and for the first time in their lives the children are free to speak openly of honour, history, the eternal, and love. And indeed, love is another topic Chizhova explores, mainly through the rather unconventional relationship that develops between F. and her pupil, our narrator.

Chizhova's clipped style proved to be an ongoing challenge. Russian grammar allows for the omission of pronouns. Questions and verb tenses are formed without auxiliary verbs, while definite and indefinite articles are not present. This means that Russian is naturally less wordy than English, neater, shorter, and – in Chizhova's case – elliptic. I have sought to mirror this as much as possible, with short sentences and the omission of personal pronouns wherever admissible, and I hope this rather staccato effect serves to keep a racy pace without sacrificing meaning.

In other sections, however, Chizhova changes tack, alternating these clipped passages with protracted, potentially cumbersome sentences (take, for instance, the novel's opening paragraph). Sometimes, these simply had to be split in English.

Another slight modification I introduced was speech marks. In the original, the combination of curt phrases and lack of punctuation made verbal exchanges hard to follow. By adding "-" I hope the reader will keep abreast of these quick exchanges.

I would like to take this opportunity to thank my husband Dmitry Ermakov for his invaluable contribution to this translation, and of course to Elena herself for her many helpful suggestions.

Carol Ermakova
North Pennines, Spring 2017

Little
ZINNOBERS

THE WITNESS

Now at forty with – if we are to take the sages at their word – the productive part of my life coming to an end and giving way to the contemplative stage, I am of sound mind and memory, qualities which she admired in herself, so I shall meekly set about writing her story, the story of her life, a small part of which was lived before my eyes, the larger part of which is known to me through her tales, which *in this case*, are a reliable source. However, having hardly begun, in other words having resolutely said what I was saying, I feel the need to give further explanations, since almost every word of my first long but relatively laconic sentence is already germinating deep within. Sprouting little roots. Perhaps my character is at fault here, or maybe it is the contemplation that comes with my age. Contemplation, it seems, is no stranger to imagination and is capable of transforming my first and overly long sentence into a pot of peat, into which, shortly before Easter, having scratched out little hollows with my fingers, I drop some wheat grains, so that they will sprout and take root in time for the Feast. A word is a little grain, with a little shoot and a little root.

Or maybe I am betrayed by my habit of comparing myself to her, a habit quite illicit, yet of which I am fully aware. This habit has taken root so strongly that I myself (and no other phrases or words have any bearing here) stand like a sprouting grain, her fingerprints on its burst husk. Sprouted, but ears never formed. Well, who expects an Easter grain to bear fruit?! To form an ear, you must be tossed into the soil of a real field, a field riddled with voracious weeds, so that you wrestle with them under the real, cruel, life-giving sun so that, victorious, you shoot up triumphant ears. Or you lose. In other words, that busy life on which people squander their most glorious years engulfs you, so that, having crossed my current threshold, they look back on the years they have lived with either bitterness or pride, wallowing in well-earned contemplation, regretting what never was, or savouring their accomplishments. Both are beyond my reach.

But don't be misled by my confession that I was not graced by the sun. I was graced by a different sun; other, harsh rays caressed my wheat ears. My life could not be called idyllic—the epithet 'idyllic' does not/ cannot be applied to my life—at any rate, not without a strong dose of bitter humour. And even if an idyll could be hinted at, then only to the exact extent to which she herself permitted idylls. She did not permit them at all, generally, with a harshness not easily married with her tact. On paper. But in life, these two – harshness and tact – were firmly fused: the unshakeable cornerstone. I will not excavate the reasons why my roots did not get their fair share of fertile soil; suffice it to say that, as I prepare to devote myself to the contemplation that my present age permits, I understand and accept it is unearned. Instead, let me continue my comparison with the Easter shoot: twin grains sometimes find their way into pots of peat, and they sprout with the double shoots of pride and bitterness.

She never taught me meekness. That was probably the one thing she would never have attempted to teach me. She was not meek herself, not in the slightest. Had she known what would become of me, she would have nipped both shoots in the bud without more ado. Then they would not have united, twining into a single shoot: meekness. She simply ran out of time. So, ironically, it was she who taught me meekness, thanks to the slowness of her fingers, a mission which had defeated all others, try as they might to instil this quality in me with heavy-handed methods.

Here I must mention one peculiarity: I can no longer speak her name. I blame this entirely on myself. Her name would trip with casual ease from a hundred lips, lips which have not yet lost that ability. But mine… For many years, they were no exception, but now my lips are locked tight, retaining only the pronoun, and having transmitted only one letter to my hand: F. My eyes, though, which read her postcards, were more familiar with the letter Ф,[1] for that is how she signed them, until that last day when, taking her own photograph instead of a postcard, she changed her signature.

A froth of pink lilac, the colour of the dawn. Every year the bush under her little balcony increases its breadth. The balcony is small, like everything else about her flat. The empty balcony, painted white, where she would stand and wave goodbye to me. She looked so small, dressed in her large pink cardigan. We had been talking about something, and, as I walked away and glanced back, she continued the conversation, leaning over the rails slightly, calling out: I am a witness. And quickly pounded her chest.

I can recall that whole conversation if need be, though I only *remember* one phrase. Just before I left we had been talking about most mundane matters (I'm already beginning to recall), which means we were speaking Russian. But the high words, the balcony words, were uttered in English. Language is the simplest way of explaining. I always memorized whatever she said in English. She was equally fluent in both languages, but her Russian was slightly washed out at the edges, like a watercolour. Her English, however, was like a fine, delicate pen and ink drawing. Apart from a few school years, I never replied to her in English – maybe out of fear of damaging those fine pen lines – so our dialogues were usually Anglo-Russian: my Russian oil painting and her English like a fine drawing etched on top.

So be it. Let this duality of language be the reason I remember that balcony again and again, and then after it, those places where she – I want to say – 'lingered.' No, she never decorated them; her walls were always bare, but now, years later, I remember the bareness of those walls like the emptiness of a white screen. The whitish smoothness of a canvas brought to life by her presence; now that the film is over, the screen is blank.

....

[1]   Ф – Cyrillic form of 'F'.

That's why I see, and will always see, the white balcony: the crooked door and the little wonky cupboard that she laughed about, tapping her head with her finger in an English gesture: 'crazy.' My eyes, my weak eyes, won't be covered. Even if they grow dry, or red, even if little black dots fly or white poplar fluff and yellow snowflakes float above the city scrub. I am a witness. Witnesses don't cry. They stand on white balconies on the very top floor.

NEW WORLD

Her mother was a *dvornik*, a road-sweeper-cum-caretaker, and never learnt to speak Russian properly. Both in good old St. Petersburg tradition, considering her nationality. Hence the Russian language spoken by all those around the daughter, both inside the communal flat and outside, was not so much a mother tongue, as an 'other tongue.' It was her mother's mother tongue which resounded above her cradle. Russian, not native *from birth*, became so later. The mother spoke to the daughter in her own mother tongue but the daughter, having reached the age of self-consciousness – i.e. about six – responded to her solely in Russian. The mother took this for stubbornness, mulishness, and maybe she was right. But, even so, it was a particular stubbornness which had nothing in common with the ordinary stubbornness of daughters. Language was dictated by environment. A phenomenon known to emigrants and their children, who are familiar with this stubbornness.

Her mother was born in a distant, non-Russian village and dodged the label 'immigrant' only because St. Petersburg and her native land were part of the same empire then, and when her mother entered this world, no-one alive was responsible for this. Be that as it may, to *some extent* her mother was still an immigrant since she never mastered the imperial tongue well enough, and so stood little chance of ever getting an easier or cleaner job. The daughter was not an immigrant, neither historically nor in fact, but the mother's life, so like an immigrant's, inevitably left its mark on her own. They lived – and here it is not a St. Petersburg tradition but a Leningrad one which comes into play – in a small room in a large, semi-basement communal flat. The mother's life, so like an immigrant's, kept the daughter forever on her toes. She was the mother's ears in the world around her. The mother could not pick up the whispers, rapid mutterings or words spoken 'into thin air' in the communal kitchen. The mother did not ask, of course, and the daughter did not pass the conversations of others on to her, but whereas in normal – i.e. monolingual – families a child does not listen in on the conversations of adults, silently relying on its parents for that, here, the daughter could not rely on her mother, linguistically. In a world which spoke a language not quite accessible to her, the mother could not fulfil the role of mediator between daughter and world. The daughter met the world head on. Being the younger of the two parties, she was obliged to converse with the world in its own language.

At the same time, the world was unfolding through the vastness of the Russian language, which she met head on, without maternal mediation, and the Russian language itself became the world. Actually, it was merely a fragment of a much larger world, but she had no inkling of that back then. Like Columbus. Due to the limited knowledge of the Europeans, who had not yet reached the necessary historical age, Columbus's world did not include either of the Americas. Columbus set sail for known shores but discovered unknown ones. Be that as it may, the cry: "Land!" held a sharp joy, independent of the land to which it referred. It was joy at land itself, *in a pure sense*. And, growing up in *such* a family, it was *this* kind of joy she knew. At the age of six, she came across *The Canterbury Tales* by Chaucer in a Russian translation. It was 1940, the pre-war winter. Reading it induced this joy, and she understood: everyone should know Chaucer. Small in terms of age as well as constitution, she had to climb onto a kitchen stool – where else but the kitchen could she read this aloud to *everyone*, so they could listen and laugh? She read it to them just as Columbus had told his compatriots of mysterious lands he had seen, of the New World he had discovered. I imagine they listened half-heartedly, not slackening their kitchen bustle for even a second: lighting the wood stove, splitting wooden tapers, boiling the washing in cauldrons and rubbing it in basins, shuffling potatoes in frying pans and clattering as they washed up in the sink. None of them, I suspect, turned from their bucket or basin to look at her, to sit and listen. Yet she took no offence; yes, she was opening a new world for them, but they, with their basins, jars, and frying pans, were her world, too, a world once large but from which she would sail away aboard the St. Mary, then sail back. Had she not sailed away and then returned, she would never have suspected that, before becoming Mary, one must long and patiently bear being Martha. That is how she began: under the rumble of basins, the crackle of frying potatoes and the roar of logs burning in the stove. The winter of 1940 was rowdy.

It was the next year that a silence worthy of Chaucer fell. The voices and basins quietened as the months passed, the roar of the stove faded into hungry memory, and the thrumming of drops in the metal sink changed to the measured drip of a metronome. That winter, she read Pushkin's *The Captain's Daughter*. To herself. Shining eyes met her there, eyes that bewitched her. She could not read about these eyes aloud to them: the *blokadniki*[2] had their own idea about shining eyes. Just as Columbus's compatriots had had their own ideas about 'shining', too: the glitter of gold. She went hungry, drank hot water and became deceptively plump. This deception tricked a terrifying man with shining eyes; she ran from him through the city's wasteland. The *blokadniki's* idea of shining was correct.

Having finished school – I know next to nothing about her school years – and having learnt that others' concepts, however correct, remain alien nevertheless, she decided go to university. This decision was a gargantuan leap out of the mother's past. Had her past listeners, barely able to read, heard about this earlier, they would have considered her either crazy or a heroine. It was not the kind of act which provokes jealousy; you can only

....

[2] A reference to the Siege of Leningrad which lasted 872 days from September 1941 to January 1944. Known in Russian as the 'Leningrad Blockade,' a *blokadnik* is someone who lived in the city at that time. The siege caused devastating famine, with over 600,000 residents starving to death. Cannibalism ensued, and children were particularly at risk, although only 44 cases were officially registered.

be envious of something within the realm of possibility, and for them, in their semi-basement flat, this was well beyond that realm. Her deed – for the decision was followed by the act – inspired impartial amazement, brief gossip, and alienation: she was becoming 'an apple from a different orchard.' She succeeded first time, and this successful attempt, while not exactly reconciling certain aspects of life around her, became something akin to an antidote, as if, once and for all, it gave her certainty: that which is important is possible. Ever after, though never tolerant of vileness, when faced with it, she would, as it were, swallow a secret potion known only to herself: "Even so…"

There were no longer any St. Petersburg lecturers left in Leningrad University in the days when she matriculated, for a variety of reasons. Still, among the random people who had replaced pre-revolutionary professors on the principle of natural selection in a proletarian state, from time to time, one did come across their students, who had managed to receive knowledge first hand. Besides these, there were also lecturers who succeeded in siphoning and furthering knowledge by themselves, thanks to their own efforts, intelligence and talent. Unlike students for whom the university bench was a forgone conclusion, or whose parents had booked a place for them mentally, so to speak, as sons of the landed gentry were once registered in the regiment, she never could *get used to it*. The propensity which affects all students to a greater or lesser degree – namely, that one cannot permanently rejoice in what comes to pass partly thanks to your own efforts, yes, but nevertheless 'according to plan'– had no hold over her whatsoever since the trajectory of that astonishing gargantuan leap from the mother's past continued far beyond the university gates. The run-up required had been herculean, congenial, so where other students were *already* walking, she was *still* flying, unable to touch down.

In the eyes of the above-mentioned rare lecturers, this flight was a quite natural state; they were themselves flying, flitting in the scholarly empyreans, and what shone in her eyes did not need to be put to the test. She studied as though she were still running through the city's wasteland, fleeing from the blockade cannibal, the only difference being that in her childhood she had been running away, whereas now she was running towards what she saw beyond the wasteland, and it was coming more sharply into focus with each university year. They were teaching her as though they were standing under the saving shadow of the building she was headed for and could see that man behind her. This trajectory was more than enough to burst open the doors of the First English School, flying in from the street straight after graduation, which, again, was unheard of: prospective teachers for this school were selected from higher echelons, almost at the level of the *raikom* party committee.

COVENANT

I was six when my younger sister was born. Right there, in the maternity hospital on Vasilevskiy Island, she caught golden staph. Or to be precise, they infected her with it: all new-borns were bathed in the same tub. As far as my mother recalls, this was neither irresponsibility on the part of the nurses, nor carelessness on the part of the doctors. Later, when mothers and babies found themselves in the Paediatrician Institute Hospital, the doctors treating them justified the actions of their maternity hospital colleagues as tantamount to a scientific experiment which fell to the babies' silent lot. You might expect this explanation would have fanned flames of indignation, but 1963 was still a very 'scientific' year. Space exploration, physics, 'big chemistry'—they all spawned their heroes, so the explanation passed as acceptable. The contagion was methodically purged from the children's blood during the three summer months, but the conquered disease left its mark: for another ten or eleven years, right up until around 1974 when I finished school, it made its presence felt, tracing symmetrical rashes on my sister's little arms and legs, or, in acute attacks, a painful, enflamed crust on her face. It was called diathesis. They dried it out with 'brilliant green,' so from time to time my sister went about spattered from head to toe in symmetrical green spots. The scientific experiment undertaken by the maternity hospital doctors left its mark on me, too, although I ended up not in the Paediatrician Institute Hospital, but at the kindergarten summer camp. Before the maternity hospital doctors' 'voluntary experiment,' as our parents put it, I was a stay-at-home kid, I stayed home during the long summer holidays.

The kindergarten to which I was assigned had a summer camp in Ushkovo, a *dacha* village on former Finnish territory. Wooden billets nailed to the trunks of Finnish pine trees were a reminder of the days when Finnish cuckoo snipers climbed those same trees. We learnt about those strange cuckoos from our camp mother's elder daughter, who lived with her mother in the little plywood cabin-cum-barn in the furthest corner of the camp. We had a very vague impression of the pine cuckoos. The mother, Larissa Lvovna, worked in our group for older children in shifts (morning/evening), taking turns with another camp mother, Nina Ivanovna. But we loved Larissa Lvovna more, firstly because her daughter befriended us, and secondly because in the evenings, when it was her shift, she would sing songs with us: about a cricket behind the stove, about a little brown button, and about Lyonka Korolyev. When Larissa Lvovna took the evening shift, and it was she who woke us after our afternoon nap, the dormitory would ring with shouts: "Hurray! Larissa Lvovna!" She never cut short our boundless delight. Quite carried away, some of the children, hiding behind the chorus of voices, would change her difficult patronymic, yelping: Larissa Vol'na![3] She did not put a stop to that, either. Larissa Lvovna was expecting. Her daughter, who would chat with our group during her mother's shift, let us in on this secret, too, so as we sang about little Lyonka Korolyev, we would shoot sidelong glances at Larissa's belly; the daughter had briefed us. The ditty about Lyonka seemed linked to this belly, as if Larissa were carrying a baby boy fated to perish in the war. She did indeed give birth to a son, in the autumn. Nina Ivanovna was old and did not sing songs with us, but we loved her all the same because she would tell us about Communism.

In the mornings, after breakfast, holding hands in pairs, we would form a crocodile and set off, beyond the camp grounds to the sea, the Gulf of Finland. Along the sandy track past the high wooden enclosure fences of other grounds, then along wayside ditches, their stagnant water covered in

---

[3]   A pun on the surname: Larissa Vol'na – Larissa is free.

lamellar duckweed. The air was heavy with the smell of wild rose bushes wilted by the sun. Small stones crunched under our sandals. The long double needles of the Finnish pines stuck into our soles. We would cross the main road, stamping the needles we had picked up into the weak, sun-softened tarmac which smelt of tar. Beyond the strip of tarmac, a vista of sand dunes, lying in ridges at the edge of the Gulf. Nina Ivanovna would point out a spot for us in the shade under the pines. Using some method known only to those in the medical profession, the nurse would calculate the most auspicious time and allocate us some brief moments of sunshine.

The older group lived in an old, two-storey house just like any other house in any Leningrad resort. The boys' dorms were on the ground floor, the girls' on the first. Before retiring to her quarters, the camp mother going off duty would pop in to wish us all good night. First the boys' dorm would quieten down, then we would hear the creaking of wooden stairs. We were already lying in bed, our hands obediently folded. She would do the rounds of the dorms, then sit herself on the chair in the central corridor. The doors of all three dorms opened onto that corridor, so, settled in her vantage point, she would listen as we fell asleep. Both camp mothers observed this ritual to the letter, no personal touches. Each sat, consumed by her own thoughts, but while the thoughts of Larissa Lvovna, which most likely hovered over her future little boy, were so personal she could not and would not share them with sleepy six-year-olds, it soon became apparent that Nina Ivanovna's thoughts in that dusk hour could quite innocently be shared with children tired out by the long, bustling day. "When I sit like this on this chair," she began one evening in a quiet, melodious voice, as if beginning a fairy-tale, "I am thinking that the beautiful time called Communism will soon arrive." She said this with great conviction, as though she were talking about something certain and close at hand, like the dawn of the next day. As if we had but to close our eyes, slip through the darkness in our sleep, unnoticed, and a new happy time would dawn by itself. "Close your little eyes." We listened to her, eyes closed. "This will be a time when everyone is happy: you, and your parents, and your camp mothers." "And how about kindergarten? Will there be kindergartens?" "Yes, yes," she would assure us. "But I don't want kindergarten!" "Then there won't be. There will be kindergartens for whoever wants them, and not for anyone who doesn't." "How about going to summer camp?" "Everyone will go to summer camp." "And Mummy?" "Yes, and Mummy, and all the mummies." From then on, when it was her shift and Nina Ivanovna sat herself down on the chair in the central corridor, somebody would always pipe up: "Please, tell us!" So again and again, adding new details and always referring to science, of course – as though that reference could strengthen the dreams of six-year-olds – she would tell us about that future time, a time akin to our dacha days, smelling of sun-baked wild roses, soft tarmac tar and the fresh water of the Gulf.

After waiting until everyone had fallen asleep, the camp mother would head for her little wooden cabin, leaving us to the night nanny, who patrolled our dorms like a night-watchman, then lay herself to sleep on the sofa right by the main entrance. I closed my eyes. For a while, dreamy inertia would conjure the sandy tracks, green burdock above the ditches, the uneven crowns of the tall pines – everything which tomorrow would bring, if I could but slip through the insignificant night-time. Night-time encroached on my eyelids with every second, ready to close in, but at the very last minute, it swerved. Because that other time would come, the time of *my* night nannies. Clad in white gowns, plump, their faces flat, almost indiscernible; 'faceless' as I would put it now. They were like the kindergarten cooks. The cooks never came out into the dining room. I saw them cooking, once, stirring something in huge cauldrons marked with red letters and numbers.

The night nannies didn't sit in the chair in the central corridor the three dormitories opened onto. They didn't need this common vantage point, since all the children were asleep, waiting unawares for insignificant night-time to pass. The night nannies were mine, teaching none but me. They would sit on the edge of my bed so lightly it didn't even squeak under their plump, faceless bodies.

Pull your nightie as high as you can, right up under your armpits. Lie on your back carefully so as not to wet the covers. Now you can fall asleep, but not with the light, unnoticeable sleep which carries you to the morning; no, with the short, brief not-until-morning sleep. But should you sleep through to the morning – the night nannies think neither of their children nor of Communism – both the other nannies come, the day one and the night one, and both start shouting that you wet the bed again, that you're a freak, not like other children. "This one only knows how to piss herself! Look at her! Take off all your piss-drenched stuff, and scram! Now we've got to wash everything after her! Eh, bloody freaks!"

Now I'm waking up, my hand pats something wet. Be careful, don't wake anyone. They'll laugh if you do. Slip out of bed, blanket to one side. Rejoice that your nightie is dry, rejoice that the window is open and the night is as dry as the nightie. Rejoice that the window ledge is low enough to clamber on to, rejoice that your legs are dangling out of the window, that your hands are holding the sheet. Patiently, not letting your eyes close, wave, wave, wave your wet stain until it turns yellow. Whatever you do, don't close your eyes, you have neither parents, nor nannies. Until it is dry, until the yellow stain, until their inevitable pale dawn, until the dance of the autumn leaves, until you see stars… So you sit in fear and trembling in the open window, the ground below your feet, the sky above your head, the boys below, the girls behind, and you don't dare fall asleep because the wet stain still shines tallow yellow, and no-one but us will come to you, because you are a freak, but we are compassionate, and so shall it be forever.

They would leave with dawn's first light, and I would climb down from the window ledge, deftly spread the sheet, and fall asleep. When the sun rises, they are not by my bed. I sleep utterly freely, unnoticeably, lightly, waiting for the inevitable morning – with the others. They saved me again, and will not return before nightfall.

A DARK VELVET ROSE

I suppose it is only now that I can fully appreciate the reckless courage of the official who first invented the unwieldy name: "Middle School Teaching a Range of Subjects in a Foreign Language." No doubt he himself spoke no other language but Russian, so, for him, all other languages were in fact not 'other' but precisely *foreign*. Those spoken in *other* countries. Maybe he dreamt of visiting that other world, that world beyond the borders, beyond the limits, taking the First Moscow Festival of Youth as its blithely thought-up model. Or maybe always, for as long as he could remember, he had been dreaming of learning to speak another – any other – language, just as the quietest children secretly dream of becoming cosmonauts. He dreamt, but had no faith in his dream. Well, OK then, maybe not him, but someone else, someone like him, dressed differently, maybe, moving his lips in a manner never seen before, gulping sounds understood not by everyone, but only by those select few like himself. Or maybe his dear child arrived at the seven-year threshold[4] and he took the risk of laying his own unfulfilled hopes on this child. But what range of subjects did he have in mind? Why was he not afraid to announce his dream in such a cumbersome fashion? Didn't he know that – in a roundabout way – words come true? Who can say?

But this time he put all his energy into it. Personally, not delegating to anyone else, he unfurled the map, scrutinised his Oktobersky *raion* neighbourhood, and made his choice – right at the edge, almost in the water. Only one street separates the school from the River Neva, and well, that's just

....

4   In Russia children start school at seven. The academic year always begins on September 1, with much aplomb.

[27]

Galley Street. Called it 'Red,' of course: old names are tantamount to foreign ones. On the other side – New Holland – an island behind a strong wall and poplars. Blockade bomb raids left a gap between the old houses. At the beginning of the sixties it became a stain on urban development: they filled the gash with the school. Once a year, on September the first, classes were lined up down below, around the perimeter of the schoolyard. Ten pairs of 'a' and 'b.' The form teachers beat down the noise, and almost six hundred pupils swelled the ranks for Maman's entrance. She would appear on the balcony above in a long, lowcut velvet dress that reached down to the floor. Two men strode behind her, keeping a respectful half-step from those velvety shoulders. They were the heads of the English and Russian departments, now and forever. The head of English Language Studies, Boris Grigoryevich Katz, to the left, forty-fivish, a Jew and a diplomat, the embodiment of tact, as we witnessed once in his tears of love for us, and often in his restrained concern for the school, and once and once only in fear for himself. To Maman's right, the head of Russian Language Studies, Sergei Ivanovich Belikov –forty-fivish, Russian, owner of a long auburn fringe he would toss from his forehead with an elegant, Yesenin-like gesture, who loved and spoilt us, and whose knowledge of Russian literature was only as broad as the school curriculum. In the far reaches of the balcony, a place was kept for the Secretary of the Party Committee. Or Dame Secretary, to be precise. Three came and went during my watch: one plump and soft, the two others scrawny but not tough.

And even further back, right against the brick wall, hung the school standard. Or waved, depending on the weather, with the guard of honour standing beside the pole. A velvet standard behind velvet shoulders. In some way, that standard was a relic of other times, times we had not caught. In and of itself, it would have been an ordinary and almost unnoticeable element of the school ritual. The low-cut dress, however, a relic from even more remote times, could not go unnoticed. What's more, the standard's recent past – precisely because it was unremarkable – was defeated by the dress's remote past, although for us, standing way below the balconies, the dress served as more than a compelling symbol of far-off times, whose distance was underlined by the standard's velvet. Doubled, duplicated and yet compromising itself, that velvet introduced a clear ambiguity into this ritual repeated year after year. To our young eyes, this ambiguity seemed fancifully incongruous, yet we sensed it could hide depths still unclear and, as such, premature.

I no longer hear the words of the speech gushing down from on high, repeating year after year. They were not even words at all, since even as they were being spoken, they were devoid of any meaning worthy of the full and undivided attention of six hundred pairs of ears. That is why, listening and not listening, the flock amused themselves on the quiet. A light estrangement, the result of our three-month summer break, meant we could throw sidelong glances at our neighbours – glances laden with promise. Maman probably did not notice the flippant rustling in our ranks. From on high, she could see the rather wide schoolyard planted with wilted little trees that bloomed for an hour with the little white and red flowers of our pinafores, shirts and ties. Ephemeral flowerbeds destined to disperse with the first school bell. Their brightness could not fail to gladden her teacherly, almost motherly, eyes. It was an autumnal garden, and she – a dark velvet rose – towered above it majestically and ambiguously, and her voice was sweet as honey.

From her very first day as head, Maman treasured the "school's honour." For her, this honour was not just a matter of overall academic prowess but also of how the school *adhered to traditions*. Some of these traditions had already been introduced by the previous head – a plain but authoritative woman who died in 1964. In other words, in our very first winter. Rumours that Polina Ivanovna was murdered by the ambulance crew filtered down even to us first years. It was said that the doctor mistook a heart attack for poisoning and pumped her stomach, and it killed her on the spot. Incidentally, nobody bothered to ask why the headmistress should suffer a heart attack. It was while Polina Ivanovna was head that a custom – unheard of at that time – was introduced. I am referring to the appraisal interview procedure for entering our school, as a result of which both our classes, 'a' and 'b', were the first *selected* classes. Later, she introduced another strange custom, observed meticulously during Maman's early years, too: half an hour before classes began, the headmistress herself and one of the heads would stand in the archway separating the vestibule from the long school corridor. Each pupil had to stop and make a light bow (for boys) or curtsey (girls), and could only proceed once he or she had received a gracious nod from both sides. This traditional bow was also expected of us when we ran into *any adult*. It was, however, not always without mishap. Once, in my second year, running down the stairs, I bumped into the whole trinity: Maman, flanked left and right. They were processing towards me and, trying to curtsey as I ran, I tumbled down the stairs head over heels, followed by three dumbfounded pairs of eyes. As I was picking myself up, Maman stared at me in dumb fright, rooted to the spot. This custom later dwindled to the habit of saying 'hello' to all adults, and it was funny to observe some hapless *parent* wandering along the never-ending school corridor as the crowd pouring towards him shouted greetings in chorus, and he nodded at them from side to side, flabbergasted, like a discombobulated *van'ka-vstan'ka*.[5] Truth be told, on the whole, parents were not much liked in our school. They were met with exceptional politeness, of course, the teachers kept them *in the loop* as they say, but this loop lay beyond our hallowed ground; when it came to business, the gates would shut, as if someone proclaimed: "Be gone, non-believers!"

....

[5]   Van'ka-vstan'ka – a very common children's toy, similar to a large Weeble.

THRESHOLD

Now it is time for me to get down to business, to my tale of what actually happened to her, to us, to our world. To our little world, if you will. Don't be deceived by my use of this epithet. I belonged to a world which commands my immutable respect, cancelling out my use of the epithet I used. This respect is linked with a quality our world embodied to the full, a quality the big world cannot boast of: integrity. Those belonging to the big world only know of integrity from hearsay, or from books, and maybe that is why they always seek to discredit it. I don't have the strength to fight them.

Having briefly mentioned our little world's integrity, I must also note that in no way did this mean uniformity. Our class was never a tightly knit unit. It was made up of three groups, clans or castes which co-existed without overlapping. Membership was determined firstly by the parents' social standing, and secondly by our own individual talents and luck. The groups were spontaneous aggregates. Children of the intelligentsia in the highest, technical kids in the middle, and in the lowest, those whose social standing was irrelevant since everyone saw they were dolts and fools. Now I think that those in the higher group recognized one another through particular words and phrases drawn from the abstract conversations of their parents – conversations which had nothing to do with day to day work or domestic affairs. These particular expressions were like scraps of paper, their jagged contours matching as soon as they are brought side by side – or put together. A kind of pass. Or password. But there were no such conversations in our families – I mean in mine or in Ira Eisner's; she was my closest friend.

For the sake of fairness, I don't want to exaggerate the predetermined nature of our divisions. Yes, the groups did form in the lower forms, but right from the beginning, the barriers between them were not impenetrable. In other words, theoretically at least, it was possible to gain entry to a higher group, although there was no well-trodden path for such unlawful entry. Anything could happen. For instance, one girl whose birth right determined She belonged to the second group, immediately entered the first when her mother went to Yugoslavia and returned with cheap but unbelievably beautiful women's boots and dresses. Her best friend rose through the ranks behind her because she was the same height; they were the tallest girls in the class.

Now, looking back, I must admit that I, too, had such a chance once, but I blew it. I had the best handwriting in the class, and, as it transpired much later, one of the girls in the highest group was rather in awe of it. Taken by my calligraphy, she attempted to lift me to her heights. This attempt was made in our first year, and coincided with the most important event in my life. Or, perhaps, this most important event actually became some kind of detonator for the explosion which never followed. You see, before then, I used to wear thick cotton stockings which hooked onto my belt by means of metal fasteners hung on rubber. The stockings were short, so bare legs and fasteners flashed from under my dress. That summer of 1967 my father went to Czechoslovakia on an assignment, and brought me back several pairs of nylon tights – blue, green, red, and sea-green. And one more dark blue pair for me to grow into. On the first of September, I arrived wearing these tights, and that clinched it. Before the month was out, Larissa Yurchenko came to me in the break with an entry question, the reply to which would have been obvious to any 'higher' girl, but which had me completely baffled. "What would you choose, a French fur coat or a sheepskin jacket?" I had no idea what a 'sheepskin jacket' was, so I mumbled miserably: "French fur coat." And thus, I was decisively sifted out of the candidature. That year, any fool 'insider' knew you had to choose the sheepskin jacket.

These divisions, which had hardened by the sixth year, did not apply to copying homework, slipping answers in class, or taking others' questions in tests. There were no star pupils in the higher group. Their attitude to studying was tainted by a gentry-style laziness, while the rest of us never allowed ourselves to let down our guard, hoping perhaps to compensate this social inadequacy with a pleb's diligence. Our time was exam time, when the eyes of higher and lower alike begged us for help.

Of course, in those days of our rather shuttered existence, we didn't really ponder the characteristics of our little world and the larger world, limiting ourselves instead to tentative professional aspirations, tempered to a large extent by sober evaluations picked up from our parents as to the chances of entering this or that college. The very notion of college formed a sort of a line, the border or threshold separating us from the larger world. This threshold went by the name 'matriculation,' and it dazzled us, blinding us, preventing us from making out the prospects opening behind it. Simply put, to a large extent 'matriculation' was a goal in and of itself. We never discussed what would follow. I can remember only one case which could be called an attempt to peek beyond that threshold. Irka and I were walking home, probably in year six, when our conversation turned to 'matriculation.' "I'm leaving after college." She said it out of the blue, very seriously, which is why I immediately understood *where* she would go. I remember I began trying to put her off, heatedly, as if it had to be decided then and there. She listened without interrupting, but her eyes were elsewhere. I realized she already regretted telling me, but I didn't have the good sense to stop. I hurtled ahead, coming up with more and more new reasons. Judging from the expression on her face, however, they were not new to her, as though someone before me, maybe even she herself, had been repeating this ad nauseam from all angles. She waited until my onslaught abated, until all my reasons dried up, and only then did she speak herself. She did not refute my arguments, nor did she explain anything. Lightly stepping over some kind of threshold my arguments were jostling against, she changed the subject: "You know what

I often think about? Granny and Grandad lived here almost all their lives but their Russian was still only so-so. Their parents couldn't speak Russian at all. If my children are born there, their native tongue won't actually be Russian. I always think about this chain, and I'm somewhere in the middle. A kind of translator – if they should all meet one day." I didn't know what to say, and she, of course, did not expect a reply. She changed the subject, quickly, without suspecting that this strange conversation would stay with me for ever, so that twenty-some years later, I could connect another chain, my own, which, for me, became one explanation for what happened to all of us. Although in our general case, it was not only about language.

Irka, by the way, was right to change the subject.

PICKING A POET

I think, for the time being at least, these intricacies of social development went unseen by the teachers. They grouped us by friendships and subjects. The choice of guests for name day celebrations was put down to friendship. Progress in studies was put down to natural potential and diligence, in almost equal measures. Which is quite right. Yet I, from my vantage point, insist on another angle only because of an incident which occurred in our 6 'b' form, and which became the prelude to a tangible, long-lasting division besides which the 'personal content' of our birthday parties provided but a rough estimate.

In and of herself, she wasn't worth a penny. Anastasia Fyodorovna, our Russian language and literature teacher at the time and secretary of the School's Party Organization, took it into her head to include five-minute poetry readings in her lessons. The idea was met with enthusiasm, but the genuineness of this enthusiasm was tempered by the desire to cut down grilling time since, if handled skilfully, these 'five-minutes' could be stretched to twenty. As for Anastasia Fyodorovna, besides educational aspirations natural for a literature teacher, she had her sights set on a series of events which could easily be noted in her Party logbook. And so, our interests happily coincided, a state of affairs already halfway to success. Gladdened by our amenability, Anastasia suggested we put it off no longer but, right there and then, pick a poet for the next lesson. Having laid out the boundaries laconically, almost in the form of a crossword, she left the choice of candidates up to us: the poet must not be in the school's current curriculum. She expected to have the final say, of course. The din was unimaginable.

"Yesenin, Drunina, Vanshenkin!" yelled the 'middlers.' "Mandelstam, Pasternak, Akhmatova!" bellowed the 'highers.'

How well I remember the expression on her face as she patiently nodded at all our shouts, quietly knocking her desk with her wedding ring. In her heart of hearts, she was with 'us' of course, but 'they' were more forceful. Anastasia, however, preferred not to interfere. Perhaps she was afraid of quashing our zeal with a premature intervention. Or perhaps she failed to see anything dangerous in this stand-off, either for herself or us; it was a family matter, so to speak. Or perhaps, even more simply, like the 'highers' who put them forward so vociferously, yelling their names, she hadn't read the poets they suggested. But: French fur coat or sheepskin jacket...? If this simplest explanation is correct, then the debate becomes quite abstract and groundless. Or perhaps she had in fact read them but suspected none of us had and was hoping we ourselves would not like this abstruse nonsense. Be that as it may, Anastasia Fyodorovna tried to defend the correctness of our opinion, but the 'highers' shouted us down.

We didn't have any Pasternak at home. I had to order a copy at the Youth Reading Hall on Fontanka. I read it as though it were written in a foreign language, worse than that: strange words crunching sharp shards which lacerated my diligent memory as, chosen at last, I memorised: *It's with your laughing picture that I'm living now*, with whatchamacallit wrists and joints...[6] Have to learn it by tomorrow, can't read poetry from a piece of paper! Can't believe Fedka really likes this, kept yelling he was the best poet, can't not know him... *hand mashes mandarin peel*, if you move the comma, what do you get – a mandarin hand... Perspiring from this waltz,[7] I have to take the crib sheet with me, I'll rehearse again in the morning.

Fedka Aleksandrov sat at the next desk leafing through a book. I recognized it at once. Same as in the Publichka library. Only he'd brought it from home. I go first, crib sheet in hand. Read without looking at it, managed to finish

6 Poem by Boris Pasternak 'Your Picture' ('Zamestitel'nitsa,' 1917).
7 Reference to another line from the poem: '*and air with the sweet sweat of fresh waltzes laced.*'

memorizing it in the morning, fit the shards together. Anastasia was nodding, buried in her desk. I went back to my place, stuck the crib sheet in my pinafore. Fedka put up his hand. Guilty smile. Or so I thought. Smiling, he walked between the desks. Couldn't choose, he said. Too hard, such wonderful poetry. I'll read from the book. Anastasia did not object. Before reading, he turned a few pages, tossing his head back, book held at arm's length. Anastasia stared at him, mesmerized, like a mouse staring at cheese. He read, drawling the words, flapping his hands, softly clicking his fingers. Anastasia squirmed but bore it. One minute, two… six… Folk were bored. The urge to laugh was overtaking everyone bar none. Strong, stronger than any division. Barriers crumbled: light little bubbles popped here and there. She knocked her wedding ring on her desk, out of habit most like. The giggles subsided, also out of habit. Silent mirth reigned. She no longer reined us in. Watched, gleeful; like watching a clown. Probably thinking she'd acted correctly, children should understand for themselves, then it would stay with them. The reader threw glances over the book, slipping up more and more often. Didn't get to the end, tossed his head, clicked his heels in a bow. Clumsy and crooked. Everyone laughed. Anastasia leant over the register, laughing. Fedka peeped under her hand. Returned to his place, smiling victoriously. The mark was generous. No -one raised their hand. The five minutes were up. In the next lesson we read Drunina.

The photo I live with is not laughing. It gazes at me tenderly.

I still remember them by heart, and don't like them, afraid of these brittle verses as if, once memorised, they had poisoned me. I come across them sometimes – they are quoted. Each time I explain away my distaste: I forced myself to learn them. Even though I know this is not true: with fear and meekness, I forced myself to learn much of what I hold dearer than life. Maybe some subtle poison seeped into me then – along with the dust of the Youth Reading Hall, through the sound of someone else's wedding ring knocking on wood. Golden band on the nameless ring finger. I caught 'flu once. The night before I had eaten a whole pan of fried marrow. The smell of fried marrow still makes me sick.

AND THE SOLE GAZE

After the winter holidays, our English group was left without a teacher. Lidia Alexandrovna's husband was recruited to Egypt for the Aswan Dam Project. No time to select a substitute teacher. Lidia Alexandrovna was probably keeping her family plans secret until the last moment, fearing a jinx. As is customary, our group was split in two and sent to other classes: one half went to Valentina Pavlovna, the other to Boris Grigoryevich. I always went to B.G. since my Irka was in his group. After a month, he fell ill. I remember that day. We were sitting in threes at the desk – there was always a shortage of desks in English classrooms. Still as mice, we were hoping to be left alone, forgotten. But our hopes were shattered about ten minutes into the lesson. The door burst open. Sashka Guchkov flew in like a devil on a broomstick. "Look sharp! They're coming! With the Head!" The door slammed and opened again. We stood up. Those at the edges were standing to attention in the passageways. Those in the middle were jammed in, bulging over the desks. In walked a small woman, an improbably small woman. With a theatrical wave of her hand, she closed the door behind her. No sign of the Head. The woman told us her name – strange to our Russian-English ears – and began speaking in English. The noise quietened down. None of our teachers spoke English like *that*. It was not that they didn't know the language – our knowledge was far worse! Maybe it sounds strange, but the English we were used to was no different from maths or literature: English for the second grade, English for the sixth grade. It was cut to our size, or for us to grow into. The teachers taught us in the same way as parents buy clothes.

She spoke fluently and fast, not in the slightest afraid we would not understand, as if she knew in advance we could not fail to understand. Barely looking at us, she was telling us some story of her own, going over to the board from time to time and tracing some English word in quick, white chalk. No translation. We had never heard any of those words before, and she had prior knowledge of that, too. We watched them emerge from under her hand, white, and that was enough both for her, and for us, as though she entrusted them to our eyes more than to our ears, as though our eyes had already met these words and would recognize them, she had but to write them down. Her English was light and joyful, with swift jokes, heels high and narrow. I was about to make some comment to Irka; distracted for a second, I saw her sullen face and averted eyes, like back then, during our conversation. As if Irka, turning aside from my reasonings, was continuing that conversation, but not with me this time. For a couple of seconds I was still hovering on the threshold, an uninvited guest. Then I turned and walked away. To become eyes again, the sharp eyes of a hawk. Looking straight ahead, now at the board, now at the small woman, standing tall, taut as a bowstring. She did not see me. After all, why should it enter her head to snatch any one from behind the desk in an overcrowded classroom, single out of the present for the sake of some uncertain future? For that, different eyes were needed, eyes which would look at both of us from afar. Such eyes were unknown to my twelve-year-old self, and I did not know how to distinguish. I could only hearken to the voice: "You will be with her forever." The bell rang. She stopped short, mid-sentence. She used the bell as a threshold she was unwilling to cross. The bell gave her that right. She went over to the teacher's desk, for the first time that lesson. Everyone lined up by the door, still smiling after her story. Everyone said: "Do svidaniya" as they passed, and she replied to each of us. Calmly and nonchalantly. She did not care at all whether she ever saw us again or not. She stood just as tall, but I already saw the bowstring was slackening. Everyone walked out, only I walked forwards.

She was watching me coming towards her, and with every step I was becoming smaller and smaller so that in the end, finally, she could only make me out with difficulty. She, on the other hand, was becoming bigger. Her narrow nose was becoming longer, her cheekbones sharper, her smile emptier, leaving no hope. It was still not too late to simply say: "Do svidaniya." "Will you tell us more?" I don't know what made me ask. I was alone, but could it really be that, in that moment, the only moment in our whole life together, she did not know what I *already* knew? I asked, and grew big again, bigger than her. She winced, finding my words dreadfully coarse. She had to summon all her strength to restrain herself. I stepped back, not quite realizing what had happened but already shuddering, regretting what I'd done, and then my childhood nannies, fear and anguish, rose up behind me. For the six years I had been studying everything under the sun at my own risk, there had been no sign of them. But now, ah, how deftly they chose their moment! Swooped down to my aid from my bygone years. The rustle of wings rising over my head like protective hands, so I might understand I love her.

O Lord, why hast Thou forsaken me? I had no words, I could not speak, I was wordless. What could my wordless teachers teach me? It is the present me saying this, as I am now, at forty. Now I know a plethora of words, both Russian and English. I know words which are cleverer than me, they become 'me,' my memory, my thoughts. I know how to gulp them like anti-parasite drugs, or put them under my tongue like Validol. Russian and English – double-action painkillers. What can I know about time, about His timing? They say He is always looking down upon us, and, should He look away, He can always be recalled. But why do I still hold fast to the belief that it is different with me? For me – just one single split-second, one sole glance: that day. There is no law, no rule. Or at least, none that I can formulate. Trifling and puny. Well, let it be so: fear and anguish, and that sole glance.

Actually, I was not struck dumb. The very next day I had all but forgotten about this incident and was chatting away as if nothing had happened. Even during English lessons, I would forget about my night fears when I beheld her with my own eyes, and listen thirstily. The lessons went on as usual, she did not return to that story again, not even in passing, as if both story and white chalk had served their purpose, needed only for our first encounter, so she could look with almost indifferent eyes on *everyone* as they passed her with their mumbled "Do svidaniya." B.G. came back to work, meanwhile, and the number of English groups returned to the primordial trinity. After a long break, filled with chatter, Irka Eisner spoke to me seriously again. She had firmly made up her mind to move to F's group. Averting her gaze, Irka told me she needed *that* level of education. But how can you tell?… In the end, she persuaded me to go to B. G. with her. B.G. heard us out calmly. Maybe he was hurt, I don't know; Irka was top of the class. A precise mathematical mind, good memory, conscientious. We talked of friendship, our sentences overlapping. He agreed at once. Said he would miss her. His only condition was that we find someone to swap from my group to his in Irka's place, voluntarily. That probably seemed a simple condition to him. But not to us. We stood outside his office, numb. After all – and here neither of us averted our eyes – who in their right mind would agree to leave F voluntarily? But Irka didn't want to give up. She ran through the surnames. We agreed on Lariska Panferova. C's. Pea-brained. A friend in B.G.'s class. We lied precisely and artistically. Irka wants to transfer because we are friends. B. G. doesn't have anything against it, but he asked us to find a replacement. He's kinder, he doesn't grill you so savagely. *He* suggested her, Panferova. Lariska agreed at once.

Irka and I were jubilant. At last! Handy, too. Evening phone calls about homework.

At night, I leaked pain. Pain poured from my eyes as tears, trickled from my mouth as saliva. The pillow, soaked with pain, turned as wet as my childhood sheets. I did not get up to dry it. The terror of death – her death – drained my strength. Night after night I saw it over and over. Just as I would see it in real life twenty-five years later. The pain would dry up a little by itself during the night. By morning, all that remained were yellowish stains on the pale blue pillowcase. And that is how I cried my eyes out. After three months, my eyesight had worsened. By May, my eyes had turned bad: -7 – 6. They dripped drops in them and took me out of classes for two weeks. But I went to school and listened. I could neither read nor write. Then they prescribed glasses for me. The frame was ugly. The fear of her death loosened its grip. Now I was afraid of going blind.

A BLUISH FLOOR

In September, a new study was put at her disposal. Located in a far wing, it was tiny, desks jammed up against each other. It had been renovated that summer. Blue linoleum, blue walls. Looked magnificent on the first of September. We cleaned the classrooms and studies ourselves. There were only two cleaners for the whole school. They cleaned the Head Mistress' office, the Directors' of Studies offices, the staff room, the vestibule and the stairways. A bucket and mop stood in each classroom. The teachers showed us how to wash the floors. Deftly. That's how they did it at home: cloth in the bucket, ring it out with both hands, wrap it round the swab. Run of the mill. The women teachers demonstrated with enthusiasm, their hands getting wet and dirty. This was called 'wet cleaning.' Those of us on duty shuffled the cloth around, dipping it into the bucket now and then. Smears were barely visible on the painted floorboards. But on our blue linoleum, dry smears turned to yellowish patches. After two weeks, the original blue had all but disappeared.

"Who has read Shakespeare?" She asked in Russian, measuring us with cold eyes. Fedya's hand shot up. The eyes paused on him but did not thaw. "What, exactly?" The hand came down and clicked its fingers. "Er... what's it called...?" Silent clicking. "Romeo and Juliet." He remembered the title, smiled. "Is that all?" A terrible silence. It was addressed to him alone. The rest of us cowered. She looked at him with disdain. But as for us, who had not read even this, we were beneath even disdain. "You'll stay after class." Fedya perked up and held his tongue. "The floor has to be clean. Do you know what a clean floor is?" Now she was addressing the rest of us. "Who is on duty?" she was asking. I stood up. "As in the navy," she took a white handkerchief from her pocket, swiftly bent down and wiped it along the floor. Turned it over and showed it. To me. Grey smudge on white. "See? Do you understand?" Now she was only talking to me. I understood. She scrunched up her handkerchief and switched to English. Fedka showed up to maths just before the bell. I followed him with my eyes. He noticed and drove the smile from his face, as though his newly obtained glee had to be hidden from me of all people.

After classes I went to Auntie Valya the cleaner and begged her for some detergent powder. She led me to the storeroom under the stairs. New buckets and mops were kept there. "Wotcha gotta wash?" "The blue room." "Gotta bucket there?" "Nah, and the cloth's tatty." She handed me a bucket. "Don't go usin' too much powder, never wash it off, you won't." She tore off a piece of sacking. "Have you got some kind of brush? There's graffiti on the walls, can't rub it off with a cloth."

The blue walls were clean. No-one would dare. "Here. Wet it, put some powder on it, give it a good scrub, then rinse it off straightaway with clean water. Don't wait till it dries." She showed me how. "Here, take another swab." The new swab was a gift from her, herself. I dumped the old cloth and bucket in the toilet. Fetched warm water, a whole bucketful. Moved the desks aside. Dipped the brush in and painted a wet square, metre by metre. A dollop of powder from the bowl, kneel down and begin scrubbing. Scrub and dip, scrub and dip. Wipe with the dry cloth. Nobody had taught me that. Dry and dazzling bluishness emerged from under the yellow patches. My hair unplaited itself, got in my eyes. I pushed it aside with wet hands. The water in the bucket darkened after each square. Pour dirty water down the toilet, rinse the bucket and fill it with clean water again. Five times, six times. I lost count. All was quiet in the corridor behind me. I worked from front to back. Reaching the door, I straightened up. Aching back. Blinding dry sheen. The door creaked. "Still here? Not goin' home? I've gotta lock up." "Just finished." The cleaner glanced round. "Washed it off? Good for you. Pack up now." She closed the door. I took my shoes off and went barefoot.

All dry. My floor – clean as a bed. I lay down and stretched my legs. Not a single patch. Closing my eyes, I thought I had nothing to fear now. Now I can start reading Shakespeare.

Monday – grammar. Tuesday – textbook. Wednesday – English lit. Thursday – textbook. Friday – homework. To each lesson its own. Kipling was chosen as our home reading. About sailors. She did not accept a single answer the first time. No marks. She listened, and warned that next time she would mark as follows: 2 grammar mistakes – C; 2 unlearned words – C; slow tempo – one mark down. She explained how to learn by heart. You are given three pages from the book. On Monday, you write down any new words. On Tuesday, you look them up in the dictionary. On Wednesday, you learn them by heart. On Thursday, you retell it close to the text. *Only* in indirect speech. Direct speech is not allowed. After a month, we were all up to speed. The other groups gradually got used to it: we never show our faces. They saw us as martyrs. Irka would pick me up in the mornings. We ran vocab races on the way to school.

After class, she nodded to Fedya. That meant that he would go to the Blue Room after classes. Sometimes she did not nod, did not pay him any attention. Then he would walk to the door, glancing back over his shoulder, waiting for her nod. Irka and I discussed it on the way home. Fedya held his tongue, strutted. Irka had already read it. She came across Shakespeare at home. Not Romeo, admittedly, but Hamlet. She promised to coax it from her parents, bring it for me. Yesterday F. called Mishka Dudintsev. He hadn't read anything at all, just shared a desk with Fedka. Irka was vexed. I would never dare. On Monday, Irka raised her hand in class, announced she had already read Hamlet. F. heard her out, indifferently. Parents lent me. Pasternak's translation. These words didn't lacerate the brain, didn't crunch like sharp shards.

The detergent powder I had scrounged had run out. I had taken the brush home that first time. Those on duty washed the floor with a cloth, and not every day, only when Fedka and Misha didn't come. By the time my turn came round, the light blue floor was yellow again. Now I always carried detergent powder and a scrubbing brush in my satchel. And waited.

It was Tuesday when she nodded to me. My day had dawned. I came after classes. She was sitting in the corner, writing. I pushed the desks together and took out my brush, fetched the bucket of water. As before – square by square from the window. Swish, swish, scatter powder, scrub, rinse, fetch water, square after square. Wet knees. She didn't look in my direction, just sat and wrote. I crawled over to the corner. She stood up, went over to the window. Her steps left marks on the washed floor. Crawling on my knees after her, I wiped it dry. In the toilet, I poured away the last bucket and looked in the mirror. Red face, dishevelled hair, dark patches on my knees. I came back, put the bucket in the cupboard, shoved the brush in the bucket. No point in carrying it with me. I would have cried, had I dared. She stood up, took out a white handkerchief. I thought she would bend down. I didn't care. But she didn't bend down. I was standing by the door.

"Sit down."

I had been at it for two hours. These were her first words. I sat at my desk and hid my red hands. She opened the record player and took a record from its sleeve. Knitted her brows, raised the needle, lowered it slowly, and walked to the centre of the room.

There, there, there – as though someone were approaching me, three soft steps from afar, many, but as one, but broader than one. Her hand is raising, opening, and the voice – her voice, but different. I had never heard it like that, not even in English, as though it were not a voice but something other, more painful, higher, *inconceivable*, descending on the sounds like the needle. The sound flinches, but the voice flows over it, as if floating over water, sound by sound, barely touching them.

When in disgrace with Fortune and men's eyes
I all alone beweep my outcast state,

And trouble deaf heaven with my bootless cries,
And look upon myself and curse my fate...[8]

I don't understand, I don't know all the new words, I have not learnt the new words yet. ONLY some, but I don't need them to understand. I sit, clenching my red hands, flexing my fingers again and again. I sit, clenching all the way up, to my throat, when her voice, her not-voice, something I have no words for, retreats, steps back, one step at a time, her hands descend, sounds unclench my fingers and *they*, fused into one, manage to take off, break free from my red hands trying to hold them back. Slow shiver, and there, on high, everything is being torn like a veil before me: *they* sing out that which I have no words for, which I never name. High heels to the record player, the hand deftly raises the needle. "That is a sonnet by Shakespeare. I wrote it down, for you." High heels to the desk with the sheet of paper. She gives it to me. My hand red, hers small and white with bluish veins. Veins of blue blood. "Learn it, and we'll try together, you and I. There are three sonnets in this cycle, I want you to read them together. The first and third for you, the second for Fedya." The desk was bare now. While I'd been scrubbing, she'd been writing.

For a whole month now, day after day, I'm standing in the Blue Room, at the desk. She is in front of me. Record player under her hand. Lifting the needle up and down. Often at first, with almost every word, since my voice doesn't behave, teetering in her hand like a frying pan on a detachable handle. Fingers clenched, arms wooden, throat wooden. My stupid throat. Everything I'd learnt before – irrelevant. Day after day, she stands in front of me, her hands hold my voice, veins of blue blood before my eyes. Just the first line. Then the second. Day after day. Lessons pass unheard, nights pass unheard. We read in turns, she, me. Each word a sound of its own. Her turn, the sinews in my throat tightened. My turn, must watch both throat and face.

....

[8]   Shakespeare, Sonnet 29.

Must follow the music and her fingers. She is patient. I didn't know anyone could be so patient. I am patient; there will be no end to my patience. She never consoles. Guides the needle back. One line at a time at first. She takes the needle off and doesn't put it back. I made it to the end. She's probably thinking two whole months have passed. I look into her face. Shadows under her eyes, she's worn out. Sitting motionless. Beckons me, sits me beside her, hugs me. Now she consoles me. "Now you read it at home, by yourself, to memorise it." She takes the record off and puts it in the sleeve. Now I can be trusted. At home, I take out the record. *My* piece of Gluck, played to whiteness. After that, blackness. Fedya's will come in between. His future whiteness, in between.

I am sitting in the corner, moving my lips. Fedya's at the board, she is opposite. Opposite him this time. No one pays me any attention and that is good. I can listen as she reads, as she did for me, earlier. After a week, my lips hit the words.

Sonnet 71
No longer mourn for me when I am dead
Then you shall hear the surly sullen bell
Give warning to the world that I am fled
From this vile world with vilest worms to dwell…

She reads patiently, patiently guides the needle, but her face shuts down with each passing day. I see how he is trying – starts hopeful each time. She barely interrupts, lets him recite to the end. Then recites herself. Again. He misses. Misses, and misses. Again and again. Apologetic smile. I see it. He is reciting about himself, about his own death. She doesn't want to see his apologetic smile. That smile will ruin everything. After two weeks, she hands his sheet to me, points, and I take the stage. My violins, my intro. Fedya watches on from my corner. She doesn't explain anything, but I don't need her to. This is not about me. It's about her, about her death. I am her lips. I speak with her lips about her. I would not dare say it about myself. Not like that. Whom would I dare to console on *my* death? On her death, she consoles me. There is only one word of mine: *for I love you so* – but it's *so* mine, so nocturnally mine, that I am not afraid to recite it. She signals to me to stop, and stands up. Lifts the needle and puts it at the end of Fedya's …

But be contented when that fell arrest
Without all bail shall carry me away
My love hath in this line some interest
Which for memorial still with thee shall stay… [9]

Her face brightens. She reads to me about herself. She is alive. She comforts me in advance. I have survived her death because, in that moment, she knows that I shall have to survive it again one day. *For I love you so* – these are not her words, these are my words. She cannot say this properly. Not now, nor for many years to come. But she will. *Do not so much as my poor name rehearse.* She will say it, and then I will never be able to say – rehearse – her name again.

....

[9] Shakespeare, Sonnet 74.

LITTLE ZINNOBERS

As far as the District Department of People's Education (DDPE) is concerned, our school is the pride of the District, a blissful little show island of window-dressing. As far as our school's administration is concerned, the DDPE equals the Ministry of Foreign Affairs: they send numerous foreign delegations to us, and we receive them with due honour. As they are led through the classrooms, the educational process is demonstrated to them. We got used to it long ago. The door would open and B.G. enters with a knowing smile. A Russian smile. A thin stream of about twenty people oozes in behind him, smiling foreign smiles. The lesson wasn't interrupted. The strangers were given the chance to study Soviet school children in their natural habitat, and that 'natural habitat' was displayed simply but artistically. Good pupils raised their hands chummily, bad pupils didn't – to keep from sin. Evidently playing good ones, too, just on the lazy side. The teacher's voice would ring out more clearly. If it wasn't an English lesson, B. G. would translate in a whisper, keeping the guests in the picture. After about ten minutes, evidently already fully taken in, the smiley guests would tiptoe out, leaving behind gifts: our desks would be decked with heavenly manna – chewing gum, pens and necklaces. B. G. left last, bequeathing us an absolutely normal smile as a farewell gift.

Unlike B. G., Maman did not play guide to the foreigners. She made friendly overtures to the head of the DDPE, on whom our annual renovations, new furniture and linguaphone cabinets depended; the natural habitat where we were usually displayed should be laudable rather than natural. Nevertheless, that was just the backdrop. Maman quickly came to recognize this. The Shakespeare theatre F. organized became the trump card. A new era dawned for us: we became Maman's favourite children.

"Dear friends, I am the compère of a small collective within the framework of the Robert Burns Club for International Friendship. It is our tradition to greet our friends with a small concert. We are, of course, not professional, but we shall try to do our best."

I am standing in the first floor landing. In front of me, benches. On the benches, an English delegation. A very important delegation. In the front row, Maman. Beside her, several middle-aged English ladies in lace collars. The less fancy audience – jeans, sweaters, beards – in rows behind them. A perfect Shakespearean theatre. My English intro is over. Benign smiles, light applause. F. is in the corner by the record player.

First I announce Lena Tronova. Classical dance. F. puts on the record, Lenka floats in on her toes. Dances superbly. Light figure in a rustling tutu. The guests are taking photographs. Continuous flashes. Lacy ladies nod: Russian ballet. Maman whispers with her neighbour. Along the lines of: in the USSR, children study ballet from early childhood. The lacy lady is impenetrable. I notice something not altogether lacy about her, even then. Jeans and sweaters applause enthusiastically, the lacy ones just gently tap their palms. Maman throws B. G a meaningful look:

"An Ideal Interview with our Greatest Actor."[10]

I announce something I have never seen, what they stayed behind for after classes. Fedya, a great actor, Misha, a journalist. An interview: "And so, you are about to appear in Shakespeare?" "I would rather put it…" Fedka is snooty and inspired, "that Shakespeare is about to appear in me." An explosion of laughter. I laugh, too. Mishka is walking on respectful eggshells. The great actor presents a new Hamlet to the public: not in black but in brown velvet. This is a revolution. They speak fast, too fast for me. But this is not for me – it's for the foreigners. Fedka is holding a skull. A real skull

....

10 Stephen Leacock, *Frenzied Fiction*.

from the biology lab. The audience giggles. He stands up from the stool, throws himself on the floor, crawls on his belly, legs convulsing: "I crawl slowly forward, portraying by my legs and stomach the whole sad story of Yorick." Laughter crescendos. Mishka's open mouth. Fedka leaps up. His back to the audience, he twitches his shoulder blades, here it is, Hamlet's passionate grief at the loss of his friend. Mishka is like a dog on its hind legs. The Great Actor is modest as never before. Already condescending to the rapture, he declares that actually, in reality, he is about to present the public with something larger than Shakespeare. "How shall I express it? Something... Well, in fact ME!" Slowly, as if felled, the journalist falls to his knees and crawls backwards on hands and knees. Applause. Long and continuous. Effusive. With a quick glance, I take in the most important ones. F. is in her corner. Looking through the window. Maman is laughing with everyone. B. G. is surveying the hall, half standing. The lacy lady is smiling politely, putting her palms together. Soviet ballet or Fedya, it's all one to her. I am clapping, but butterflies are already fluttering in my stomach, because now I have to announce myself. Shakespeare's sonnets to the music of Gluck. They are waiting for me to leave – they know me as the compère. I stand, waiting for the rustle. F. is behind me. Good Lord, such emptiness! Just like my stomach. The rustle and my voice, wandering after the violins.

Velveteen silence. I don't see anything. I only imagine I see their faces. How could I, with my poor eyes? I just seem to see polite puzzlement on their faces. How can they fail to understand? It's THEIR Shakespeare after all. They are putting me off. If I dared stop I would yell at them that they are disturbing me. Above the hall, above their heads. They can no longer bother me. I start the third sonnet and lower my eyes. I didn't mean to look, I glanced by chance. Fingers. A white lacy handkerchief. She's crying, ripping it with her teeth, ripping the lace. Very close, at arm's length, and I can't be mistaken, not even with my poor eyes. I alone can see this. And F. If she is looking. The others cannot see how the chief lacy lady cries and shreds her lace with her teeth...

They are going straight to him, passing me by, paying me no heed. In ones and twos. Beards, jeans, sweaters, lace. Surrounded. Shaking hands. Clamouring, all at once. Triumph. He bows and nods: my name is Theodor. He is tall and handsome. I know it, I know he is more handsome than all of them. Thrusting pens, pens, souvenirs, badges. He is smiling, thanking them. Pockets full of presents. I look round. F. is sitting in her little corner, looking past everyone. She has short, gingery hair with a centre parting. Flashing gold, lock after lock. She runs her hand over her hair, softening the golden sheen of those locks. I stand, twiddling them in my hands. My presents – two rollerball pens, blue and green. A man and a girl passed by, gave me them, thanked me politely. Girl in a short pinafore with a zip – from throat to hem.

Maman is waving her hand, beckoning me. I look round. F. is sitting at the window. Golden sheen, again, or so it seems. One golden lock after another, again. Her hand doesn't go there. Neither seeing nor hearing. Standing in a threesome: Maman, the lacy one, B. G. She's crying, of course. Eyes red. Clutching the shredded hanky. Not at all lacy. She's ripped all the lace with her teeth. I see the shreds. Maman hugs me, gives an imperceptible nudge.

Her English is very fast, now she is nervous, almost swallowing her words. I understand; I'm used to understanding when it's fast. Amazed, she says, didn't expect anything like it, didn't expect such things were possible in the USSR, propaganda is propaganda, everyone lies. "With this music, how did it occur to you? To bring them together, as though they were written for each other." She waves a small box. "I recorded it on tape, now I'll listen to it all the time, I want everyone to hear it." "It wasn't me," I want to get away, she was talking about putting it with music, I must get away. I look round, searching for F. She's not there. The corner is empty.

The delegations started showing up more frequently. Not a week went by without B.G. giving a polite knock during some lesson and nodding to us three from the door, announcing the arrival of the next party. Our threesome would stand up. Forced to interrupt class, the teacher would watch as we quickly tidied away our textbooks and follow B.G. Everything paled into insignificance at the news of a delegation. They could even pluck us from a test. The compliments and gifts showered on us became commonplace, no longer setting us aquiver with joy. We shared our gifts with our classmates – Fedya with the 'highers' and I with mine. Our return was awaited, our skiving privileges forgiven not entirely selflessly.

At the end of the concerts, F. would dole out short, harsh critique. Swiftly reciting the lines where each of us 'hadn't quite made it.' Her critique was a spoonful of tar in the barrel of our glory, but it was special tar nonetheless, and we gladly gave the whole barrel away for this spoonful of tar. The taste of the tar was the sweet taste of our rehearsals. Sometimes she left silently, without a word to us. That meant everything was OK, we had performed as we should, nothing to discuss. Sometimes, after yet another concert, F's face would become particularly withdrawn and she would call one or other of us, so that having worked for a couple of hours, she could get us back to the previous level from which we had slipped. "It has nothing to do with either the guests or Maman. No-one. You must *keep the bar*. It has to be unfaltering." Sometimes, after particularly lavish applause and a lush harvest of compliments and gifts, F. tore it all down, mocking our gestures and intonation with particular pleasure. Or sometimes, it was the opposite. The foreigners left, thanking us coldly and politely, but F. would suddenly admit that today she had listened herself enrapt, this phrase in particular, and her face would exude delighted amazement. She never asked what compliments we received, let alone what presents. Twice I tried to talk to her myself. The first time after that first performance, I found her in her study. Summoning my courage, I told her about the lacy lady. She said she'd seen her crying. Then I said the lacy lady had spoken about bringing music and sonnets together, saying it was a miracle she had not expected to witness in the USSR. F. listened utterly indifferently, as though it had nothing to do with her. It was only when I pronounced "in the USSR" that her face suddenly took on the same frightening aspect as that time I had walked between the desks. Her narrow nose lengthened, and her cheekbones sharpened in a second, and the half-disdainful smile with which she was listening to my tale of the lacy lady's compliments faded away at once. "USSR. Indeed! A great Zinnober!" I didn't understand but didn't dare ask. There was one other time when I came to her myself after the performance and told her I'd been given lipstick, and since I, of course… And I held it out to her. She took it, nodding her thanks.

THE ENGLISH SCHOOL IS ME!

Maybe she never asked us any questions because any questions she might have asked us had already been put to our predecessors from the First English School, where she worked for over ten years from the end of the fifties, before she was transferred to us. She liked to tell us about that time – the first time – although those reminiscences of hers did not really serve as illustrations for a case in point; they were more like a mental return to some golden age, inaccessible to us. The phantom of the legendary First English School hovered over us throughout our allotted years, the seventies. Compared with that golden age, ours was an iron age. Compared with her previous visitors, our DDPE guests, guests from the District Party Committee, methodologists and occasional foreigners were mere road sweepers. That was her 'bon mot,' and she would use it liberally in her conversations with us, decorating all and sundry with it, indiscriminately. She would decorate any of us with it, too, by the way, if there was good cause.

The First English School was the ultimate in cronyism in those days. The children of some Tovstonogov[11] actors studied there, including one of Smoktunovsky's children. Smoktunovsky[12] had just starred in Kozintsev's film *Hamlet*,[13] but the film was received badly; the intelligentsia preferred

....

[11]   A reference to Georgy Alexandrovich Tovstonogov, director of the Gorky Bolshoi Drama Theatre, Leningrad (now the Tovstonogov Bolshoi Drama Theatre) from 1956-1989, one of Russia's most highly-acclaimed theatres.
[12]   Innokenty Mikhaylovich Smoktunovsky (1925-1994) is known as the 'king of Soviet actors' won several awards for his acting both on stage and for cinema.
[13]   Grigory Mikhaylovich Kozintsev (1905-1973), highly acclaimed Soviet theatre and film director.

the scent of the Taganka Theatre,[14] spiced with political musk. Not F. To her, Vladimir Vysotsky's[15] stretched sweater and hoarse, 'modern' voice *yelling* 'To be or not to be' were all offensive. She heard the dictates of modern times in those yells, and she held both (dictates and our modern times) in unswerving contempt. She was drawn by something left over from times past: a trace which she could recognize instantly. Or more precisely, not just any trace, but the *genuine* – i.e. incorruptible – trace of the past. She came face to face with Smoktunovsky once, just before he left for Moscow. She was walking through the school, he was coming towards her. They all but collided in a doorway. He stepped back politely, letting her pass. She intended to proceed, but then, looking into his eyes, she saw something which (as she explained to us many years later) lingered in them forever, something from *his* Hamlet, *the only genuine* Hamlet. And that trace, that eternal something, compelled her to step aside and let him pass. Had anyone else performed that gesture, it would have been nothing but a simple manifestation of admiration for a wonderful actor.

The glorious First English School declined after she left, paled into insignificance; in our day, no-one in town had heard even a whisper of it, and her favourite pupils-cum-actors had all 'aged,' as she put it. She imbued this word with a much more frightening meaning than the physical consequence of time's passage. From time to time, she would shake our souls with tales of her previous pupils who, besides the burden of their age, had taken on a capacity wholly mysterious to us, namely the capacity to share details of their none-too-successful family lives with F. With noble disgust, she would quote the current – *road sweeper* – phrases of her former girls. Quote, and listen to our laughter. Yet she never pretended we would turn out any

....

[14]   The Taganka Theatre in Moscow, founded in 1964 by Yuri Lyubimov, was constantly in trouble with the Soviet authorities for its more progressive, unorthodox approach to theatre, and Lyubimov was eventually stripped of his Soviet citizenship and exiled in 1984.

[15]   Vladimir Semyonovich Vysotsky (1938-1980), singer-song-writer famous for his unmistakeable gravelly voice, rousing ballads, and often irreverent lyrics. Also a prominent stage and screen actor.

better: the same thing will happen to you, absolutely the same, you won't even notice it happening. We believed her, of course, since we were used to believing her. Believed, yet didn't believe, since we took her former students, our predecessors, for everyday dolts lacking intelligence. "The English School is wherever I am." She rarely rose from her bed any more, could certainly no longer leave her house. I reproduce her words with absolute accuracy, but, committed to paper, they seem slightly distorted; her intonation is missing. Her genuine intonation turned these words into the semblance of others: "the English school is me." She would pronounce these words much later, two decades after our working days with her were over. An outside observer might have taken this formula of hers for arrogance, but, actually, it was absolutely accurate, with an accuracy which extended far beyond the boundaries of literal meaning.

It's unlikely she seriously thought a cardinal change in the audience for her productions (Tostanogov actors in the First English and DDPE foreigners in ours) was some new, enigmatic sign of the times, which, once recognized, meant much could be fathomed. She worked with us, achieving something she alone could achieve, and loved us in the Shakespearean images she herself created, since she knew fine well we were doomed. Doomed and sick, fatally ill with the illness of time, we would never be so fine. Ageing – or rather, what she meant by that word – invested her love with a special meaning, an additional meaning, and her love was never reckless. She never deceived herself on our account, nor did she ever deceive us, though she clung to this thought stubbornly. To an outsider, it might seem she were inveigling us not to age. And maybe she was indeed beguiling us, knowing the futility of her guile. Yet still she continued to 'heat the streets.' The latter, her own phrase.

The tender infirmity of our youth held us hostage to certain shallow passions – love of glory, pride, self-importance – passions which gradually became poisons seeping into our blood, and our blood was at the mercy of time, of time's particular, deadly corpuscles or bacilli. Was it not she herself who let taste us these poisons, from her own hands, holding them out on the tip of a dagger, or a rapier (to use our Shakespearean props)? But when F. stood nearby, on guard, she could reined us in, harshly and mercilessly. Doled out antidotes. A trueborn oriental sovereign, she measured out the correct dose of poison so that later, when there was no-one to measure it, it would not kill us instantly. For us, she preferred prolonged ageing to instant death. She did not stand on ceremony when she chose her potions. She used strong ones – last resort remedies, like a doctor who knows all her patients are doomed. Barracks full of the doomed. Bitter experience told her that, strictly speaking, no-one would recover. Just as our predecessors hadn't – the mythologically superb pupils from the First-since-Creation English School. Yet she went about her task with tragic stubbornness, as though she had sworn a special Hippocrates oath. She would only give up on the dead. On those who, having finished school, left by themselves. At fifteen, we could not fully share her tragic premonition. Nevertheless, the last years of our youth, of our school life, were accompanied by the sense that something inevitable loomed ahead.

Or maybe time, which she was at war with, is just a tempest, swapping the signboards? Maybe this crafty, puny enemy is in fact playing tricks on me, muddling me? Muddling the its signs to prevent me from witnessing against it. Holding a firearm to my head, hanging on the walls in others' rooms, standing in the corners in others' studies, locking others' wrists in handcuffs. How can I bear witness if I am frightened? The weights of the little cuckoo clock hanging above the dining table, the large mantelpiece clock which perished during a bomb raid together with the house into which we had not yet moved, the heavy, onion-shaped silver watch belonging to my grandfather who left the country around forty years before my birth, taking it with him, the delicate ladies' watch on a golden bracelet traded for a goat during evacuation in the Urals... They all show a different time, a time long gone. I would not lay a finger on any of these deadly firearms. So what right do I have to raise my hand at the witness stand?

"Baker's." The sign hangs over the glazed tiles of the baker's shop. We drank coffee with condensed milk standing at the high tables covered in greyish plastic, eating seventeen-kopek rum babas and eight kopek *bublik*-bagels. I was here with F. once. And I am a good witness after all, for the devil is in the detail. I remember the prices, and the stamped down snow on the pavement, and the wet wooden shavings on the floor smudged by the huge mop strokes .... Look, there I am, standing in the square at the Palace of Labour. Time has already changed the signboard above it, hung up something new, something my bad eyes cannot make out. My eyes see something else. For not all words are the same. Only those demanding labour and love light up and remain, and then some of them are spared the fate of *incarnation*; strangers' hands won't touch them. To strangers, they will remain discarnate, though actually they will become *reflections*. They will retain everything: the everyday weariness from which they were born when, day after day, from rehearsal to rehearsal, other words – our reflections' predecessors – were repeated dozens of times by her lips and by ours; they will retain the moment when the street grew as hot as midday summer and when, finally, everything was to her liking, and we ourselves became her reflection, Romeo and Lady Macbeth, Malvolio and every soldier in Henry the Fourth. They will retain deadly hopelessness, because we will age, whereas 'reflection' – well, it is a word which becomes harder and harder to write down with every passing year.

CRISS-CROSSING

Shortly before New Year, just a couple of weeks before we broke up, F. told Usenkova and Perova to stay after class. They sat in the second row, right behind us. F. delights in their beauty. Says they are like heroines in an American western, the blonde and the brunette. But I doubt any of us, heroines included, could really appreciate this compliment. F. also says Usenkova looks like Catherine Deneuve, only prettier. Anyhow, she called them both after class and the next day, one of them blabbed: F. gave us a scene from Twelfth Night. The fuse was lit. The news spread like wildfire, reached her ears two days later. Instant explosion: explosion with no explanation. F. called Lenka Blank and me after class – she *happened* to be sitting at my desk that day, Irka was ill. F. did not delight in our looks. From her hands, we received sheets which had already passed through the hands of our predecessors, along with a warning: be ready for rehearsals after the holidays. F. did not mention the need to keep our lips zipped, rightly assuming that, after what had happened, ours would only open under torture. I am Viola, Lenka is Maria, the maid. F. gave the role of Malvolio to Kostya. Not much time, she said, the Day of Theatre is in March, other classes are getting ready.

Rehearsals for 'the Twelfth' began in mid-January, after the holidays, and straightaway we ran aground on the first phrases. Mine was first. I had to enquire in a noble tone. Then Lenka's curtsey and reply – a deceptive spatter. The scene developed fast: after the two phrases we got stuck on, Malvolio appears with an idiotic smile, dazzling in his wide, canary-yellow garters, criss-crossed. My task was simple: noble posture, absent-minded curiosity and surprise, with a pinch of indignation. Maria had to play on two fronts: concerned sympathy when her mistress was watching, and giggling delight when Ma'am looks the other way. Paramount: light, swift transitions. Light transitions eluded us. We walked to and fro, like clockwork, replaying the reel of the first phrases: countless times, back and forth. F. interrupts each time, shows Lenka true deceitful spatter. Transforms as she does so: I look into her face and her ease surprises me. As though something clicks inside, throwing up an image: eyelids twitch, lips smirk. Lenka listens and nods. We retreat, enter anew. At the third rehearsal F.'s patience evaporated. Resolute, she swaps us over – castled. I didn't like it. Who would like to be castled, changed from noble countess to giggling maid? But now, surprisingly, it takes off. I curtsey and giggle. *It* clicks in me easily: smirks its lips, winks.

Most of the time F. coaches them. Speechless Maria is left to her own devices. While they are chatting, I choose my moment to giggle to my heart's content, but if Lenka so much as throws me a glance, I cover my mouth and freeze, penitent. F. barely looks in my direction, it seems, so I invent pretexts to speechlessly scurry to and fro, light and swift. No, she is looking after all, says: fancy! You're a born maid! She says this with gay, reckless ease and looks at me, but not with her usual sonnetian attention: quickly turning in my direction, she catches my fleeting, speechless contrivance, enhances it with a single gesture, infusing it with additional aplomb, which I adopt at once – straight from her hands. This *fleeting work* cost us nothing. Both of us – she and I – are dealing with something easy and simple which I already possess. It manifests, surfaces, F. has only to set the tone, enhance a gesture, a turn, a glance. I don't like the role of Maria. After my sonnetian triumphs, I am worthy of higher things. The audience will look at *them*.

In February, with the props almost ready, we turn to costumes. F. jotted down the sketches herself. In a show of unprecedented understanding,

Kostya's parents gave four roubles. A trip to Gostiny.[16] We buy pink satin, green calico for camisoles and yellow atlas ribbons for garters. I sew the trousers, his sister, the camisole. At home, in a wardrobe, I unearth a Red Riding Hood costume: red bonnet with flaps – maybe Dutch, maybe monastic – and an equally red waistcoat, hemstitched with decorative white braid. They give me an old sheet for the skirt and sleeves. Good, says F. Lenka's mother is so taken by the idea of a sheet that she donates two, both thin and see-through with age. We dye them with blue cotton dye, but either we didn't stir it diligently enough or the dye was old: they came out blotchy. It'll do, says F.

She's in raptures over Kostya's costume. Author of the pink breeches, I'm pleased. But Lenka and I exchange words: had they given us money instead of sheets, who knows whose would have come out on top.

---

[16]   Gostiny Dvor, the main department store.

INCOMPLETE CIRCLE DANCE

On weekdays, the assembly hall is the dining hall. We transform it, dragging benches and chairs from all the recreation areas, piling tables on top of each other. Chairs stand in the gallery, too; on weekdays, it is from up there the foreign delegations are shown Soviet children, feeding. Conscientious, the children pretend they are not being watched. And – credit where it's due – the delegations pass above us, duly moved. They are not permitted food. In extraordinary cases, Maman offers them cognac in her office.

Transformation was inherent in the design: on the right-hand wall separating the kitchen from the dining hall there's a fully-equipped stage, covered by dark red velvet curtains. The velvet falls in generous folds – enough for ten of Maman's dresses. During festivities, the stage curtains open, drawn apart by cords on either side. And here the hidden flaw in the construction comes to light: the stage muffles voices. Or maybe it is not the stage but the velvet folds, soaked in heavy kitchen smells. Be that as it may, only the Pioneers' repartees ring out loud and clear, shouted out in a ringing chorus as if the dark velvety curtain, stripped of any honourable, red-bannered destiny, was playing tricks, revealing its secret preferences. F. discovered this flaw at the very first dress rehearsal she organised a couple of weeks before the Day of Theatre. After listening to our muffled mumbles for five to ten minutes – Shakespeare *does not sit well* with velvet – she raised her hand, interrupting.

There was a counter to the left of the stage. Auntie Galya, the dinner lady, stood behind it on weekdays. Behind her mighty back hid the kitchen. To the right, just beside the door, was an alcove, with the entry to the scullery lurking in its depths. Dirty dishes were taken to the alcove. According to the planner's plan, the food should have circled the stage in a kind of closed circle dance: out from the kitchen via the buffet then into our hungry hands which took the leftovers to the pre-washing alcove. I wouldn't swear to it that the circle dance always came full circle. F. took all this in, then rejected both stage and curtains. We set about moving the tables and freed a large section of the hall, which became our stage. F had figured it out. She gave the order: come out from the kitchen via the buffet, play your part, and exit into the scullery. The same incomplete circle taken by the food.

There were no tickets, of course. But there were *specially* invited guests, which meant there was a seating hierarchy. The first bench was reserved for the administration and their guests. Behind them, teachers, released from their pedagogical duties. The central section was occupied by pupils, leaving the farthest benches for the actors' parents. Those who combined parenthood with high position – in other words, those of high standing whose offspring studied in our school, and were Maman's pride and joy – sat next to her in the front row. Games teachers and their retinue of school sports stars – our school prided itself on this – sat in the gallery. In the right wing, right by the door to the scullery, sat Auntie Galya and the dinner ladies. Now, thinking with hindsight about *our* whole story, I must admit that there was an oddness lurking in this monstrous gathering of people – boys dangling in bunches from the high dining room window ledges. All scenes, with very rare exceptions I shall deal with later, were in English. For most of the audience, however – and the audience grew from year to year with each Theatre Day – English was a closed book. They were deaf in English, so to speak. Nevertheless, the majority of those who were not specially invited guests simply could not imagine staying away. Just try and stop Auntie Galya, for instance! Actually, it is precisely Auntie Galya who could be called the embodiment of that deaf-dumb oddness – not some abstract, passive embodiment, but the most active one. Year after year, each and every one of us exiting the stage via the alcove for leftovers under thunderous applause would fall into Auntie Galya's embrace. She cried and kissed us all, indiscriminately. She understood not a single word nor showed so much as a hint of respectful admiration for F. – i.e. not recognising any merit of hers – Auntie Galya found another solution for herself. Through her power, absolute within the confines of the dining room, she enforced a new order: before evening rehearsals, we could count on free hunks of bread, always doled out by Auntie Galya's hands. In other words, running ahead lexically, she was our bread sponsor. Of course, in her hierarchy, we (and all other pupils) stood one rung lower than the teachers; unlike them, we were not allowed to enter the kitchen by ourselves to fetch food by ourselves. And two rungs lower than Maman and the directors of studies, whom she served personally, bringing them food from behind the counter. In some different reckoning system – here Auntie Galya reasoned more rigorously than any physicist – we outranked them all, standing almost higher than Auntie Galya and the kitchen staff themselves, who did not pay for bread. In this system of reckoning, the kitchen staff did not pay anything for dining hall food; but, according to their own understanding at least, they received it not *for free*, they *earned* their daily bread by their hard labour. As for us, we received our after class bread *not for work* – Auntie Galya didn't care about the trials and tribulations of our rehearsals – but solely thanks to her warm-hearted choice based on what you might call a certain exclusivity, the magic of our tongues, repeating wonderful and incomprehensible words which she heard but once a year, sitting in the alcove by the empty sink, released from its dirty dishes, the magic of the tears which we drew from her normally dry eyes but once in her difficult kitchen year. In short, for her, we were 'God's little birds,' and, like the birds of the air, we had every right to receive our daily bread gratis, knowing neither worry nor care.

Installed in the kitchen, we discussed the situation briefly. Can't peep from behind the buffet counter, they'll see you in the hall. Have to sneak behind the stage. We opened the curtains a slit, observed from behind, all eyes. Year Six skipped out first, Valeria Pavlovna's charges. Tom Sawyer. The curtain, heavy with our eyes, did not waver. F. sat in the second row, far left. Never, neither then nor later, did she remain in the wings, left us to our own devices. I think she knew about our curious ambush. But although our eyes returned to her face with the regularity of a pendulum, she gave nothing away. She seemed to be looking slightly to one side, but we could see she was listening to the text adapted to year six students. Thackeray's Vanity Fair began. After that, three witches. From our ambush, all we could see were dishevelled wigs. I could hear the applause rained on the witches from the kitchen.

The Shakespearian Theatre is being announced. I see my father standing up, making his way to the very back, to stand behind the last row of seats, as on the photograph. The old sanatorium photograph in the album. He is young there. A hazy memory, then I don't see anything more. I walk ahead, crossing empty space, stop in the middle. Standing, blind and deaf: I neither see nor hear, but I sense F. sitting at the end. I don't dare look. She warned us deliberately: no glances. The hall is silent. In the silence, I recite. Curtsey. Passing through, I take Fedka's skull from under the counter. They saw it. In the hall behind me, giggles. I don't watch 'the great actor.' In the kitchen, in front of the mirror, I don the red bonnet, listening. All quiet at first. Then giggles. Then guffaws, from all sides, louder and louder. I peep from the corner. The hall roars – so much for foreigners! Fedka crawls on the floor, arms and legs twitching. Mishka is flying on tiptoe. I no longer see my father: the sanatorium photo is ripped – the back row has jumped up, climbing onto the window ledges; desks creak, arranged in a barricade. Everyone is roaring, as though on cue. Teachers, understanding not a word, high ranking parents, all laughing raucously like ordinary mortals. They understood why they had come. Girls from the upper classes yelp, hiding in their sleeves. I spot Fedka's father out of the corner of my eye.

The assembly hall has never heard such applause. They come out to take another bow. Maman claps with gay abandon. I already know *her* expression. Pale cheeks, bluish shadows, yellow, lips tightly pursed. She is looking away, as though she herself were not part of this laughing hall, the hall which she herself has staged to laugh so rowdily! I cannot finish my thought, no time, Lenka is two steps ahead of me in her dress with bluish blotches. I see only blotches, blotches on the floor I didn't wash properly. My white and red follows the blue. The hall is hidden – heat haze. I giggle and crouch down, they are already laughing, laughing, guffawing. Hiding behind my sleeve, I listen to the hall. It is easy to giggle since –just like everyone else – I am them. I hide among them, my giggles drift amongst their unbridled guffaws…

Lenka and Kostya bow out. I'm curtseying to one side. Right in front of Maman. Sergei Ivanovich smiles, tossing back his fringe. We head off to the scullery. Auntie Galya meets us. The steamed faces of the kitchen staff, laughed to tears. Passing the sinks, we are in the kitchen – come full circle. F. is already there. Crept along the wall while we were taking our bows. "Sit down. The rest later." We wait for everyone to leave. Then we leave for the bluish study. I look at the floor on my way: clean, no blotches. Not bad, she said. "Maria was the best. Are you listening? Your Maria is the best! You realise nobody noticed that? They never will," she repeats. I understand.

Back home, I asked my father. He liked it, especially Fedya. "How about me?" I raised the question I would never put to anyone again. "Of course, but Fedya, well…" My father stands for fairness. "They used to call it melodeclamation. Poetry to music. Beautiful. It was quite common, especially in cinemas, before the film. Your Mum and I used to go." I understand: he was young then, as on that sanatorium photograph, would stand in the back row… It's ripped now. On Monday, Fedya came up to me and said his father liked me very much. His father is a director, now he is directing a play, not in Leningrad but in Arkhangelsk. A professional production, he said. Hadn't expected it of course, but well, we couldn't take the credit. "It all comes down to the teacher. Nothing *of yours*. I won't heap praises, or you'll end up like Poppet Zinnober." "Who?" I asked, automatically, and regretted it at once. I hadn't asked her then, about the lace one. Now he will pull a disdainful face. "Little Zaches, Great Zinnober… I haven't read it yet. Dad says it's a tale where they praise someone who didn't deserve it. A frightening tale." "And what about you? Did he like you?" Fedya nods and shrugs. "Mine liked you, especially my father." "Really?" he smiles, pleased.

I didn't go the Publichka to read it. I thought I should at first, but then didn't. Frightening, his father said. I didn't feel like it. Just didn't.

The Fairy Rosabelverde. By no means a tall woman, with very short hair, whose face no-one on this earth would consider flawlessly beautiful. When, as was her habit, she looked away, immobile and strict, as she listened to the words we pronounced from the stage, her face evoked a strange, sometimes eerie sensation. Pale cheeks, bluish shadows, yellow, pursed lips. In all my long years, I never dared glance in her direction while I was on stage, but I always knew about her other side, where, listening to us, she gazed with her fixed, formidable stare, discerning something eerie behind the words which she herself had put in our mouths, one glance at which pales the cheeks, purses the lips and forces the bluish shadows to darken. She never called us poppets. A small fairy, short hair, with a gingery glint – or OK, let's say 'golden' – combed our hair day after day, turning it into wavy curls. She fed us with her own food, like a bird – from beak to beak: from the throat, from her hands. She loved us and adored us, but there was more doom than hope in that love, for she knew so much more about her poppets than her beloved authors from the Age of Enlightenment knew about theirs. The reality which had fallen to her lot: deceptively plump, blockadian hunger, the pitiful cessation of her previous pupils which, due to her fairy pride, she never called betrayal yet treated as such, our vile story, to which I will come sooner or later – that reality must surely have taught her there are forces in this world more powerful than enlightened education. Otherwise, why should she grow pale as she looked at the hall raging with guffaws? What was it she saw in this comradely laughter which startled her so much that, during all the years which followed, she only returned to Shakespearian comedy once, and even then, she directed it in such a way that no-one in the hall took it into their heads to guffaw. They giggled, laughed, and had a good time, yes. Everything but *that* guffaw. Now I shall never know for sure, never know from her lips, whether, paling at strangers' guffaws, she understood where it was all heading, whether she understood what would sprout from it? Could it be she *always* knew *what* would sprout from such guffaws? If she knew, why did she allow it?

An evil she-dwarf. That is what one of the dethroned poppets called her, after twenty-five years of active life, and three years after her death. Food takes its own course – the incomplete circle dance of Zinnober poppets, hand in hand: from the kitchen via the buffet, into the hungry hands which automatically carry vile, unfinished leftovers to the scullery. This circle dance can never come full circle.

LEAVING AND RETURNING

Our status changed after Theatre Day. Rehearsals became a valid excuse, accepted by all teachers without exception. It was enough even for The Chemist and The Literati to just come up, make a serious, penitent face, and declare that yesterday, due to rehearsals… The teacher would nod, accept. We were clever enough not to overdo it. None of the teachers *ever* reported this to F. or complained about us, although, in all honesty, they had every right. Either they were a little afraid of her, or genuinely believed it was our right. She, however, certainly did not think so. And we would never entertain the idea. Home reading, lectures on English and American literation, preparation for dictation – everything was completed rigorously. Although there was one isolated incidence in Year Nine when, despairing of her failure to rein in Irka and myself, The Chemist approached F. and complained of us chattering in class. Worse, she was evidently relying on teachers' solidarity, hoping to temporarily suspend us from rehearsals. Until such time as… This was madness on her part. Had she limited herself to a simple complaint, F. would have obliterated Irka and me from the face of the earth, but – God bless The Chemist Varvara Gavrilovna! – this phrase saved us. F. said not a word to us. But to Varvara Gavrilovna… She offered her help, saying she was ready, *temporarily*, to change places with her, and maintain discipline in her classes, if Varvara Gavrilovna for her part would kindly take on her, F's, responsibilities. "Rest assured, if I come to your class, it will be silent as a grave, and it will be silent for as long as I am standing over that grave." A little later, F. played out this story in a skit, not mentioning any names, of course. It was that famous skit she once organized for the teachers. No students were allowed, but some details leaked out via Svetka, The Geographer's daughter. F. and B. G. played out various little scenes from school life, in Russian, and the teachers laughed fit to bust their guts. She forced them to guffaw in Russian, threw them their Russian laughter like a bone.

She loved words. How could she have learnt so many languages besides her native tongue otherwise? Russian, English, German, Italian, Spanish, and Arabic, which she spoke as a child. She learnt Arabic when her mother evacuated her to her own native village near Kazan at the end of the war. In her mother's village, at fourteen, she was a believer, praying, repeating *surahs* after her Granny. Granny was old and almost blind. F. gathered goat dung in the steppe with other girls and stoked the stove. The little goat dung pellets dried in the steppe sun had no smell. She would slip a dry ball to her Granny saying it was a dry sour cherry. Granny would nibble, guess, laugh and wag her finger. The God of Arabic *surahs* soon vanished. All that was left of Him were wide, washed out Tartar trousers, drawn at the ankles; water jugs for *namas* washing – several times a day: tall, with a single handle, bending their long, bashful necks when carried through the yard. It is shameful to meet a man or a boy when you are carrying *such* a jug. Jugs, Turkish trousers, scraped wooden floors, the smell of the steppe – the steppe's dry grasses. Yearning, she spoke of the smell of the steppe before her death. Her perfume smelt of the sun and the steppe.

She loved words. Grammar less so. She took it as something self-evident. I can't remember a single case when she set us some grammar rule to memorize, not even one in the school curriculum. Initially, of course, she must have discussed our numerous grammatical mistakes. I say 'must have' because, oddly enough, I have no memory of such discussions. I only remember *how* she corrected mistakes: with a short, swift, furious glance. Her empty eyes staring somewhere in the far corner of the ceiling, she would listen to our endless retellings, piercing them with her fierce glances, sharp and swift as needles. The tortuous pricks of fury were frequent at first, then ever fewer, until she rarely lowered her eyes. After about two years of constant training,

Irka and I learnt to catch and pierce, too – faultlessly. She noticed once. Now, having nailed a mistake, F. would throw a quick glance at us, too. After that it stuck: mistake, and three pairs of eyebeams cross, hers and ours. Pages and pages of home reading, we retold Salinger and Hemingway, but somehow, imperceptibly, we got the hang of it, not during retelling, of course, but on some other pretext. She rarely allowed such exercises in her presence; only in special cases. For instance, when yet another group of methodologists or teachers would show up to learn from her experience. Then, with her complete complicity, we would put on a show without so much as a hint of a smile.

I see it clear as day: a group of women enters our class importantly. The classroom is already a language lab. We are sitting in ones at specially equipped desks: on/off switch, headphones, microphone. On her desk, the control panel. The visitors sit with us, in ones. We put on the headphones, bring the microphones to our mouths. The teachers bend over their notebooks, studying the lesson format. We are retelling the next three pages of *The Path of Thunder*. Tragic love story of Sarie and Lanny, a black lad and a white girl. Finished. Switched off. Short comments. F. gives marks. No going over mistakes. Move on. "Now we'll have a little chat about one very interesting matter," she begins in slow English, her voice clear and quiet for the guests' benefit. "The topic is," her tone is almost tender: "Why Fieta left her native village for Cape Town every year, but always returned." They note the topic down in their notebooks carefully. Doesn't look like they've read *The Path of Thunder*. Fieta is the local prostitute. Extremely wide hips, fat thighs, a gaggle of kids from all sorts of men from the port. Every spring, she leaves for Cape Town but every autumn she returns to the village with another child in her belly. By the next spring, liberated from her burden, she starts to feel bored. We are encouraged to discuss why. Possibilities are soon flying thick and fast: she went in search of love, wanted to have a lot of children, left to earn money, hankered after the bright city lights. In short, the topic is inexhaustible. The teachers are dumbfounded. Genuinely. This isn't even uni, just Year 8. F. listens to each new proposal seriously, without smiling. We are ready for battle, hands shooting up one after the other. The teachers listen with growing personal interest. We discuss the problem, casting our net wider and wider. F. is listening respectfully. Only we can see the laughter ripening under her serious demeanour. The topic draws the women in, it's developing, like a film, as in the cinema. They're already at a loss for vocab, can't follow our hypotheses literally, word for word. We are getting carried away, faster and further. F. listens attentively, head slightly to one side, but I already see what the animated methodologists cannot see – her anguish. "What did he just say?" A fast, hot whisper in my ear. '*My*' woman is tugging at my sleeve, asking me to translate. I'm raising my hand, I have no time, a thought has already ripened – about loneliness. "What did she say?" *Mine* buzzes like an autumn fly. I translate the gist quickly and briefly, so as not to get distracted. "I got that, please, translate in more detail." Good God! I can't do two things at once! Who's the teacher here, for goodness sake?! With a sigh, I begin to interpret simultaneously. She's nodding, nodding. It's my turn, I raise my hand. I jump up. About loneliness. An empty haze in F.'s eyes. "What have you just said?" *mine* asks. I translate. Now, looking around, I see *we* are muttering into *their* ears. F. observes this process with growing interest. We are carried away: back and forth. The bell. The women stand up reluctantly. Pack their empty notebooks. They would gladly carry on listening. They leave, single file, flushed, as in the cinema. B. G. is the last to leave. He had been sitting quietly at the back all lesson. In the doorway, he turns, gives us a devil-may-care wink. Softly, so that it won't be heard in the corridor, he says to us all: "Well Done!!!"

"Overall, not bad, Kostya. Three grammar mistakes. Fedya, tempo, simultaneous translation, good." "Is it true?" Fedya half gets up, "What do you think, why did she keep returning?" "Is it important? They were slicker with these gimmicks in the First School, generally," she smacks her lips as though remembering something tasty. "More erudite. Parallel examples from literature. They would begin all highfaluting, but ended up heaven only knows where…" She snorts with laughter, flapping her hand. We're a bit embarrassed. Looks as though we got carried away. Like the women.

"THOSE BORN
IN THE DEAF YEARS..."[17]

At the beginning of May, before the annual exams, She handed me a sheet of paper with a new cycle – this time, to Massenet's music. Learn it, she said. Meanwhile, she began dance rehearsals. No-one but the participants themselves knew about them, of course, as usual. I found out by chance: stumbled upon their rehearsal. It happened like this. During the last class, F. called me into the corridor; opened the classroom door a crack, apologised, sought me with her eyes. I got up, went out. Tomorrow, 9 am, English delegation, she said. Alert everyone. Iron the costumes today. The costumes are stored in the cupboard in her study. Stuffed in any old how after the show. Nowhere to hang them, taking them home's not an option: delegations arrive out of the blue. Ironing costumes, that's my task. I normally do it just before the performance, standing in her study at the desk at the back, waving the iron about. Her other groups are used to me, pay no heed: iron away, why not. Well, they do notice, of course, just pretend not to: fancy, an actress, ironing! F. stands in front of them as she stands in front of us. But I always think: She chose us. She behaves differently with them. She's kinder to them. More severe with us, and swifter. With both disdain and praise. She looks at them with the tender eyes of a teacher, like B. G.'s group.

I went to her study after class – no longer the blue one. They gave her a study on the same floor as Maman and B. G. The girls arrive a bit later, after

....

17   Poem by Alexander Blok 'Rozhdyonny v goda glukhie'. See discussion of the poem in Afterword, pp. 224-225.

about ten minutes. She lets us pop into the dining hall before rehearsals. She doesn't go herself. I really don't know when she manages to eat. Arrived and paired off. She goes to the record player, switches on some music. I haven't heard this instrument before. Sounds like an upright piano but harsher. The viscous sounds curl like lace, as though someone were knitting, spinning them out from their fingers. Two couples – all girls. The steps are careful, quiet, pointed, not ballet-style. Together, apart, arms like branches, touch palms, briefly, hot. Soundless clap. Left to left, crossing over. "Head back, look straight ahead…" They obey, eyes meeting. Over and over, many times, like sonnets. The needle torments the sound, stretching, weaving the lace. I am forgotten. Happiness. I iron slowly, tracing every seam. Stretching the lacy sounds with the iron. She stops the music. "The ladies should have high hairlines, as though they were trimmed. We'll comb them back. We'll tie the partners' hair back. Don't let your eyes waver." The ladies are Natalia and Lariska. The partners are Marinka and Vera. Slowly, slowly, all fingers and thumbs, I hang the costumes on hangers. Blue, parrot-like, red and white.

They sit at the desks discussing costumes. Lilac, she says. Sharp, narrow neckline, criss-crossed with lace. Double sleeves. The lower sleeve tight, the upper one wide, with slits to the elbow. She shows them in a book. They get up. F. throws a short, impatient glance in my corner. Finished washing, scrubbing, ironing? At this rehearsal, I am no-one. I stuff the iron away, drag my satchel behind me, leave. I'm walking along the corridor. Behind my back, behind her door, *this* music. There, behind my back, they pair off again. There, the most important place on earth. Yet I am not there. If I'm not there, then I shouldn't be. I want to curl up in the corner, bury my face in the blind wall. If not there, then nowhere.

In Year 8, our five minutes of poetry started up again. Anastasia wasn't too keen, but we insisted. Probably rued the day she thought it up. And now she can't really argue with us. Mandelstam, Gumilyov, Petrarch. We consult F., she tips us off. Once Fedya mentioned Yevtushenko. Reads well, F. said. Anastasia warned: correspondent from *Pioneers' Pravda* will come to the next class. It's Gumilyov. "Should we change?" Anastasia asks sweetly, hoping for our cooperation. "Maybe Yevtushenko instead? You like him, don't you? It's not too late." We protest loudly. A week later, Olga Tkachyova brings in the *Pioneers' Pravda*. She is chairman of the pioneer squad's council. They must take notes. A whole article about us. We read aloud. Gumilyov by the by. Just children reading poetry. Apparently, the correspondent got talking to us after the class. Correspondent: "Do you like poetry?" Fedya Alexandrov: "Of course! How can you not love such moving verses: 'No people are uninteresting, their fate is like the chronicle of planets...'[18]?" Fedka's face, a flabbergasted caricature. "What, is she stupid or deaf? I didn't... She never asked! I would never..." Laughter. "Yeah, I always wondered," yells Fedya, "Why the folk they write about in the papers are always such idiots!" "Idiots, yeah – look who's talking! 'Moving verses'!" Slavka yells even louder. "Stop yelling, I'm not deaf! And what's all the fuss about?" Now Anastasia chips in. "Why do you think you look like an idiot there, Fedya? You like Yevtushenko. Why are you getting hung up on the words? Moving. Yes, they are indeed moving." No more ruckus or laughter; now we're hissing like snakes. Usenkova stands up, straightening at her pinny. "Fine. But even if they are good, we didn't say that. And we never will. You are defending her as if you had written this yourself." Now, finally, it's quiet. Olga puts the newspaper aside. We are no longer laughing, shouting or hissing. Anastasia sits like a puffed up toad, all red. We took the article to F. Thought she would be indignant. Just shrugged, disgusted. That was the end of the five-minute poetry readings. Anastasia didn't dare mention them, and we didn't bring them up. A month later, Sergei Ivanovich took over our class. He was Director of Russian Studies.

Sergei Ivanovich is a particular fellow. Shortish, blond, almost always dressed the same. Trousers already shiny. Likes to show severity. But his severity doesn't last long – he's terribly kind. Sergei Ivanovich is in a bit

---

[18]   First line of the poem 'People' by Yevgeny Yevtushenko (1932-2017).

of a conundrum. Director of Russian Studies in an English School – a dubious position. He is Maman's second deputy, after B. G. He shoulders the timetable, which has to be negotiated, as well as all specialist teachers except the English. He strolls through the school smiling. He's on smooth terms with B. G.; their orbits don't collide. No-one ever sees them together except when they are escorting Maman. During Russian lessons, S. I. likes to give vocab dictations. He dictates fast and furiously: be that as it may; never expect help from anyone, anytime; electrification, participate, thrifty... He never repeats. Missed it, didn't hear – your fault. Sergei Ivanovich likes authors who are in the curriculum. Knows a stack of quotes. Teaches us to reply as expected. *For matriculation.* "So you think they are sitting there on the other side of the Neva just waiting for you with open arms?" his epic intro about university. Teaches to answer as one ought: "Toss in the theory, then follow the text." Sasha Guchkov at the board: "Sergei Ivanovich, and then?" S. I. is sitting snugly installed behind the first desk, his usual perch for questioning. "I've already told you, Guchkov, what's not clear? Toss in the theory!" "But I can't just toss it in," Guchkov groans. Laughter slowly bubbles up in our ranks. "What do you mean, you can't toss it in?" S. I. turns to the class indignantly. "Just drop it in, like this: 'Dikoi and Kabanikha are birds of a feather...'"[19] And he gives a large sweep of his hand, tosses his fringe. S. I. never tots up term marks mechanically over the weeks. He just knows who deserves what end-of-term mark. Starts getting ready shortly before the last day. Calls us out one by one if our marks aren't quite up to scratch. Warning: "Beware, test tomorrow. Out of the blue. You're heading for a D. Questions on Blok: "I would forget about courage, winning..."[20] "But Sergei Ivanovich," whinges the one being warned. "Does it have to be *that*? I don't like that poem." "Why don't you like it? Splendid verses!! The pearl of Russian lyricism," S. I. frowns, getting upset for real now. "I want 'Those

---

[19]   Characters from Alexander Ostrovsky's *The Storm.*
[20]   Poem by Alexander Blok 'O doblestyakh, o podvigakh, o slave...'

Born in the Deaf Years," the warned one digs his heels in. "OK," S. I. agrees at once. "This is also a pearl of Russian lyricism. Beware," the conversation restarts as though nothing had happened. "Test tomorrow. Out of the blue. Questions on Blok, 'Those Born in the Deaf Years.' Out of the blue."

An American is on his way to us. Not with a delegation. Alone, in person. He teaches Russian in America. F. warned us in advance. He will take our English group for a whole term. "What about you?" a soft, sorrowful moan from the desks. "I shall sit in. B. G. chose your group. 'For special merits.'" A subtle smile. Thin as a pole. Grey. Wavy hair down to his shoulders. He sits down at the teacher's desk, takes out his tape recorder, introduces himself. In Russian: "My name is Henry Krohman. How about you?" We stand up one by one and introduce ourselves ceremoniously. "You can call me Uncle Henry. That's what my students call me." Lenka speaks up: "That's not how we do it. We usually use the patronymic." "It's easy," Irka encourages. "What is your father's name?" "So," we shout in unison, "It's Henry Karlovich." He's delighted. Says he'll tell his students. In Russia, he had a patronymic.

His Russian is strange. Like walking on stilts. "Any questions have you to me?" We glance at F. She maintains a benign silence. "Henry Karlovich," Fedya, pronounces very distinctly. "What do your students like to read in Russian? Which literary works?" Henry listens hard. "They not so good. It is not enough lessons. Maybe, university, in university. They read *dialogues*," he switches to English. Just one word. Embarrassed, maybe. Then in Russian again: "I have recordings. I will can switch on." Rustling. "Wanya," a girl's brittle voice, stilted Russian. "Where are your waliiiinki felt booooots?" Long silence. "They are on the stove." This is Wanya, sing song voice. Otherworldly, funereal silence. "And what do *you* like to read in English?" We reply. The list is growing. It throws him into a trance. "Then what can I teach you?!" That's the end of his Russian, apparently. "No need," we come to his aid. "We can just chat. Or you can check our retelling." "May I?" F. stands up, comes to the teacher's desk. "I have watercolours by the painter Sadovnikov," she spells out the tricky surname, syllable by syllable. "If you don't object, I will give them to the children, they will tell you about Leningrad's famous buildings.' Henry is beside himself. We are taken aback: unprepared. F. hands round the watercolours. Phew! Something on the back: date of construction, architect. Henry listens. Evidently remembering Wanya in his Walenki-felt boots. "May I?" he addresses F. "I will give all the children top marks." "Please do," F. is the embodiment of hospitality. "Tell me," Uncle Henry cannot contain himself. "The children prepared these narratives in advance, of course?" "I'm afraid," F. replies, "That this is the first time the children have seen these watercolours. In general, it is a pleasure to work with them - no matter what you give them, it will be the first time they have seen it." She speaks in Russian, only for us. Henry doesn't pick up on her jibe. He didn't expect anything of the kind. He thought it would be as it is in America... At the end of the lesson, B. G. pops in, excuses himself, asks how the lesson went. "These children! Such children!" B. G. smiles modestly. Both leave. "Why did he keep going on about valenki felt boots?" We want to discuss this immediately. "Well, not everyone can be such Shakespeare specialists as you are," F. cuts us short. "Some don't read Shakespeare at all. You won't either, when you grow up." F. gathers up her watercolours. Our colourful tales about valenki felt boots are a hit with the other groups. Uncle Henry and his Walenki floor everyone. "And his English is pretty odd, too, kind of, I don't know – throaty," says Fedka. "What's odd about that? Who is he anyway?" "German," Mishka speaks authoritatively. "Why should he be German?" someone defends him. "Who else? Chinese? Krohman. Uncle Karl...And Karl... stole coral from Klara, and Klara stole a clarinet from Kurt." "Wonder where he managed to learn Russian," giggles Slavka. "Bet he was captured, POW at Stalingrad." "Yeah, that's it," nods Fedka. "That's where he found his beloved valenki, the dream of his military youth."

Day after day, Henry Karlovich sits before us. We are already used to it. Him, too. About time to switch to 'uncle.' He records all our lessons on the tape recorder, one after the other. "When I go back to America, I will put them on. Or they won't believe me." We retell, ask questions, compose dialogues. No more showing off – settled into routine. Sometimes Henry asks us to read something to him in Russian. He keeps a special tape for that. His favourite is Blok. Says he will put it on in his classes. Let my students listen to the beautiful Russian language. They won't understand, of course. Too few hours… He doesn't smile. We are sorry for Henry. What kind of life is that – droning on about your Stalingrad valenki year after year?

SEDUCTION SCENE

"Seduction scene," she says. We've already learnt our parts. Kostya is the Duke of Gloucester, I am Lady Anne. Today is the first rehearsal. F is filling us in on what has gone before and what is yet to come. What has gone before is the murder of my husband, Prince Edward. What is to yet come is my wedding. The Duke of Gloucester – she calls him Richard – is thirsty for power. A murderer. I am the means. I am a widow walking behind the hearse. I hate him, I hate my husband's murderer. It's a very dangerous feeling, she says. You must learn to love it. So that everyone will believe you. Gloucester is ugly, a hunchback with a withered arm. I understand this in my own way: the ugliness, hunched back and withered arm must become indiscernible for my weak eyes. I hear in my own way. For you, the girl with the weak eyes, only the voice remains, the doubly sweet voice of an ugly man; the speech remains – the fine, flowing speech of a hunchback; and the mind remains, the keen mind of a man with an arm withered from birth. She is not asking me to forget his wickedness. She is telling me about his death. "A horse! A horse! My kingdom for a horse!" In *Russian* tales it's a half kingdom, but in English chronicles it's a whole one. She gets up and acts it out herself. She is playing his death scene for me, so that I will know why I should *come to love* him, and for what. So there I am, standing and watching. I see a hump growing on her light, fragile body. A contortion, the name of which I don't know, cripples her arm. Her arm jerks upwards, withering. With her voice, booming like a hollow hump, he yells, ripping her mouth. The hump is the mark, the slit for the arc of the arrow you let fly. Ah, the sweetness of aiming at the hated hump. There is nothing sweeter than the fidelity of a villain when the villain is loyal to you alone. Defying the whole world. Meaning you are the world. Now I know why I should love him, and for what. Horror is my final innocence. I will scream this hatred into the eyes of this toad, right into his mocking, deferential eyes. Love in a black body, in a black glove, hunching his hand into a fist. My hands in his hands; in the fingers of a murderer as he plucks the bud. Do you understand what it means when you spit into a man's face? She is speaking to us sternly and seriously.

She has a difficult time with Kostya. It is not easy to teach him to play a villain. He has soft, kind eyes and he looks at me tenderly. This well-mannered, sporty boy must play a limping devil. Only she can succeed here. He walks me home, carrying my schoolbag. It's difficult for her but easy for me. It's easy for me to spit, to love and to hate as I look into his pure, trusting eyes. It's just as well she chose him for me. Had she chosen Fedya instead, I would have been embarrassed. We are going to F.'s place for ten o'clock on Sunday morning; there is not much time left until March when we are staging Richard. A snowy field. Sparse, lanky apartment blocks. We have to walk along a cemented path. The top floor. We're too early. It's twelve minutes to ten. We are standing near the window. Kostya's hands are warm. Mine are icy cold. He always has warm hands and mine are always cold.

She opens the door. We come in timidly. Her perfume. And such a smile! Tender and homely. We take our shoes off, sit down, drink tea to warm up. Biscuits, nuts, raisins, dried apricots: a glowing feast. Are you cold? Pity, I had a bottle of cognac yesterday, I would have splashed a spoonful in your tea. But one of my students came by, from the First English School, and we drank the cognac together. By the way, she looks at me closely, he played Richard. He's a chemist now, about to graduate from the technical institute. She tells us about that other production from the past. She talks of nothing but Richard, not a word about Anne, as though she had died. I am not thinking about anything, just sitting and drinking tea. She is talking to Kostya, and teasing me. No, I am thinking after all. Thinking about how her Richard came, her student from the First. About how she offered him cognac. That means he didn't age, after all. Maybe we, too…

I am yelling and lunging, yelling and lunging, yelling and lunging. She is wincing: "Only stray cats lunge like that. You…" She takes the sword from my hands. "Look." Good lord, how she shouts! Gloucester gets up. Now it's his turn. She touches the tip of the sword where my hands should be. "Then bid me kill myself and I will do it," she says with a sneer spiced with passion. A word in exchange for a life. I know this is my last chance. I cannot see her, but she is there. She is standing next to me, whispering, as if from afar. My very last chance. You only get one chance with evil. You have to throttle it that first time, when it gives you the chance.

A TALE OF DISEASE

Fedya said there are many superb modern authors. Dozens of masterpieces. She said that in all the proceeding centuries, only a few dozen masterpieces had been written. So why should there be such an incredible peak in our lifetime? I can prove it, he says. Bring them. Vasily Aksyonov, for example. "Well, all right, bring it, I'll read." "Well," Fedya hesitates, "You've *already* decided it's no good." "Surely you don't really think I am capable of rejecting a masterpiece just to win an argument with you?" "Ah," Fedya lightens up, now he's sure she will read honestly. "I'll bring you loads of really great books." "How many is 'loads'? Five, ten, a cartload, a wagonload?" He thinks: a cartload. We listen attentively, without laughing. He counts them out: Belov, Voznesensky, Solzhenitsyn... "So you think they will all," she leans on the table with the tips of her fingers. "Still be read in 100, 200, 1000 years?..." "No doubt. They show our time." "If they are in the cart, don't bother, I already know *them*." "They show modern problems, what concerns people of the twentieth century," Fedya is getting heated. "So what is it that distinguishes people of the twentieth century from all others?" "Uncommunicativeness, for example." "Uncommuni-nowhat?" We realize she's teasing. We laugh together, against Fedka. "People don't know how to be with each other, everyone is inside themselves." "A wonderful explanation," she says in all seriousness. "Only I don't understand what is so bad about being inside yourself. Is it better when you go outside and lose yourself? It's utter crap..." She shakes it off her fingers. "But you must agree, it's a problem." "It is not a problem," she cuts him short. "The intelligentsia hold these authors in very high esteem." "Who? I don't understand this word." Her lips are white.

"Intelligentsia." Fedya is at a loss. "Educated people who are interested in everything." "*Every*thing?" Her eyes are dark with fury. "Everything means nothing! Only idiots are interested in *everything*." "But still, everything is… in its own way," Fedya is at a loss faced with such fury, already retreating, tired. F. is standing in front of us, taught as a bow. Looking past Fedya, past us, past … "If they are curious about *everything*, let them satisfy their curiosity *everywhere*, anywhere but where I am." The bell. The lesson didn't even begin today. We leave tired. I think Fedya is brave. I couldn't. I'm also thinking it would have been better if she had proved it to him. Proved it to everybody. And to me. I am walking along the corridor, following my chain of thought. A kind of pain, ache, joints.

The next day I fell ill. Temperature of 39.5. They rub me from head to toe in vodka mixed with vinegar. Tuck the blanket under my chin. Cotton wool walls. Rough, cotton wool sounds. Rubbing against each other. No time to be ill. Rehearsals during the school holidays. I lift my arms out. Dry as a fly's leg. The occasional car rummages around with cockroach whiskers. Big, dry cockroaches. My throat is big and dry. If I speak, it's like Henry Karlovich. He passes by in high white valenki, looking like a partisan. A partisan speaking German… Henry Karlovich smiles: he has a patronymic. I read Blok to him. Because they are both German. *Those born in the deaf years ta ta ta of their, we are children of Russia's frightening years da da da never mind…* I'm heading for top marks. This is not Henry but Sergei Ivanovich who's grilling me, out of the blue: *From the days of war, from the days of freedom, blablabla there are reflections in our faces…* The blanket is flat and heavy. *Let there be above our deathbed…* A withered ball below the ceiling. *Those who are more worthy, O Lord, O Lord…* She will depart now. They enter, rip off the blanket, pour water over me.

Holidays, then the weekend. The district GP doesn't come for a week. I'm already coughing; sitting coughing, lying coughing, sleeping coughing. My ears are deaf, bunged with cotton wool. The GP discerns double pneumonia. Can't cope at home, requires injections six times a day. The ambulance takes me to the children's hospital on Lermontovsky, eight per room. Me and some small kids. They let their mothers visit during the day. Mothers are allowed from 9 – 11. At night, me and the kids are alone, neither doctors nor nurses. The doctors sleep at home, the nurses somewhere in the hospital not far away. During the day, the mothers chat, wash nappies under the tap, hang them on the radiators. The mothers are very busy – never a free moment. Not allowed to take hospital stuff home, not allowed to bring your own things here. Washed-out nappies smell. In the evening, the mothers take turns to come to me, put oranges on my bedside cabinet, oranges I won't eat anyway. The mothers don't know how to just ask. They think it's more sure with an orange. First they were asking, but now they don't, just put them one on top of another, like an orange mound. I will keep an eye on them. They whinge, you understand, it's useless to ask the nurses. I've already been here for a long time. So long that I know in advance. I only have an hour. They'll start crying in an hour. First Fedya. He is nine months old. During the day, they give him intravenous injections. His veins are small, it's easier to inject in the head than in the arm. They find one by the temple.

I climb out of bed and walk. Swaying. Pull him out of the cot. If I put him in bed with me, I might drop off and squash him. He's small and sickly. I walk and walk, back and forth, round the beds, as if at a rehearsal. Now I will put him on mine and sit myself next to him. "Tell me." Little Nadia is waiting, whispering so as not to wake anyone. She and I are adults. She's four. They brought her a week ago. This is already the second week I'm telling her about Shakespearian theatre, about Richard the Third, telling her his story. Sometimes I speak in English. Ask her, 'Do you understand?' She nods, quietly and solemnly. I fall silent, and only then does little Nadia fall asleep. I walk to the mirror, stand in front of it with Fedya in my arms. My face is covered with boils from the injections, little islands, like mould, colonies of mould – neat, greenish-pink. The nurse says I've gone mangy. In the mornings, they smother me with Brilliant Green, like they did my little sister. I know: it is for when there is an infection in the blood. So, me too. Brilliant Green rubs off. Stained pillow, greenish-brown.

Arkady Efimovich said: Little Nadia will be discharged tomorrow. She's stopped coughing. Don't want to leave, she tells him. She cries when he's gone, whispers she won't leave me, she'll stay with me and listen. The mothers gather round her, comforting. You'll see Mummy tomorrow, they repeat their main comfort pitch. This is our last night. Fedya is all cried out. We call him Fedora's Grief.[21] "Yesterday they handed me a letter from her." Little Nadia listens; she knows who it's from. In her letter, she calls me Lily-of-the-Valley. Arkady Efimovich says I'll be discharged in about three weeks. The letter doesn't mention the Day of Theatre. So I understand: no Richard this year. If there is no Richard now, you see, there never will be. If I stay in the hospital, she will not be able to rely on me anymore. She will think I will get sick at any moment; I am unreliable. Little Nadia mutters, falling asleep. I realize something has to be done, but I don't understand what. They come for Nadia in the morning. I go out to say goodbye. "There she is, there she is, the one who was telling me..." What can wordless, healthy Nadia explain? Her mother looks at my frightening hospital face, greenish-pink. And looks away. "Yes, yes, fine, hurry up." Little Nadia turns away, trying to get into her sleeve. She is already forgetting about me, a few more steps and she will never remember. I don't care. Now I know what to do. I have already decided everything. If I start today, it will be over by Monday, one way or another. On Friday, the doctors go home for the weekend. Doesn't matter, he'll be found, they have to find him. When they bring lunch, I turn my face to the wall. I will not touch food any more. The nurse chunters, clearing up. "You're already all mangy. If you don't eat, you'll turn into a freak." Nothing new. I sleep. They are used to me sleeping during the day. The nurse brings supper. Doesn't want to take it back, shakes my shoulder. "I won't eat," I reply without turning my head.

....

21   Reference to a tale by K. I. Chukovsky about a slovenly housekeeper.

Now the nurse on duty comes. Touches my forehead. Why don't you eat? Don't want to.

Lamp above the door, bare wall lamp. Fedya isn't crying. He's already cured, they don't inject his head anymore. I stand up and drag the stool behind me. Put it in front of the mirror. Pull down my shirt, climb up. I stand in front of the mirror and look at myself – all of myself. Scraggy torso, ribs, nipples, collar bones, dark, thin legs. The mirror cuts off my head, they could put any on. It's hard for me to stand, one more day and I won't get up. I am responsible for this body which cannot be relied upon. Boils on my cut-off face. The nurse said they'll disappear before you know it. That means the ribs will disappear, along with the legs and everything else. I won't miss them, won't miss them once they're gone.

Breakfast is taken away again. I'm already unable to get up. My ribs and legs have almost disappeared. I hear them trying to persuade me before they take it away. "Maybe you don't like hospital food? Would you like mine? A cutlet? Shall we call your Mum, get her to bring you lunch?" I don't want *anything* from my mother. Not even my body. They discuss. We should call Arkady Efimovich, she might die. He shows up towards evening. "Why don't you eat? Think I won't find a way? Ever heard of force feeding?" He strokes my hand. To love, someone else is needed, someone kind. I already know that. "I won't eat *anything* in the hospital." "But you might die." "You said, three more weeks. I won't stay that long." Now everyone is listening, listening to how I talk to him. "How long, then?" "'Til Monday. One more day. I'll leave on Monday." She's tired of the kids, the mothers whisper, especially Fedya, he cried every night, she carried him in her arms. "Why didn't you tell me?" He grasps at this straw. "Where were the nurses...? They should have..." He flaps his arms, he's a gentle man, he knows where the nurses were. "I want out." Out, he repeats. He sits and thinks. Thinks for a long time. A glow on his face. A sickly glow. "OK, I'll let you out, set you *free*." He leaves, comes back, hands me a piece of paper. "Here. I signed it. You keep it. I'll come to say goodbye," he says gingerly. He never came. The next day he fell ill and stayed at home. "Arkady Efimovich is a gentleman," laughs the nurse. "Asked me to give you his respects. That's what he said: give her my respects."

A greenish streetlamp over the road, stripes fan out on the snow. The windows are sealed with masking tape for the winter. Smell of nappies from the radiator. I know how to open doors. Victory courses through my veins, the golden juice of the mothers' ripe oranges which I did not so much as touch. I go to the bedside cabinet, pull open the door. Tributes from inconsolable mothers. A mountain they had carried to my bed. Dark fruits on the blanket. Thick-skinned fruits, for my fingers had lost their strength. I dig into the thick skin and tear up the mothers' oranges, grabbing them with my nails. I don't want to look at myself in the mirror. Neither with a baby nor without. Ever. A half orange on my palm, I bring it to me teeth and dive into it. I don't bite, I press and suck. Suck it dry, like a predator, like a Venus flytrap. I suck out my prey so as to toss away the empty skin just as I threw aside my body, dried up and freakish. Yellow juice drips on my hospital gown. Dries into yellow stains. These stains cannot be washed out. A stain on the chest, and on the hem. Yellow. Mother's blood.

I VOUCH FOR YOU...

One week before her death she granted me unimaginable grace. She was sitting on the sofa that day, leaning back on the pillow. I was sitting nearby on a small bench, exactly as I usually did when we were discussing our own affairs. This conversation, however, was special. It didn't jump from topic to topic as had become the norm over the last years we shared. She had called for me that day. The topic held us in its grip, swallowing all our energy: tormented us and sapped our strength. We needed to reach an agreement about a certain matter, and we two were the only ones who could. Afterwards, we were sitting, smiling fondly at each other, when she suddenly suggested I ask her *anything*. She said she would reply to anything, anything I asked. She knew what she was doing. She had confidence in me, just as I had in her. She would have replied, but my lips didn't open. I shook my head, and she smirked. She knew when to bestow gifts. Perhaps, had she shown me this grace the day before, before our conversation, I would have asked her about many things. For example, *did she know in advance* that by making her children the best she was also making them the very worst, the best and the worst simultaneously. As if she were swinging the pendulum, tossing it so high that, swinging back, it would inevitably reach the highest point, or more precisely, the lowest one. She was no nanny, but a doula, dragging good and evil out with forceps. She found it out herself, later.

Or maybe I would have reminded her about the story of the nymph Thetis who I secretly and illicitly considered her predecessor. Herself immortal, she strove to make her child immortal, too. Otherwise, why did she put him to the test of time's fire, a fire which would inevitably consume him? Not having so much as a single iota of faith in her own immortality, surely she did not believe in its divine power? If a child is tested during long nights and fed during the day with the ambrosia of special, *innermost* knowledge, you can make him invulnerable, rip out time's sting, save and preserve him. How many times did victory seem within her grasp, yet the heel which she held between her fingers was always jerked from her hands by a force alien to her: parental love, natural and undemanding. And the child who had gulped immortality trod the common path leading to death. Worse than that, another mortal child, burnt by the proximity of the immortal, would later turn to this world with only malice and contempt.

At the first rehearsal, our scene was hellishly bad. She stands toying with the pointer as if it were a handle, stony-faced. She let us play it out, didn't interrupt: ominous omen. White, tortured lips. "We don't have much time. We have to recreate it, starting from the beginning." During the week, she rehearses Henry, Macbeth, dance, my new sonnets. A cycle about love. Only about love. I don't like this cycle. Richard is on Sundays, as usual. During the week Kostya plays Prince Harry, the tavern scene.

On Sunday Kostya brings a velvet camisole. She sits on the sofa, stroking the velvet. Small hand on black chasing the nap. Black, grey – colour obeys her hand. Anne follows the coffin – deep mourning, of course, but nevertheless we'll make light – light turquoise. Black and sky blue. She draws a sketch: high bodice, slit sleeves. The neck is open, narrow décolleté, white fabric under the cuts. Inner sleeves tight, hugging the arm. At home, I rummage in my mother's stores. Buttons, press-studs, old beads. There is a reel of long Czech thread, father brought it from *that* trip. Mother sacrifices it without a word: pneumonia. No old sheets. Gleaming turquoise satin from Gostiny Dvor. Bodice, high gathered waistband, stomacher of white guipure lace. Satin, of course, not velvet, but has to be folded on one side. I embroider the waistband, round and round. The cuts are bound by pearl beads.

I don't want to go to the polyclinic. Sonnets, costumes, Richard – no time for physiotherapy. Our scene comes together quickly. Sometimes I feel weak. Remnants of the illness roaming around inside. I keep it at bay so she won't notice. My face is clean, the scabs disappeared on the second day. Only weakness remains. I hold onto the window ledge, as I did in the hospital. I turn around. Kostya two steps away. He looks away, averts his eyes. I am waiting. The eyes return. Grey from the grey courtyard, as though she had stroked her hand over the nap. Were it not for this weakness, I would have understood without words. He is waiting for me to understand. My eyes grow dark, blacken, going against the nap. "You are so beautiful," he is saying. "So light, so weightless, so weak, especially now, standing at the window after your illness." I am waiting quietly and attentively. He is saying: "I love you." This is smoothed velvet, a tender, greyish sheen. Said, and waiting. How can I reply to *these* words if, every Sunday, I hear other words, words which make my heart sink, burst? Those words are roaming in my blood, and he doesn't know what else is there. My blood is hospital-coloured – the colour of the yellow juice. Other words are in me, those immortal words for the sake of which I rose from my wretched hospital bed, and turned away from my wretched body. But for my knees, I would have come to him and said, yes, I love you. Just like *these* sonnets. I could have said it easily, for love is something else. Love is her, and not him.

The Day of Theatre dawns. The night before, terrible weakness. Was ironing the turquoise dress. White underskirt, white shoes, white hoop for the head. Hair will be loose. She wants it that way, so it flies. In the morning, I cannot open my eyes. Must think it through. Slowly and carefully. If I let on, they won't let me. If I go – pneumonia. Again. Hospital. Injections. Kids. I prop myself up on my elbow. Her. Richard. What did you mutter in front of the hospital mirror? Let those fear, those who fear death.

She is looking at me. I came to hang up the costume. If she hadn't noticed, I wouldn't have let on. She is saying: "We should push the chairs together in the corner. You lie down, and stay there until the performance." She doesn't suggest I go home. Doesn't offer a choice. Groups come one after the other, changing lesson after lesson. Furtive glances into my corner, eyeing the costume. If I am lying there, that is how it should be. She leads her lessons in a quiet voice, almost a whisper. They reply even more quietly. Leave on tiptoe. In the breaks, she comes. Puts her palm on my forehead, shakes her head. I prop myself up on my elbow, lean into her. Last lesson. Now I have to dress up. Now everybody will come. I get up, leaning on one arm, crawl out from the chairs. She gives me a long look. No trace of tenderness. Calm and collected. She looks at me from afar for the last time. At my temperature, at my forehead, at my birdlike weakness. They will be no more, because I shall be no more. There will be Lady Anne, Lady Macbeth, Richard, Falstaff, Prince Harry. She will look at us as she looks at herself. No tenderness when one looks at oneself.

I see only the back. Long, narrow. Shirt down to the floor, enveloping the feet. Long arm, long fingers. In the hand, a candle burning in a heavy candlestick. Slowly lowered to the floor. Lady Macbeth wipes out the stains, scrubs the blood, focussed. Clock strikes. It's time, with a quiet, firm voice. Hell is murky! What is there to fear? Surely a soldier isn't afraid? The narrow back straightens, perplexed. The palm opens like a weak flower. Who would have thought the old man could have so much blood! Puts her hand to her face, sniffing, sniffing the rotting smell, rotten blood… Mustn't scream. Must be quiet. A scream would terrify the fearful. Voice hoarsening. Banquo is dead. What's done is done. I close my eyes. Mustn't look anymore. Otherwise I can't do – mine.

They pass me, one after the other. Into their scene. I don't listen to their voices, try not to listen. Bursts of laughter. Different laughter, not like last year. She did it differently. She doesn't have to catch them any more. Before, we were for them; now, they are for us. They tumble into the wings, faces on fire. Distant, estranged eyes. Kostya is smiling the smile of the prince, looking past me. Marinka's white teeth, the predatorial teeth of a tavern keeper, head thrown back, hand pressed against her scarlet dress. I see what is left in their faces…Red reflection.

First bars from her corner. I am ready. Empty inside. I am speaking to them, convincing, exhorting, speaking about glorious love with the tender voice she used. About the glorious love which I don't know, about the sweet one stepping over the earth.[22] Maybe young Lady Anne stepped like that because she loved the husband whose coffin she followed – in rage, in turquoise, in pearls. I want to be different, sniff my rotting hands, console my soldier, hang his soul with my stained hand, but I shouldn't frighten them. I console them all, speaking again and again of the tenderness I don't believe in. Folding my hands at the last bar, I grant them my empty heart. They believe me because they want to be consoled. She ordered me to console them.

We stand, bowing. My knees bent, head lowered. Empty. Eyes won't be dazzled. I look right into Maman's perplexed face. She applauds, arms outstretched. B. G's eyes are shining, spellbound. I turn to Kostya. Give him my hand. He looks at me with tenderness, looks into my empty eyes. The body returns. Pain in my back, calves trembling. The ceiling is as high as the sky. They hang in clusters from the gallery. Nobody cares about my illness, his love, or that I can throw off my body like a shell. We leave, go to the first row. Slow harpsichord. Two couples, hand in hand, light and beautiful. Two pinkish dresses, two pinkish capes. Maman calms down, consoled, smiling at the lightness and beauty. Step back, bow. Hands touching, momentarily, precisely, swiftly, like breathing in and out. Here, slowly melting, there a little faster, like short sparks. Simultaneous slow and fast: slow wrist, fast fingers touching. Maman is wrong to be consoled: this is not a dance; it is something for which I know no name. Neither men nor women, moving and not moving, touching and parting. Empty eyes, dancing in emptiness. The harpsichord doesn't fill the space: there is neither passion nor melancholy nor

....

22   Veiled reference to Sonnet 130:
I grant I never saw a goddess go;
My mistress, when she walks, treads on the ground:
And yet, by heaven, I think my love as rare
As any she belied with false compare

pain. Angelic touches, angelic backs and faces. Only the chains connecting the eyes are not yet angelic – don't let go, don't come undone. The sore emptiness of departing pain, all but gone. Last wave of the hand, heads turn and look away. I shoot a furtive glance. Maman applauding, delighted. In her palms, joyful relief – it all ended well. With pink beauty.

I walk along the embankment. Still light. People come towards me – men, women, children. Drawing level with me, they raise their eyes to me, surprised. That's right. No-one at home. I go to the bathroom, the mirror. Good God, I forgot to wash it off! Thick layer of white powder, like chalk. Thick black stripes over the eyelids. Blue shadows up to the brows. No wonder they looked… I was walking along the embankment as Thetis! I laugh, turning on the taps, guffaw, scooping water. Rub the face with the towel, check: reddened cheek, reddened eyelids, joyful eyes. No temperature whatsoever. No trace. Nothing. I laugh: no more hospital, no more injections, no more mothers' kids. Unfailing medicine, marvellous medicine, true medicine.

My parents did not attend the Day of Theatre. Dad was away on business, Mum at her accountancy course; she goes four times a week. Kostya's parents were there, I didn't see them but he said they came. On Sunday, Lyubov Georgievna calls my mum. They talk for a long time. I don't eavesdrop, do my homework. A week later, the parents meeting. My Mum has a course again, but she skips it. Returns pleased.

On Monday F. keeps me after class. I sit at my desk, she sits opposite. Brows knit, voice calm: "Kostya's parents came to me, talked about you." Stops me with her hand. "They are worried about your relationship. Only the highest respect for you. I wouldn't permit otherwise." I see her mouth quiver momentarily. "Kostya's father said he spoke to Kostya. Said whatever happens, it's *always* the man's responsibility. He said he and the mother have nothing against friendship." But the children are already grown up, so they asked F. to observe, and have a tactful word if necessary. Again, a momentary quiver of the mouth. "I told them I vouch for you. They accepted my guarantee, saying, in that case, they have nothing to worry about. Then your Mum came and asked me to make sure," something changes in her voice, "That you eat before rehearsals." "What am I supposed to eat?" I think she will hit me now. "Anything – bread, salad, cutlets – anything I could eat if I didn't spend all my time with you, from morning until night. Your Mum said you leave home without breakfast. I promised her to keep tabs, but to *you* I say: I don't have and never will have time to take care of your lunch. I am not a mother. But if I find out you have come to rehearsal hungry, I'll suspend you. Do you understand me?" Not a mother. I understood.

It's not up to me to judge whether the sheen still shone in my eyes. Maybe not, possibly because there was nothing special left in my classmates' eyes. Everything as before: foreign delegations, home reading. The sharp transition from Richard to parental concerns was gradually forgotten. We were busy with a new DDPE initiative which the school administration launched into with particular enthusiasm. A series of KVN's[23] dedicated to the Republics of the Union. The DDPE hoped to kill two birds with one stone: to introduce school children to the ethnography of the USSR's nations, but to do this in a jolly and resourceful way. Our parallel Year 8 classes – a and b – got Kazakhstan. We scoured the library for Kazakh verses, which, incidentally, needed no jolly or resourceful intervention on our part: they were already ideally suited to decorate any KVN. The DDPE ladies probably had not counted on this. KVN homework called for daily rehearsals. They passed cheerily and haphazardly, with analogous results. There were no *real* rehearsals. F. looked tired. No talk of Theatre Day, as if it didn't exist. She was indifferent to the KVN rehearsals, stifled any

---

[23] KVN - 'Klub vesyolykh i nakhodchivykh' or 'Club for the Witty and Ingenious,' a live TV show in which teams compete by responding wittily to the host's questions and performing funny sketches. Although KVN teams were usually taken from schools and colleges, the game became a huge Soviet social phenomenon, one of the longest running TV shows. Launched in 1961, KVN was suspended in 1972 due to censorship concerns, but took to the airways again after Perestroika, in 1986. More recently, Boris Yeltsin and Vladimir Putin have both attended KVN games.

mention of them with aloof calm. We rarely saw each other. She arrived earlier, did not make an appearance in the dining hall. Left straight after her classes. During the breaks, she stayed in her study, locking it from inside, and didn't set foot in the staff room. She limited socializing with her colleagues to a polite 'hello' and 'goodbye.' Even these brief greetings, it seems, demanded a strength she didn't have. Because – and I noticed this for the first time – she accompanied them with slight bows, an excuse to hide her eyes. As if she were bowing to emptiness. She only made an exception for Andrei Nikolayevich, the English language teacher, who had appeared in our school at the end of September and, having readily responded to her invitation, played Falstaff in Henry IV. In his thirties, he seemed to be a man of no age.

He took our group for technical translation. Despite his extensive technical experience, he liked it even less than we did. We would come up with such pearls as 'naked train conductor running along the carriage' instead of some more befitting electro-technical terms. After laughing with us, he would put aside technical wisdom, leaving it up to our homework conscience. Meanwhile, freed from the ridiculous necessity to broadcast about conductors and semi-conductors, he would produce some book and read aloud some modern writer. He was particularly fond of Fazil Iskander. Unlike F., Andrei Nikolayevich held some modern writers in high esteem. Nevertheless, since he ranked second in our hierarchy, authors loved by him were automatically placed below authors loved by her. Generally, you could strike up a conversation about anything with Andrei Nikolayevich without fearing harsh, disdainful rebuffs. About lunches, for instance, or about KVN. We had but to ask him for help compiling our KVN assignment, and he would join in at once with university enthusiasm. We wrote our famous harem scene together. At the preview, B. G. and our form teacher – who blazed red at the mere sight of Andrei Nikolayevich – laughed until they cried. All laughed out, B. G. *asked* us not to include this scene in the programme.

Andrei Nikolayevich was not like a teacher. In the four years between graduating from university and appearing in our school, he had worked as a translator abroad. Extremely portly, yet quick and energetic, he sported a full, thick beard, never-before-seen foreign jackets, a diplomat-style briefcase full of new books which he bought up in incredible quantities on a daily basis, and a huge golden ring with a black stone on the ring finger of his right hand. Initially, F. never missed a chance to poke fun, mercilessly, at his habit of mentioning his business abroad, his omnivorous taste in books. However, the touching admiration with which he treated her from the very first day worked its charm. Her jokes became kinder, all the more so since, once he noticed the target of her humour, he, too, began laughing at himself, and then suddenly explained that his frequent mentions of his life abroad were simply due to his scant life experience. "What else do I have to remember but university and my time abroad? That's all I've seen. As for books.... Even as a child I dreamt of collecting my own library. Guilty as charged – I like to have a book in my hands." This was accompanied by such a mischievous wink that F. laughed heartily. On a par with us, he obeyed her directorial indications unquestioningly. Not immediately, I admit, but after a decisive conversation; she interrupted the rehearsal, invited him to step out of the classroom. And he became a magnificent Falstaff, the best I ever saw.

Status quo was finally established. By spring, they would often leave school together and take long walks in the city. Having left us to our KVN rehearsals and parental care, she discussed her further theatrical plans with him. To outsiders, they made an unusual couple. He corpulent and heavy, but walking next to her with a light, wide gait. He, gesticulating enthusiastically, as though reinforcing his developing thought with slightly tipsy, exaggerated gestures. She small, like a little sparrow, walking on sharp stilettoes a half step ahead, listening to him with respectful interest. From time to time she would throw in a phrase and the conversation would change direction. Sometimes she spoke herself, and then her gestures became precise and free, as at rehearsals, and her feet carried her away to most unexpected places.

Once she climbed a park bench; in another instance, she deliberately climbed a ramp, re-appearing in a jiffy atop a stone dome where she finished her monologue.

As is usually the case among a predominantly female workforce, their relationship did not go unnoticed and soon led to rumours. Rumours circulated among the teachers. (I firmly exclude Maman, B. G., Sergei Ivanovich and our female maths teacher.) The women who taught the younger classes set particular store by these rumours, as did certain English teachers who were not privy to the more significant events of school life. As for us – and I stress this – we did not gossip. Our attitude towards F. ruled out conjecture of any kind, and that automatically extended to include anyone drawn into her orbit. Echoes of this gossip must have reached F. and Andrei Nikolayevich: some female teachers excelled in tactless teasing. However, both he and she treated the ladies' out of place jibes with slight disdain, a disdain which stemmed from their broader and bitterer experience of contempt – the inevitable experience of those deaf years. They never touched upon this themselves, out of a refined sense of tact, but on occasion – admittedly only when F.'s strength had returned – they might allow themselves to let their hair down and brazenly play along with the gossipers. Once, after leaving school, they were heading towards Theatre Square when they noticed Valeria Pavlovna coming towards them, just where the canal bends. They exchanged glances – by then they understood each other without words – slowed their steps and, standing on tiptoe, F. tenderly adjusted his scarf. The changed face disappeared round the bend, and they laughed for a long time, clutching the cast iron railings. Sometimes they visited the tiled bakery to drink coffee with shortbread, but they each paid for themselves. They didn't visit each other. The walks they both enjoyed sometimes stretched into the evening, and as he put F. on the tram to her house from Moscow Gate at dusk, A.N. would exclaim: "To the opera house, Cabby!" and F. would laugh and wave to him from behind the tram's glass window. Maybe it was thanks to this humour in their conversations that

F. was able to regain her strength after that monstrous, fruitful tension in which she held herself and us during rehearsals. Their discussions ranged far and wide, and, with the same lightness with which they exchanged jokes, she could easily and directly reply to his questions, all the more so since his questions were simple. I can easily imagine these light and natural transitions because, to some extent, Andrei was my predecessor. Or more precisely, the predecessor I knew personally. The comparison is somewhat strained since our common connection to her was not a sense of humour: she invariably denied me this, despite the fact that, with the years, I did learn to joke in her presence in a way which made her laugh. In her talks with Andrei, on the other hand, F. was to some extent *my* predecessor because, as soon as I finished school, I married him. I mention this merely for the sake of correctness, since it is the purest case of genuine transfer of affection.

The parents needn't have worried, neither mine nor Kostya's. The fear which sent them down the wrong track led to a dead end, and the track was not left by my footprints. My dead end is different. I never loved anyone else as I loved her. I loved her always, and it was she herself who, one week prior to her death, found the only possible way out of this dead end, having changed the signature on the back of *that* postcard. The new signature unified her hard, Judaic arrogance with Hellenistic enlightened insight into various kinds of love. This way out was born of my suffering, of my life-long love. However, if I might *really* look back, i.e. look at it *historically*, then this unification poses no paradox: the Judaic and Hellenistic traditions were two equally potent sources of Christianity. In the historical sense, these sources merged when the time came. She, however, did not secure time's support. "If I ever decide to be baptised, you will be my godmother." That is what she said to me once, in all seriousness, about a year before her death. Even now I dare not name this phrase, uttered out of tenderness, in anticipation of possible events. She slipped it under my tongue like a dry sour cherry. But it was no dungball from the steppe where she had tricked her untrickable Granny; this was a real dry sour cherry, dried out under Allah's sun.

Nevertheless, who in their right minds could keep a straight face listening to my speculations about people's passions? They would say: shame it turned out like that, but, hand on heart, what way out did you have, except your paltry plays, your passionate and fruitless acting, and that means – step aside. It's not for you, little actress, to debate the origins of Christianity. Know your place – your actor's place lies beyond the church yard, beyond the consecrated ground of the cemetery. You were and still are a freak, an ugly daughter, and we don't give a damn about how you peer in the mirror searching for some likeness to your sworn *mother*. Yeah, yeah, I nod, it is not hard for me to bow my head before the people's court. This court does not have the final word, and even if it did, I would have said: your fingers, beating in applause, always end up sticking into the sky[24] as soon as your palms are parted. Your fingers do not know brief brushes with unbearable emptiness.

· ·

[24]   Russian expression meaning 'to get it wrong, make a mistake.'

BANISHED FROM PARADISE

In the spring, radio voices[25] began broadcasting Solzhenitsyn's "Gulag Archipelago." Father listened to chapter after chapter, pressed up to the horribly howling receiver. I was busy with my own things and did not pay any attention to this event of course, but the foreigners who became more frequent in our school with the approach of spring mercilessly drew us into conversations about Solzhenitsyn, wanting perhaps to enlighten us. At a loss in the face of their persistence, we turned to F. Without proffering her own opinion, she suggested an evasive answer: we haven't read that work by Solzhenitsyn. I cannot say for sure whether F. discussed Solzhenitsyn with B. G., but despite his generally responsible and cautious attitude towards politics, he did not brief us on this matter. Even if he was tempted to do so, he happily suppressed it, out of a sense of self-preservation, perhaps: by that time, we were already privileged, so to speak, and had he unleashed a political discussion, he would have been forced to conduct it in earnest, which, considering our political foolhardiness coupled with his rich life experience and respectful attitude towards us, could lead could lead everyone into the rough. An intelligent man and a Jew, how could he not have been on Solzhenitsyn's side?

Political discussion cropped up nevertheless. With the physics teacher, though, oddly enough, who took upon herself the thankless task of saving our souls. Lyudmila Petrovna was a well-built, resolute woman, kind and decent in the womanly way: a good housewife, responsible mother and a

....

[25]   Veiled reference to Voice of America, BBC etc. which began broadcasting into the Soviet Union.

devoted wife. When she was young – in our time she was around forty – she became a Komsomol enthusiast, responding to the Party's cry to join the Virgin Lands Campaign, and for the rest of her life, she loved to reminisce about that romantic time. Fedka triggered the conversation. He just raised his hand and announced that his Grandparents listened to the radio every day with rapt attention – chapters from the new book by Solzhenitsyn – and they say it's all true. Lyudmila Petrovna listened well-meaningly and began to reply along the lines of: this is not the whole truth, and as such, not quite the truth, because Solzhenitsyn throws the baby out with the bath water. This baby was the enthusiasm of the Soviet people, which has no historical analogues, and which allowed us – and this is how she put it: "us" – to complete the industrialization of the country, win the unprecedented war, and successfully realize our grandiose post-war goals. At this point, Irka began hissing in my ear: what, can you successfully realize without realizing...? Fedya stuck to his guns and gave other examples, remembered from snippets of Solzhenitsyn. In the end, they each stuck to their guns. Although they did allow each other to express themselves freely – Fedya by simply asking the question, Lyudmila Petrovna by joining in so frankly. To us, Fedya's position seemed a strong one: his grandparents were behind it. In other words, he was talking not so much on his own behalf as on behalf of those who would be horrified by his wagging tongue. Their recollections were as personal as Lyudmila Petrovna's experience of the Virgin Lands Campaign, and that is why their discussion went beyond the confines of a debate between teacher and inexperienced pupil. We sat, agog, following the contortions of their discussion, which was, in some sense, a discussion between the generations. Lyudmila Petrovna did not try to deny the grandparents' tragic experiences. She said frankly, yes, that happened, but you shouldn't forget the other side of the coin. Details of the discussion did not leave the confines of the physics lab. The Administration was busy with KVNs, which were going ahead full steam in all classes, as well as with the new American teacher who appeared in our school; in keeping with the newly-established tradition, he was attached to our group.

The appearance of Stanley Lavrentevich (his father was Laurence, the rest is a technicality) did not bode anything political. He appeared in our group just as meekly as the memorable Henry Karlovich, although, unlike his predecessor, from the very first day he startled us almost more than we did him. For Stanley spoke incredible Russian. When, well-oiled, we recited long chunks of Shakespeare, Marlowe and English classical ballads, he replied with huge passages from Dostoyevsky. Compared with Henry Karlovich and his Walenki and the other foreign guests' tralala in Russian, Stanley seemed phenomenal. Unlike Henry, who now seemed a rather comic figure, Stanley didn't bother to check our homework; having evidently decided once and for all that *such children* do not require petty chaperoning, he delved instead into linguistic subtleties worthy of any university lecture theatre. F. had initially sat at the back desk as usual, but now she joined in the discussions more often, so our lessons gradually developed into a dialogue between them. We followed their twists and turns with genuine delight. Her purest English pronunciation and his energetic American braided into delicate designs, complimenting and contradicting each other. Their friendship and mutual admiration were blooming before our eyes; very soon, both F. and Stanley felt light and free enough to allow themselves jokes, which were initially aimed at their differing pronunciation. Stanley liked to show F. photographs of his family – wife and two children, snapped against the backdrop of a magnificent house – and several times, always in the presence of B. G., he fished for an invite to her home. F. painted this scene for us: B. G. would turn both his eyes and the conversation aside. In such cases, F. would smile at Stanley and he wisely smiled back. For our benefit, F. gaily painted an image of Stanley's impossible visit to her little one-roomed flat. "Please, do come in. Yes, the flat is small, but comfortable, five rooms." And she counted the doors: front door, toilet door, bathroom door, kitchen door and door to the balcony. It was twenty years before Stanley made it to her flat.

A. N., an enthusiastic supporter of enlightenment (incidentally, he saw F.'s work as nothing but enlightening) suggested we take Stanley on tours of places connected with Dostoyevsky. He himself joined us on these walks. We scaled the stairs in the footsteps of Rodion Raskolnikov, which led us to the door of the old moneylender hag, and read the idiotic graffiti left by those who had been here before us: Rodion was here. Or discussed how well Fedka would have suited the role of Raskolnikov: light chestnut hair, greyish eyes, his blazer the colour of a greatcoat, collar turned up. Fedka strained every nerve, threatening to kill the old hag, and, following the text, he counted the steps down to the one under which Rodion Raskolnikov kept his sharp axe hidden. Once we went out in search of the Marmeladovs' flat. Two local *muzhiks*,[26] very Dostoyevskian (Stanley went into raptures at the sight of one of them: "Oh, Russia hasn't changed at all, essentially!"), readily gave a knowledgeable reply about the sought-after flat. Stanley experienced a period of well-earned happiness, the crowning glory of many years of painstaking Russian studies, an apotheosis he never dreamed of attaining. Our group switched freely from Russian to English and back and Stanley felt as though he were in linguistic paradise, where the lion lies down with the lamb.

In short, we became friends with Stanley for the time being, not noticing that B. G. followed him like a shadow, albeit smiling and bashful. After a month, F. kept us back after class and announced: the DDPE had issued a warning to B. G. and he had warned her. It had become known via certain channels that, due to the nature of his activities, Stanley was connected to a Western publishing house which distributed anti-Soviet literature on the territory of the USSR. The DDPE expected Stanley to set up *distribution* right in our very school. The highly experienced DDPE ladies reckoned he would mostly likely begin by leaving it around in the bathrooms, otherwise why would they force poor B. G. to follow him even there? F. gave a snide snigger at this point but immediately returned to her serious tone: "Can you imagine how ridiculous... Especially since Stanley knows full well I cannot

....

[26]   Muzhik – a term for a rather rough, tough man.

fail to notice *how* Boris Grigoryevich is present. In short, I want you to know about it so that you won't look like complete idiots, should anything happen." Stanley joked in class, utterly oblivious. F. sat behind our backs, and only the blind wouldn't have noticed her ominous, polite silence as she looked away without replying to his jokes. The daylight lamps buzzed. We stood up and sat down, folding our hands neatly. After a week, a suffering look appeared in his eyes. She didn't go to the dining hall but handed him over to B. G. during lunch break. Stanley left without looking back. After another week, F. told us to come after class – all of us. Yesterday Stanley had come to her asking to have a talk. He said he could not understand what had happened. "Perhaps he… tactlessness, not deliberate… a foreigner, some things cannot be understood, not even from Dostoyevsky…" "Mr. Moor," she cut him short. "When do you intend to hand out your books to the children?" She asked, and he understood this in itself was mercy. "I must warn the children, you see, they don't expect it, they have grown fond of you. The children will bring the books to me and I will have to *rake over* this story. You do, of course, understand the phrase 'rake over'? I will not rake it over, so I will have to resign, leave my rehearsals, leave *everything*." "Good God! Surely you can't think I would do *this* to our children? Did I ever so much as…?" "To my children," she said inexorably. "You only need to give the command and I shall leave at once," he said. "I'll tear up the contract. I could never have imagined I would love our… your children so much. I've never been so happy." "So you will leave but B. G. and myself will stay and will have to answer *questions* regarding your premature departure?" she was asking tenderly, replaying the frightening scene for us under the bars of the daylight lamps. "No, I'll stay. You can be sure: I will never harm either you or the children." "As you please," she replied indifferently. He continued to take classes. During lesson-time F. invariably and politely joined in conversations on language. The shadow of B. G. returned to its owner. Stanley walked the school alone. I scrutinized his face and back. They were the face and back of a man banished from paradise.

After his departure, B. G. said to her and she to us, that Stanley had left all his books in his hotel, that he had "forgotten" them in his room, but at the time I was unable to determine the truth of it all. Twenty years later, Stanley wrote F. a postcard from China where he was teaching in some run-of-the-mill college, having retired on his American pension. The postcard said he would love to see her on the way from China to America. Either out of extreme politeness or out of mere curiosity, she agreed to receive him. Without so much as batting an eyelid, he surveyed her flat and began enjoying the conversation. They talked in English: Stanley had managed to thoroughly forget Russian. Overcoming her illness, the seriousness of which he never did notice, she offered him rationed buckwheat porridge and listened to the difficulties of his post-Russian life. After he left, she said to me: "Stanley has become old." I easily figured it out: it only takes twenty years to become an old man once you are banished from paradise.

After the departure of the foreigner who had been thrust upon him, B. G.'s eyes now shone with genuine tenderness when they turned to us. This was his expression when he asked us to extract a kind of preview or sample programme from the Kazakh KVN, something which could be served to *special* guests. These guests were appearing in our school with almost the same regularity as the foreign delegations, and, as B. G. tactfully and tentatively put it, were also worthy of *some* concert. We recognized them without any prompting, by default, so to speak. Portly ladies in dark crimplenes and light blouses, and skinnier men in grey suits with faces to match. Straight out of a pedagogical handbook. We prepared a programme, replacing some quips too short for A. N.'s tastes with ones we all thought were dumber, thereby learning an excellent and far-reaching lesson: the dumber the joke, the more genuine the laughter of the eminent guests. Our imitation of a cotton-gathering harvester roused special delight (or guffaws to put it simply, like the guffaws in her first Theatre Day): Sashka Guchkov grabbed Slavka by the legs and this pair paced the stage pretending to gather cotton. Utterly sick and tired of the KVN, we were particularly amused by the prophetic onset of the formal intro:

We gather again for the KVN
In truth and not in jest.
We parted early and in haste
But we're back and shall return!

So it 'returned' for the last time in the spring of Year Ten, just as *that* story was at its height. Having grown up in an atmosphere of unfaltering and absolute responsibility, it never entered our heads to refuse. I remember our deadened voices singing out jolly Kazakh couplets under the usual guffaws of the eminent audience.

I told my parents I wanted to enrol in drama school. I remember clearly, I said "want to" not "intend to:" prior to a conversation with her, I would never dare *intend*. But that conversation never came about. Even so, my mild announcement threw my parents into a panic: it could hardly have been worse had I announced I wanted to become a road sweeper. My parents didn't associate with actors. The only representative of the theatrical world they knew was our neighbour, Vladimir Pavlovich Belyavsky, but they saw him every God-given day. Vladimir Pavlovich held a diploma in theatrical directorship: in his day, he had graduated from the institute on Mokhavaya Street. Now he is unemployed and lives on an invalid's war pension from the Great Patriotic War[27] Vladimir Pavlovich liked to speak of his deeds on the battlefield, although rudimentary calculations proved that at the time military action ceased, he was barely sixteen years old. In short, a battle-weary son of the regiment. Of course, it is unlikely any of his neighbours read his medical records, but Vladimir Pavlovich's lifestyle alone was enough to make one think he was no invalid at all but a parasite and swindler. From time to

---

[27] I.e. World War II.

time he led theatre workshops in Houses of Culture, but was invariably and swiftly kicked out, so during the quite prolonged periods when he had no other audience, Vladimir Pavlovich deigned to broadcast to his communal flat neighbours, having caught them unawares, i.e. in the kitchen. I remember him well, standing under a painted wooden shelf where his pans stood with schizophrenic accuracy: in strict ranks, handle to handle. For a while, these stories saved Vladimir Pavlovich from communal cleaning duty: none of the neighbours dared bung such a big cheese in the communal rota. And so it was, until he committed a terrible – you could say 'fatal' – blunder, after which he was exiled from the communal Olympus. In our flat, there was a phone which stood in the hallway. In the evenings, when his natural God-given audience had crawled into their rooms, Vladimir Pavlovich liked to talk. Dialling the number and pronouncing the quite familiar greeting, he would sit on the stool, closing the flaps of his dirty aristocratic dressing gown, and begin his discourse on modern theatre. Sometimes he paused, waiting for his interlocutor to comment, and would then continue with renewed inspiration: Belyavsky's interlocutors were notable for their respectful brevity. The fact that the phone was occupied for a long time annoyed the neighbours. Nobody else could have got away with it, but, for now, Vladimir Pavlovich was Jupiter. That all changed, however when, unexpectedly, my mother overturned the coat stand. Or in other words, got held up in the hallway for several additional minutes. Paying no heed to her, Vladimir Pavlovich dialled the number. Mother automatically counted the number of digits. Instant insight gave her free rein, and, for the first time in the history of this communal flat, she scolded Vladimir Pavlovich, and not a simple: get off the phone, others need it, but a sharp-tongued observation: No need to sit here for evenings on end talking to yourself! Caught in the act, Vladimir Pavlovich was dumbstruck. With a Roman gesture, he closed the flap of his dressing gown, put the receiver on the hook. From that day on, nothing could spare the fallen Jupiter from cleaning the communal areas. These events sealed my mother's opinion of the life of theatrical figures. My father's opinion on this matter rested fairly and squarely on his absolute certainty (the source of which was unknown to me) that all actors and actresses were, without exception, utterly amoral. His notions regarding these more often than not unhappy folk went beyond both Greek and Roman norms, firmly establishing themselves in the Middle Ages. With an intrepid hand, my father tossed them beyond the limits of any ground sanctified by God or man. My parents' opinions converged unconditionally on one point: actress and director are apples from the same tree. Admittedly, deferring somewhat to the natural passage of time and going beyond medieval limitations, my father offered a solution: get a *normal* job and act in an amateur theatre in the evenings. A nobleman's superciliousness could be detected in this idea, but who knows how any nobility appeared in my father. Evidently prompted by him, Mother finally went to school and talked to F. along the lines that she and her husband were very much concerned about my ideas, and asked her, softly, to talk me out of them, or at least, not to support me in such aspirations. F. assured her she would never support me in this because, now as before, she never supported her students in their choice of profession, since she always considered this a completely personal matter which had nothing to do with parents or teachers. I think Mother understood the *essence* of the answer, since, from that time on, she never started a conversation about F. with me. F. kept silent, too, but she did not give me a role in *her* productions at the beginning of the new season, suggesting instead that I prepare the English ballad 'Queen Eleanor's Confession' by myself. To an outsider, it might seem she had given me my first independent task. I alone knew this was not the case. This decision, a fateful consequence of her conversation with my mother, meant something else: F. was pushing me aside, moving away from me, leaving me.

I cannot know for sure why she rejected the English original of the ballad and selected Marshak's translation instead, nor can I overlook her choice of Russian, a choice which knocked us out of Theatre Day tradition: we were set apart. The Russian into which she hurled me unified our independent rehearsals with the equally independent but very different KVN rehearsals, and this double unification (of language and independence) transformed them into the amateur hobby my father hoped for. Only Stanley thinks the Russian language is soft, bubbly and tickles the throat. Actually, it is hard, sticks up like a paling. But I'm getting ahead of myself again: initially I breathed light and free, like a diver in a good diving suit; little did I know I only had as much oxygen as I carried on my back.

Lenka-Lady Macbeth – a queen dying in sin. Kostya, her pigeon-toed and cross-eyed consort. Lenka-Olivia – author's voice, I am the criminal Earl Marshal, who would have been hanging from a pole that very night had everything turned out differently. Inviting me to the frightening and resolute deed, the King solemnly did vouch *for himself, in front of me*. He gave me his word in exchange for my help, help in a pursuit considered blasphemous in *that* epoch. Every day I hear my voice as though I am talking down the phone without having dialled the last digit. Emptiness surrounds me at rehearsals, the gay emptiness of our reasoning. Cannot give up, because she gave the command.

Shortly before the Day of Theatre, she asked to see the finished scene. We should have waited for *her* Henry to finish and come out afterwards. I was sure the Henries would leave straightaway, but they didn't. F. pretended not to notice: let them sit. She watched with benign attention. The tender eyes of a teacher watching someone else's charges. Earl Marshal, exposed, raised his hands and fell to his knees before the King who had sworn the oath on his sceptre and crown. Kneeling, I saw her laughing. She looked at the spectators who were allowed to see someone else's production – and that look was an invitation to laugh. When she had laughed her fill, and let them laugh their fill, too, she said that there was a good dollop of Eastern despotism in my prostration, which, as a tyrant and a despot as well as an oriental woman, she understands all too well, of course, but where I got it from is a mystery to her. "In England," she looks at me with disdain, "They fall more quietly... Do you understand me?" I stood up and fell to my knees more quietly. My new, English fall opened a breach in the Russian palings, and we were allowed to leave in peace. We decided to dress rehearse the scene in the hall, to be on the safe side, but the lights short circuited out of the blue. Everywhere, except in the gallery. Light fell from there like a white moon-path. Thinking it over, we decided to put the King's chair in the path of light. We told F. about this the next day, and she readily agreed.

The Queen said she could don Lady Macbeth's nightshirt and sit in it right up until the moment of her death. The King was quite satisfied with Richard's costume, which could stand in for a suit of armour. How could you crawl over the stage in a suit of armour, anyway? And it's unlikely he would have turned up at the quarters of the dying, rattling in real armour. A cloak with a hood, that's good enough. Lenka came up with idea of dyeing Olivia's bluish dress a solemn and humble black. As for me, I didn't get off so lightly. I didn't dare ask my parents. Found the money myself: stopped taking breakfast and slowly, slowly saved the solid sum of ten roubles, enough for a blue satin camisole and a blue cloak with a white lining. Not quite enough for a long monastic one, though. Compared with Kostya's, mine looked cropped: the pseudo-Franciscan hood barely covered my forehead.

Two weeks later, Maman received an official invitation from several cultural societies in the South of England. Our theatre – the scene from Richard, the sonnets – as well as its director, Maman and B. G. were invited for a tour of four south English towns at the organisers' expense. The temptation was great, so Maman started fishing and hooked a reply: the theatre can go, they said, but only with children from working class families. Without much hope of success, Maman gently asked F. to prepare Richard with a new line-up, having conscripted performers from the agreed list. F. declined, but the rumour was out, and it reached our ears. Politics, it turned out, began at birth. That winter brought together seemingly irreconcilable things: parents and politics. Now, after a quarter of a century has passed, this reconciliation does not seem so odd.

THE LAST DAY OF THEATRE

She sketched *their* costumes herself, of course. Or maybe she demonstrated on herself. With habitual ease traced the sleeves with smooth wide gestures, underlined the narrow waist with a poised gesture, with her palms, from the chest down, and caught the wide skirt with her fingertips. She knew how to wear imaginary dresses. She would have discussed the colour scheme with them, too, but they held their tongue until the Day of Theatre dawned. When they appeared, when they were delivered by car, ironed, freshly sewn, floating on air, F. blushed. They stood inside, hands held high, flushed with her joy, because now it became clear as day to *us*, who had been abandoned, that she had not been wrong to abandon us. After turning away from us, she made the right choice in turning to them: 9a, our competitors in the KVN. Their parents ordered the costumes at a real tailor's. They did not come themselves, though, not wanting to intrude. Instead of the parents who did not come, it was the majestic, indescribably beautiful costumes which stood there. For each one, yards and yards of the finest silk had been used – and that means *bought* – for each one: yellow and pale cherry for the pranksters; black with Jacquard brocade for the queen mother; white atlas and chiffon for Juliet. The pranksters' dresses were hung on hard hoops and were embroidered with small bows and wide waves of lace. They were so *real* that F. easily and delightedly pretended not to notice the fashion – the fashion of the eighteenth century. Thanks to the new parents' efforts, the approaching Day of Theatre was fast becoming sumptuous: the previous one was no match for it.

She always laughed at our ability to mix up the centuries as soon as she asked a 'historical' question. She would help us snap out of our stupor with her ironic: OK, is it *before or after* Christ, at least? But now, when the Windsorians somehow flew into another century, she held her tongue, didn't console them. She didn't console anyone at all – neither us, dumbstruck, nor them, somehow slipping up. But she noticed their temporal mistake, otherwise why would she raise her eyes and throw that quick glance which she always threw when she caught temporal mistakes? With this short, super-short glance, she was asking me: before *or after*? And I, having just been admiring their dresses, dresses of parental love and respect – wonderful, generous and mistaken – replied: *after*. My cropped Franciscan cape did not belong to any century. I had skipped breakfasts and sewn it myself. My family was not behind it. *After* I replied, and in that moment, I renounced them.

A knock at the door interrupted my chain of thought. A messenger from the boys ran in from the adjacent classroom and announced that Fedka – Romeo – had left his dark blue tights at home. Her gaze shifted from me, shifted into focus: "So?" She asked as one asks the bringer of bad news. "Is he going to hang about under the balcony bare-legged?" Sophie rose up, white as the parental atlas silk, quite forgetting her hand in her hair, plaiting pearls. I lowered my eyes and saw my legs in bright blue tights, those tights which my father had brought from Czechoslovakia, now raised to the level of Earl Marshal, in other words, to the level of Romeo. F. caught my glance, gave a curt nod and turned away. "Leave," I saved the messenger and began taking them off. And at once, belatedly, imagined the whole procession, as we walk to the assembly hall, white, black, yellow, cherry, in all their glory, and then after them, me in a blue camisole with bare legs poking out from under my blue, not-quite-monastic cape at every step. I was walking after them like the ghost of my own life – *my previous life*. A pathetic ghost who wears short hold-ups. I went to the door, stuck out the tights and hissed: "Fetch Kostya's cape." The messenger nodded, dashed away and returned a minute later with the cape and Fedka's thank you. The ghost dissipated. I wrapped myself up and Sophie's hand began plaiting pearls again. F. said that "everyone" could sit in the hall against the right-hand wall and enter the stage straight from the audience, except for Juliet, who should be in the gallery. She said it, looked at me, and I understood: her "everyone" does not include me; I will sit in the wings with bare legs.

O Lord, even now, a quarter of century later, a quarter of a century I spent on finding all the words of love, I see how they walk through the school surrounded by a wall of numbness. The little ones who were not allowed in the assembly hall froze like little pillars along the walls. A. N. headed the procession. Dressed in a brown suede jacket, with finest antique lace on his turned-back collar, starch-white flared cuffs like gauntlets. He was followed by yellow-cherry coloured pranksters decorated with bows and lace, followed by the queen mother in black Jacquard brocade, surrounded by equally black soldiers – her son's murderers. (Kostya walked with them.) Behind the soldiers, tenderly violet dancers (Irka, her moment of glory at hand) behind them, pearly-white Juliet with fair-haired Romeo. And finally, our Eleanorian left-overs. Kostya turned back, his eyes searching for me. I nodded, and he fell behind from the soldiers. I'd said I would be in the wings until the very end since Eleanor is the last. Send someone for your cape. "You OK?" he asked, concerned. I shrugged: "OK." But he placed an orange in my hand. We only lingered a moment, but everyone had already taken their places when we came in. The spectators were looking at me thinking: what does *she* have under her black cape when *everyone else* has such luxuriant costumes?! I went backstage, sniggering, because it was empty under the cape – *nothing* but bare legs and an orange.

They're already laughing. I take a peek: A.N. is embracingTaika, one of the Windsorian pranksters, round the waist, twirling his moustache. The pranksters are chirping. They push A. N. under the hopsack and sit on him as if he were a chest. He bows, taking the pranksters for their bows, twirling them like his moustache. Sophie's voice, tender as white atlas silk, tender as a pearl basket. Morning like the dawn chorus. Romeo jumps on the stage, running here and there… I don't watch any more, sit and think, let him not forget, let him bring me the tights. Who knows what will enter his love-struck head… And then I heard everything together: Auntie Galya's whisper, her sobs, shuffling of feet on the stairs he is climbing up in the darkness, clumsily, his arms outspread, as on a tightrope. He stops, afraid of making a noise. But my eyes are used to it. He looks and doesn't see: I am in a dark cape in the darkness. Sit and listen to *that* music: violet couples touch fingertips – in emptiness.

He's already made me out. He comes on tiptoes, balancing deliberately, clowning. "So?" I ask. "Wait," he replies hurriedly. "Turn round." Electricity crackles, spark-emitting tights, St. Elmo's fire, thin struts. "Here." He shoves them, scrunched up. They are terribly warm, damp from his love-struck warmth. I untangle them, hang them over my arm, waving, letting them cool down. "Did you see?" "Is your father here?" I don't know why I'm asking, automatically. I don't care about his father. But these tights – they won't cool. "Turn round." I'm speaking automatically again; it's pitch black. "Did you create Eleanor?" I keep mum, pulling on the cooled tights. His voice breaks through his whisper. The non-angelic music has ended. Now they've stopped – these *non-angels*. "My father's gone to another city," had he named the town, it would've meant on business, but he said 'another.' Ran from him as though he were Poppet Zinnober. He turns to me, looks at me, although I didn't say he could. I'm silent. Silent about my shameful fall, about how I fell to my knees with a racket, about how she laughed because I fell like a slave when I should have fallen like a freeman. I should speak, but I am silent since it is because of him that I've been sitting here all this time with bare legs. I squeeze and squeeze the orange. Just a bit more and it will splatter yellow. Everything has gone cold, now they'll announce Eleanor. Irka is already announcing, in English, what will be in Russian, as if their mother-tongue were already English. Swift steps on the stairs: "Give me the cape." I bend down, put the orange on the floor. Go down the little stairs, stand next to Auntie Galya. She dare not sob.

Moon path from the gallery. Something in my throat – something wrong, foreign: it is used to English. Russian rises up. Zinnober yourself. Lenka is leading the queen.

The queen of England she has fallen sick,
Sore sick, and like to die;
And she has sent for twa French priests,
To bear her companie.

I stand and listen to the beginning, but I hear silence. This is a different silence, not the same as for Romeo. Like the foreigners' silence when we play for them in English because the foreigners hear *every* word. Now they are foreigners, too, now we are performing *in their language*. "Good Lord!" Auntie Galya whispers behind my back. For the first time, she understands every word. I throw the curtain aside roughly, like a cape, and cut across to intercept the moonlight. Flashing the white lining, I kneel before the King. We put the capes on, cross ourselves at the high, empty windows. The King has a crucifix which he hides under the cape. Her face is pale, whiter than calico. She speaks, lips barely moving, not looking at us, approaching. Saving her soul at the cost of my death. Frozen in horror, Maman listens, riveted. I understand her: this is a school, how can you display *such* sins? I watch as he throws off his cape and hood. Maman is saved. Cape thrown aside, a black heap, cold as the blackness thrown from her soul. He hurls the crucifix. Should have thrown it at his feet, but his hand slips, swings wide, like a dagger, and I see it fly into the hall like a knife, and from there, a short *real* shout. In the silence, I fall on my knees, quietly, as she taught, as the crucifix should have fallen, like a freeman saved from death.

'An it werna for the oath I sware,
Earl Marshall, thou shouldst dee.'

Lights. Floating, returning to us: over the rows. They applaud like foreigners, because they understand each word – for the first time in three years. F. gets up, swift and light. I see her face in the light – sharp and tired. She leaves the hall. We follow her, but they still sit and watch as we leave in single file. First Eleanorians, then Henrians, then dancers, then Windsorians in their mistaken dresses, then A. N. in lace. Everyone, except Romeo and Juliet. Juliet is in the gallery, Romeo... Phew! I have to go back, pushing through everybody. Only one set of doors is open, can't enter until they all come out. Stand in front of the door like a beggar in my docked cape. I meet the eyes of each of them and toss them aside one after the other. Empty at last. The stream has dried up. The empty barrel of my glory, black as tar, is empty of this last Day of Theatre when I performed in Russian. I come to the curtain I stood behind, lift it up by the hem. Auntie Galya is sitting by the sink. Her face is flushed. "Good Lord, how I cried, at Fedya. And you – great!" she turned and praised me. She wouldn't have dared to before. Now she is saying: fancy, such a story, and this traitor-queen...

I am walking up the stairs, not afraid of making a noise. In the kitchen, rattle of pans – the kitchen staff getting back to work. He sits behind the stage eating an orange, gnawing the flesh right to the skin. "It was great! Did you come up with the light?" "By itself." "Great that you did it in Russian. I'd prefer to do it in Russian, too, so everyone understands..." Before they were for us, and now, we were for them. Language is the key. Their language made me their flesh and blood – their kitchen flesh and bone. I hand him the cape and leave, not waiting for him to finish guzzling.

"You should be more careful next time." I sit in front of her thinking: there won't be a next time, you can't show this to foreigners... "You could really hurt someone like that," she says harshly. How strange, she says, I enjoyed your Eleanor. It's difficult when you know it all beforehand – the look, the gesture, it is very rare, it happened once in your Richard, twice in your sonnets, it's rare, when one forgets everything one's seen before. And then you all finish school, leave and age. Shouldn't start Shakespeare with first years. Nor with your class, either. If I had my own theatre, she says, I would have only taken you… and Sophie. When I sit in front of her, I no longer know what hatred is. Everything which just happened to me leaves without looking back, just as little Nadia had left, following her mother. We are alone. All the children have followed their parents. All adults have aged in their turn. But I, who refused, have nowhere to go.

"I've wanted to produce 'The Idiot' for a long time. You for Anastasia Filippovna, Andrei Nikolayevich for Rogozhin. Money in the fireplace, do you remember that scene? We don't have a prince. Maybe Fedya…" She pulls a face, barely noticeably, as though wiping out a shadow. "Or Sasha Reshetin… Did you see him in Henry? That look of his? Only I noticed. Everyone else looks for something else. Even you." She is not afraid of Russian, so that means it's not true; everything I feared is untrue. She will manage, come to terms with this emptiness and fear which looms behind *it*, behind the Russian words, clear to all, coming at me from the school's kitchen sinks. She is looking past me and I dare to say: "But we could have…" Her gaze focuses as though I am a messenger, but she doesn't know which kind. "… then, and after school."

"University, daily routines, families, children. You don't know what you're talking about." She smirks. I see she has no energy left. She speaks calmly. No doubts. It is like death. The life which lies ahead of us is like death. I keep quiet. I have no proof. How can you have proof of something which has not yet happened? What could I have done, then? This is now, when so many years have passed… Could I really have caught it back then? That was our 'present tense' with her, now just a distant past tense, but already back then, something had accumulated in my mother tongue, in the language which does not have and never has had a past perfect tense. I could have discerned something frightening, which it was already too late to exorcize, fighting fire with fire.

Irka and I swapped gossip on the way home. Our singing teacher dyes her hair almost every quarter. But Marina Ivanovna paints her lips with super-red lipstick and bleaches her hair. She's the after-school teacher, but that isn't the main thing. The main thing is that she organises the political club called 'Search.' It isn't political, actually, but even if it were, it's ancient history, like Marina herself. She tracks down veterans who served with her during the war in the Red Gorka and Seraya Loshad/Grey Horse forts.[28] Marina digs them up from wherever she can, writes letters, makes enquiries, writes to their relatives. Some of them, successfully tracked down, appear in person, and we listen to their tales. Listening to them, you get the impression all they did out *there* was think, and mainly about us, their bright future. My father also fought near Moscow and Kursk. He doesn't tell stories. Once he said he threw up in the bushes after his first hand to hand combat: knife in my hand, he said, and under the knife, the crunch of something soft... I imagined what Marina would have done should he speak of that in class. If you ask me, says Irka, it's better to talk about that than about some bright future. Marina likes to talk herself, too. But not about the future. About her bright past, which is the war. If it were up to her, Irka says, she'd go right back there, dragging us all along with her. Sometimes she falls into a kind of trance, starts playing out the scenes. A real Shakespearian theatre. Psh, dialogues from the other world. And we listen to it all, sitting like veterans in the trenches and dreaming about *our* bright future – only about twenty minutes to go – while they, don't you know, converse with the lieutenant as if he were here, and Marina hasn't aged a day... Lips like a vampire's, I told you. But Irka says Marina is just bringing her appearance in line with the content – social realism. B. G. doesn't go against Marina; where would he find another enthusiast like her to boost the political front?

And then I told Irka what I'd seen: Marina cried on VE-Day. After they'd all left, both ours and the veterans. And not just anywhere, right in F.'s study. I'd gone in to pick up my gym bag, forgotten it under the desk, and Marina was sitting there at the teacher's desk, her whole face smothered in the red

---

[28]   Famous cannon lines in Kronstadt.

of her dreadful lipstick, and she's rubbing it, and F. is hugging her, consoling her like Sophie – you remember how Sophie cried after the Day of Theatre? Nightmare, says Irka.

She comforted them both: the young, beautiful Juliet, wrapped in white atlas silk and pearls, and the old, red-lipped hag who reminded you of either a she-vampire or a clown. And I hear how Irka corrects me – clown-ess. Well, OK, but still, she consoled them both – whispering, stroking their shoulders. Two dialogues, but not babyish ones, proper ones, in indirect speech. What could be more indirect than a soundless whisper... How could she *not pity* them, not believe the tears, since Marina Ivanova – who cried like Sophie, like a young, pale-lipped beauty – the lieutenant's beloved, died the very next VE-Day, leaning against the gym wall so naturally that at first no-one could believe it, just thought it was too stuffy for her... She stands there, her red clown smile shining on un-made up lips, and then falls to the floor and dies.

None of us were at Marina's funeral. Because it was already a different year, the next year, the year of our terrible, hideous story. The veterans were probably there. I don't want to listen to their words: I know, they *cannot* speak. Were it up to me, I would have listened to others: Mercutio, for instance. Let him come, alive and well, and begin speaking Russian, but as only he could speak, about Queen Mab, about that mad hag who controls life. Let him bring proof of his foresight – there, look, I warned you two years ago how it would all end. Then again a year ago, and a month ago... Yet you still don't understand, even when you are told in your own mother tongue. No-one would have believed him, even if he had brought in a hundred pieces of proof. They would have understood him literally, as we understood Marina when she came up with her utter nonsense about our fathers and her lieutenant. We took her literally and giggled behind her back because the mother tongue is an evil joke. In the mother tongue, you understand immediately; in other words, you miss the main point. If you understand immediately, that is not the main point, but it will blind you and then maybe you will never be able to understand... What is *worthy* of being understood is playing out in a foreign tongue, which is being learnt for the rest of your life – words, grammar and tenses – because that is *how* it plays. And when it plays, you will never make a mistake, you can't, because goosebumps run over your skin and you forget everything that went before. But then it leaves, and witnesses remain: she and I. Had I been able to understand this back then, I would have sneaked into her funeral, I would have pushed past the lieutenants to make sure: her lips are painted *the same colour as she painted them herself.* Red – the only will of the deceased. Just try not to paint them!!

FILTH

Vera Fyodorovna was 9a's form teacher. She can't come to terms with this fact: I would have preferred you. Always moaning. Each history lesson begins with her complaints. We – corrupt arbiters – are always on her side. Vera Fyodorovna has a stunning surname – Sheremetyeva, like the palace. Her daughter is two years our elder. Now she works as secretary to Maman and walks through the school with a huge belly. But it was Vera Fyodorovna who married, and what's more, changed her surname to Bykova.[29] Her "little a's" were a red rag for her. "So how did the form meeting go?" Slavik asks touchingly. Vera Fyodorovna immediately takes the bait: "Half didn't show up. They have a physics test tomorrow, you see. They couldn't care less that poor little Verochka waited two whole lessons for them." The physics books come out in the back desks; we have it the day after tomorrow. Snippets filter through. "And then I said to myself: Verka, you're a fool...!"

Lenka Blank changed her surname, too. Took her mother's, Barashkova.[30] Her father, Blank, had died long ago, but before that he'd been the manager of some shop, that's how they'd got such a flat. Lenka says she was still very small when he died and it was her Granny who raised her – Granny Barashkova. Of course, we all understood why she changed her surname, but no-on laughed. Well, actually, everyone is laughing, not because of why she changed it, but because of *what* was and *what* came. Like Sheremetyeva and Bykova. F. doesn't laugh. She raised her brows when she heard the surname,

....

29 From the Russian for 'bull.'
30 From the Russian for 'little ram.'

checked: "Surely not Barashkova?" Irka said she hates it, says you have to leg it out of here, get out of this country. The earlier the better. She doesn't mention Lenka, but I know what she means… She also said you get a hole punched in your face not your passport.

Irka spoke to F. For a long time. Said she has no future in this country, zero prospects. F. listened, then gave her a hug and a kiss. Then asked a single question: "Is it someone in our school…?" And Irka had answered honestly: No. I can imagine what would happen to that *someone*! I say. Yeah, says Irka, I wouldn't envy them! Now Irka visits F.'s office and they converse. Irka comes out flushed and happy. This is Irka's happiness. She doesn't tell me any more.

And then I noticed something else: F. talks with Fedya. He took it upon himself to go to her study after class, when there were no rehearsals. I saw it with my own eyes. He came, knocked, leaned on doorframe, his skinny torso swaying as he looked in with devoted eyes. But her eyes are unfathomable: empty and sick. From those eyes I understand: not a rehearsal. They spoke for a long time. I waited deliberately. Then he came again. But I didn't see that time. I just noticed: he looks at me victoriously. We discussed it with Irka; it riles her, too. She said she popped in once, and they are talking. F. is sitting at her desk, Fedka opposite, at ours. Fedka was flushed, mumbling, moved his hands like a spider, and F.'s face… "What about it?" "Well, dunno, full of suffering." I can't understand why she listens to him, then Irka says, he doesn't have a mother, you know. Lives with his grandparents. The Solzhenitsyn ones.

We bumped into each other at the door. I'd come for a rehearsal, she'd said five o'clock. He hurtled towards me: eyes burning, fingers moving like an idiot's. Threw me another victorious glance. I went in and shut the door. She was sitting at my desk looking out of the window. The window was black, completely empty. The curtains were in the wash. It was naked. Beyond the window, impenetrable gloom. She sat, half-turned, not looking at me, just looking into that gloom. The light buzzed: white luminescent lamps covering the ceiling. Whining like flies dangling with spread-eagled wings. She sat beneath them, motionless: a shell, dried out and empty. Standing in the doorway then, I thought: "He sucked her dry."

The buzzing fly light poured onto her fingers. They came to life first; I saw them twitch. She turned to me, not a glimmer of recognition. A queer sensation, cold clutched my ankles, for the face turned towards me was not her face. There was gloom in her eyes, like the gloom beyond the windows, gaping emptiness. As if, while I watched, she was returning from a place where one must not dally.... She stood up and went to the record player. The needle gave a rough lick, like a dog. Licked the tremor from her fingers.

"Devouring Time, blunt thou the lion's paws,
And make the earth devour her own sweet brood,
Pluck the keen teeth from the fierce tiger's jaws
And burn..."[31]

Terrible and soft, tender and inescapable, merciless and magnanimous, even as stonework, undulating as desert sand, hot and impenetrable, inexpressible and determined, invisible and dense, like air – her last cycle, about her adversary, the one she faced, one to one, from birth to death, like a seawall under high tide's onslaught, like a flower under the plough. Her final cycle, about Time, the longest, five sonnets set to Rachmaninov's 'Vocalise', which she passed on to me from hand to hand, throat to throat, when she returned. I read it dozens of times, and for the last time – when I returned after accompanying her body, and the spasm which cramped her fingers then reached my throat, choking and spluttering on *these* words.

Even like her voice, inconsolable like my remaining life, precise like water dripping on a stone, sharp like teeth gnawing the core, rough like a dog's tongue licking the hand, transparent like sweat covering the brow, amorous like a secret hidden from the face of death. I no longer heard words. They

....

[31] Shakespeare, Sonnet 19.

were cotton-like and squeaky, intangible like the pull of the earth, like the rustling of grass not yet grown, like sun blindness – whiter than snow. Words were devoid of feeling like injections given in a dream, because, from that moment on, I could get by without words. The language of my childhood was running from me, zigzagging as it ran, like a puppy, and something else was flowing into the empty cavity, burning like molten iron, hollow like an owl's hoot. It was fluid like dough, trickled like a thread through the eye of a needle. I was becoming fluid and runny, too, and in that language-less lightness I had to make but one last effort to understand, and I did it. I dared close my eyes and slide down, down the doorframe. I came to straightaway. She was leaning over me. Her fingers tenderly sprouting through the back of my head. I was afraid she would understand: I wasn't eating again, I'd let myself faint. But only calm love was flowing from her narrow eyes, and I got up and sat at the desk.

She sat down next to me and began talking as though nothing had happened. She said she had invited *that* Richard for the role of the Prince, the one who had finished school long, long ago. But she had called him nevertheless. We'll start rehearsals in a month, he'll take time off especially. Then we'll polish it on Sundays. "Andrei Nikolayevich will make a magnificent Rogozhin. You know, it turns out his mother is from a merchant family, and it shows – look at his fingers, did you notice? If only I could," – she put her arms akimbo, laughing at her unsuitable body – "I would play the Prince myself. Andrei Nikolayevich is a ready-made Rogozhin, you could nip to the chemist's right now for some stench-removing liquid. I love it, he says, when the pouch is full, but he can hand it out, too, if need be. The Prince is the trickiest. Shining eyes…" she says, a violet dress with lace. Hair tied back, pulled from the temples as though there's a permanent headache. They will all be overcome: the Prince by pity, Rogozhin by blood. You will be dazzlingly beautiful, so that Rogozhin is afraid of you and rages, like a bull, but the Prince will burn out like a candle flame, so that the guests look at you in terror, so that terror hums above you, so that the guests muffle their terror with foul, mean words, so that they judge you by themselves, because they don't know *anything else*. I will make sure of that! I sit and listen, forgetting myself, since now she has forgotten time. Both A. N. and *that* Richard, they are far from school kids, yet they are other adults, not those who have aged. That means it is possible after all, even later, *after*… If *it* didn't manage to take control of them, that means it won't manage to take control of me, either.

Our performances streamed on, one after the other. But we didn't play Eleanor any more. The occasion never arose, it was always either foreigners or 'city' guests who you can't really show *such* sins to, or cruise ships which would come into the port in autumn. In November, we performed at Makarov College.[32] I have no idea how they heard about us, but the College's deputy political director rang B. G. and invited us to perform. In English only. Maybe he wanted future merchant mariners to hear live English. F. didn't go. The 'Richards' and the 'Windsorians' went. Cadets met us in the courtyard. Two rooms were reserved for us. Kitchen staff knocked, offering tea and coffee. They laughed no less than ours at the 'Windsorians' while strict silence reigned during Richard. The college director thanked us after the performance, in person. A dance was announced after the interval. We wanted to leave, but the cadets pleaded persistently, so we stayed. There were plenty of city girls, but we were fought over. The cadets held their backs straight and looked at us shyly. Officers walked by, stern as a patrol.

At the beginning of December, we were invited to take part in a city-wide competition of amateur dramatic collectives. The first knock-out round took place in the LenSoviet Theatre. F. selected Romeo and Juliet and the second dance. Spectators were not allowed. A panel of about ten sat in session in the hall. Look like our DDPE, said Irka. Their leader, a woman, delivered her thanks into the microphone and announced the next collective together with the surname of its director. The performers went without names. "Like serfs," quipped Fedka snidely. Ours got through without a hitch. Round two

....

32   Now the Admiral Makarov State University of Maritime and Inland Shipping.

was held in the Great Hall of the Conservatoire. B. G. said we could all go. We turned up early and took a whole row. The jury was made up of nine people in the second row. The spectators, mostly senior pupils, sat down in clumps. F. stayed in the wings. Sophie was planted in the director's box in advance. We sat, patiently waiting out each act. Uzbek dance, girls in wide Turkish trousers with baskets of grapes; the wolf and the seven kids: large kids in miniskirts made the stage quake. 'Timur and his Team,'[33] followed by *the Gopak*: Ukrainian dancers in red pantaloons. The enthusiasm of the audience depended on who was on stage: each heartily applauded their own.

They announced the dance. Again, name of the collective and the director's surname: F's name and surname sounded alien over the microphone. The girls finished dancing, bowed. Red blotches on Irka's cheeks. Then Romeo was announced. With surnames, this time. Sophie's pearls appeared in the box. Fedka jumped on stage – in my tights. Music like the dawn chorus. Subsided. They began. He only managed to say a few words, just enough for them to understand they didn't understand. It started behind our backs – *their* raucous rumpus boiled up. Reached the heavens, waves of unstoppable shrieks and hoots, as soon as Sophie began speaking, tenderly leaning over the box. They howled and guffawed like lunatics, behind our backs. Their guffaws came rolling in clear, spasmodic waves, rising and falling, like a heavy onslaught. During the ebb, we could make out the words flying from the stage, but these words, dishonoured by laughter, no longer carried any meaning – meaningless, disgraced sounds. Guffaws quieted in one row would flare up in another, like the black death. The white faces of Romeo and Juliet, who had forgotten about love as though it had never been. There was only fear and trembling, the repulsive, fish-like trembling of the swaying hall. It was over. The white shadow of Juliet retreated into the depths. All laughed out, they applauded with penitent enthusiasm. We stood up under the applause.

....

[33]   Title of a patriotic children's book.

Sophie sobbed, buried in F's lap. Fedya stood nearby, chewing his lips. For the first time in my life, I saw the face of a dishonoured person. F. whispered over Sophie, lifting the spell of disgrace, like pain. We stood huddled together, like sheep. F. raised her eyes to us. She looked at our little flock and the shreds of tenderness whispering over Sophie retreated from her gaze. Her eyes emptied, growing impenetrable as gloom. Itching shame looked back at her through our eyes: we had returned from that place, the place you can only return from with shame. We were in that hall, and having returned, we carried its filth with us. The empty gloom thickened into stony aloofness: with a wave of her hand, she exiled us.

If you asked now, directly: when did *it* begin, what happened with all of us, I would say: long ago, before, long before… I would flick through everything, from the very beginning, floundering from one to another… But if you were to insist, again and again: when did it become irreversible? I would say: there and then, in that filthy hall, at the moment of their foul and senseless guffaws, their fish-like swaying.

SHAPE-SHIFTERS

After that hall – the hall where we found ourselves by chance, as it were, the hall we left only to be met by her empty eyes – everything happened swiftly. Swifter than you could imagine. It was as though time had bolted; she had been holding it in check by her own power, by her brave and steadfast presence alone, but now it was galloping towards a victory which – starting with that hall – was already secure. Time began spinning on every tongue, speaking in every tongue. Some days later, F. called Sophie and me and suggested we prepare a scene from *Twelfth Night* by ourselves. Six girls from Olivia's retinue, making a fool of simple Viola. Setting aside pages marked in her hand-writing, right then and there she showed us what it should look like: "Each time you bow, you see one face, as you straighten up, you see another. It has to be acted precisely: each girl steps forward, then steps back immediately. The next takes her place." The Year Eight girls she selected were handed over to me at her command: obey. We rehearsed with Sophie after classes. I went to F. alone: we were preparing Rachmaninov. F. didn't bring up Nastassia Filippovna anymore. At night, having waited for everyone to fall asleep, I read *The Idiot*, still hoping. Fedka did not go to her study any more. I found out via Barashkova that he was rehearsing something himself. We were sitting at her place discussing the last observed class. *They* came tearing along again to listen to our home reading. This time, forestalling their arrival, F. forbade us to translate simultaneously. The lesson was particularly jolly. F. cracked lambent jokes. We laughed. The guests giggled, pretending they understood English jokes.

"Come on!" Lenka said. "Those women need a dictionary for Russian, too: I must express a word of thanks for all we received... all of us..." In Lenka's rendition, the collective image came out wonderfully. "By the way, do you know *what* Fedka's rehearsing? Don't you know? Lariska is with him, as well as Lenka-Eleanor, Sveta, the boys from the a's. "Does F. know?" That was my first question. "Don't think so. He said they're preparing a surprise. Auntie Galya gave him the key for the hall." Then we discussed the New Year cake: Olga came up with a fat cone of sponge covered in cream. We're going to her place tomorrow – Galka, Irka and I. We'll need an enamel tray and whisks.

Masses of people came for the gateau, even Valeria Pavlovna who was just dashing past. F. didn't come. We took the tray with the remainders to the fridge, to Auntie Galya. I went to fetch it a couple of days later, at my Mum's prompting. The dining room door was locked. I listened, and knocked. Hushed voices, a rustle... "Who is it?" I gave my name. The door burst open. Fedka stepped back, letting me in. The girls sat dangling their legs over the stages. The boys were standing by the window. Seeing it was me, they took out the fags hidden behind their backs. No point in hiding them anyway: rings of bluish grey smoke coiled through the air. "We're rehearsing. It's a play by an American, a real, modern play," Fedka began hurriedly, breaking the lengthening silence. "I came for the tray." I was looking at him, at the smoky trails weaving up from the fingers. He waved his arms wide, looked as though he were trying to take off: "It's interesting, see. A real, modern play. Our problems. *Natural...*" He deflated and fell silent. "Wasting your time." I didn't catch who said it. "You know she's her..." Now I caught it. "And?" I asked, turning to the voice. Everyone was quiet. Something strange surfaced on their faces, as though they were not themselves but others whom I had once known and was trying to forget. They looked at me, waiting for the inevitable, irreparable, which was like my disgrace. "And?" I asked again. They didn't dare: *her* lackey, slave, servant, henchwoman, yes-woman. They just stood and looked, but the words they didn't say looked out from their eyes, and I stood before them: a wretched, bare-legged creature, clad in hold-up stockings, with no clue about proper tights since at that moment they felt like 'the highers' again, and me, well, I was the same as ever. There was no theatre, no Richard, no sonnets. Neither F. nor my new life. Everything remained as ever, in its *natural* place. They had ripped everything from me, like my tights. Fedka shrugged a shoulder. Chewed his lips for the briefest of moments, as he had when he had stood over the sobbing Sophie. In that moment, I saw he didn't want my disgrace, he wanted peace. Bluish smoke trails reached my throat. I coughed, and, covering my mouth with my hands, went to Auntie Galya's shelf; my tray was behind it. I grabbed it, clutched it to my torso as though protecting myself, shielding my stomach from them…

They were coming towards me: F. and A.N. He was leading her by the elbow. Her face was white. I had never seen *such* a white face. I pressed the tray against me like a shield. They passed by without a glance. "Hold on," A. N. spoke hurriedly, "I'll hail a car in the square," he muttered. "Don't worry," she replied softly. "I'm perfectly able to…" I dashed into the cloakroom and hurried after them, tying my headscarf on the run. Caught them near the square. A. N. was helping her into a car. Then he squeezed himself into the front seat. F. slid an empty glance at me. The briefcase fell from her hand. Snowflakes were dancing under the tall streetlamp, falling onto the blue enamel. I was standing, holding out my tray as though I were begging. The sky proffered snow. Cold metal burning cold fingers. White, alien, unrecognisable faces floated over the square. Blotches of dark clouds hurtled towards Theatre Square in the car's wake. Traces of other cars lay whipped out on the worn cobbles. She didn't call me, just slid an indifferent glance from behind the window. It wasn't until she was home that I heard her voice: she called.

F. opened the door, nodded, letting me in. Neither surprise nor joy. "I thought I heard you call me." A. N.'s outline loomed in the living room doorway. His face aglow with delighted surprise. I was pulling off my boots, stamping dirty little dribbles which I'd brought into her flat on my feet. She took me by the hand, led me into the living room, then left, closing the door.

They began speaking in whispers in the corridor. The front door banged. He had left, leaving her *in my care*. Noise of water in the kitchen. She came in with the kettle. I fell upon the hot drink. This time she poured it for me in a tea bowl. White glass lampshade flooded the walls with an even light, not a single dark corner. "Did you know?" The taste of green tea stuck in my throat, bitter. The bitter terror of banishment was rising up from my stomach. The empty space of my past spread out between us. There was no trace of me in this space marked with others' footprints. Now I had to make the first, and from that first step… "I found out yesterday. I went to the hall today. He said it's a play, American, from our time…" I rushed to fill the emptiness, but she interrupted. "From *our* time?" she began menacingly. Fedka's word, from her lips, became terrifying. "… he calculated it perfectly," she began with a half phase. The empty space began to shrink, filling up with events from my life. From under the footprints of others, which had marked *their* time, *my* time was slowly emerging.

"…behind my back, in my fairway. He knew they wouldn't dare touch him. And if they tried, I would leap to his defence. He would have shown this vileness, they would have come out after us, but B. G. would have rushed at me, and, unlike you, I would have answered: yes." She smirked with disgust. "And then, after a successful defence, I would have put my resignation on the table because, even though B. G. would not have found a single argument in support of my resignation, he would have understood everything and signed my paper because neither he nor I would have been able to go on as though nothing had happened." She fell silent, raised her cup to her lips, and swallowed.

"I summoned Fedya yesterday and demanded they show me." Her cheek twitched squeamishly. "He tried to slither out, like a snake under a fork. If he wants freedom…" She stood up. Against the dark background of the uncurtained window, her hair was fading with dimming gold. She began speaking without turning round. "I realised *this* would be bad. How else? He doesn't have what it takes. I … with him… 'til I was hoarse…." Her hoarse voice grew huskier. "That play's for a sleazy bar, not for the choosy. It's a crowd-pleaser." Then, in English: "It's about...!" She faltered. Had she begun in Russian, she would have been able to finish, but now, in English, she could not. She didn't wish to translate herself – out of pride. She let go of the window ledge, came back.

"I previewed it. For as long as I am in the school, they will not show *this*. If they consider this real life, if *this* moves them – let them be moved at the nearest rubbish dump. *Real* life," her eyes took in the whole room, "Is more disgusting and vile than anything he can imagine. But even if.... I would have shown him *how to direct this*, so that their mouths would water with greasy saliva... If he were a grown-up," she began speaking with a ringing, unsteady voice not her own, "I would have smashed his face in." Now she was speaking with her own voice, as if, having tried on *these and others* she had arrived at the words of the author: "When this child grows up, in about fifteen years, he will offload everything that has accumulated in him, so that everyone will drown in puke. Children are terrifying creatures." She fell silent and swallowed, her arm extended. In leaving *all* children, she was walking away from me, too. She fell silent again. The words she had said in that unrecognizable voice were hovering above me, alien and terrifying. The words crawled into an alien skin, turned towards me inside out; before her unsteady voice, I had known nothing about this reverse side. But the reverse side meant another life, a life in which words are not heard and tights are not shared, not worn in turns. One of us should have come out from behind the curtain, into the light, bare-legged. He or I.

"Children are shape-shifters." She said it very quietly, as though she were afraid of interrupting me. "Their faces can be so beautiful they make your heart ache, but the next moment, they turn, and their reverse side is black as pitch, since even children do not begin from zero. I don't know. Maybe if you were handed to me as babies... If you think you are an exception..." She looked me with a new expression: admiring and inimical, as though I, sitting before her, was *all* children. I had no time. Time was becoming me, flowing into me, flooding my emptiness: "Me. I'll go myself. I'll go to B. G. and tell him everything." "Oh, really?" she asked snootily. "How can you go, when they *already* consider you my...?" I knew what she was going to say next, what *they* hadn't dared say then: lackey, slave, servant, henchwoman, yes-woman. She looked at me with their eyes, as though this were our first rehearsal and she were playing out, briefly but precisely, what I must *direct* myself. In that long moment, I was all children; but she, she was all of *them*. We looked at the empty table. Pages of the modern play, the play of our time, which I was to direct in translation, were lying on it. "I know," I interrupted her for the first time, my hand holding the pages firmly. "I won't go alone. I'll go with the girls, together." "*If* you actually do," she began speaking slowly, as though thinking the scene through, "Call me before you go into B. G.'s office, so that I can be a witness." She was looking ahead, further than I could see. "Yes." Now I replied clearly, as I would had I been handed to her as a baby. Bitterness and pride sprouted in my adolescent heart. "Let's go. I'll walk you to the bus stop." She lifted her eyes to the clock on the wall, as though now, having heard my clear answer, she was starting the stopwatch.

The darkness beyond the window, that darkness which dimmed the gingery hair, flanked the footpath she led me along. The powerless light of the far-off, barely lit windows did not reach the road. Black bushes, glazed with bluish frost, stretched along either side. I walked, trying to step smoothly, but now and then my foot slipped over the edge. She walked ahead. Her feet walked this path every day, there and back, to and from the school.

LEFTOVERS EVERYONE ATE

By Year Ten, we had our tricks off pat. Of course, from a technical point of view, our linguaphone cabinet was well below par, but we became quite proficient, nevertheless. We could detect the moment when the connection was switched on by barely audible rustles and distant crackles. Vital skills in those times. Our times. Once these were detected, the one being monitored would begin broadcasting inspiration while the others would fall into rather lax mutterings. We began as ever, keeping close to the text. Irka's voice, deadened by the headphones, chimed in on cue. The voices withered as they fell onto the membrane. Only the clock on the wall in front of me was alive. F. didn't look at me, not even once. She looked ahead, above our desks, as though there were nothing but empty space – no man's land – between her eyes and their target. Threading empty words, I watched her furtively. From the outside, from my strip of no man's land, it might seem as though she were listening to one of the pairs; her eyes said as much: they held the same concentrated emptiness with which she always listened to our answers. But her eyebrows, meeting on the bridge of her nose, filled this emptiness with anticipation: her tense anticipation was directed at something else. This 'something else' scurried inside her like a little flame running along a Bickford fuse. Mechanically, I shot quick glances all around. Eight of us at four desks. No-one – not one of the pairs – exuded inspired diligence. No *listeners*. We were all broadcasting into emptiness. The dialogue finished. We would usually swap roles and begin again. "Are you going to P.E.?" asked Irka, trying not to move her Russian lips. Some thought which I didn't manage to grasp stirred in my headphones.

Once a month, girls were allowed to skip. Nina Ivanovna used to insist that those who were exempt must change into their gym shoes and sit in the hall. Tactful, the boys didn't look in our direction. But by Year Ten, we preferred to wait it out in the library. We just had to take our mark book so she could sign the back of the page. She penned the day, the month and her signature. I calculated: not even two weeks had passed since *my* record. "No." I replied, and now I know why. I turned the mark book over and took out a razor blade. During Irka's cues, I painstakingly scraped off the figure '1.' My time was corrected; I had altered it to suit myself.

"But why do you think we should meddle at all? Surely she'll sort it out herself?" We were sitting on the window ledge behind the bookcases. Elena Ivanovna left for the dining hall. My story stopped at the car, at how it had driven away. I didn't let slip I had been at F.'s "But if we just wait it out," I went on heatedly, already sensing I was spoiling it, "We'll be on their side."

"One thing I do know: neither you nor I have seen that play…" Irka took out her hanky and began wiping the window ledge dust from her fingers. "And what if she says she never asked?" Irka finished wiping her fingers. The door banged. Elena Ivanovna, invisible behind the bookcases, went to her desk. "What do you reckon, if you told her *someone* – I stressed it so Irka would understand – did *something* behind your back…Would she wait?" I was hissing like a snake so Elena Ivanovna wouldn't hear. Irka's cheeks reddened. I was taking her back to *that* conversation, mercilessly, watching Irka's head droop. "The two of us?" Irka asked meekly. "We need Barashkova, too." Irka gave a bad-tempered start. "She's head girl," I replied decisively. Having thought it over, Irka accepted my logic. We grabbed Barashkova just before the biology class. Irka spoke persuasively. There's a mess. As head girl, Lenka has to do something. B.G. is the only one who can sort it out justly. Lenka half-listened. Idiotic happiness radiating from her face; for the first time since that case, Irka was starting a conversation with her.

We came early, eight-thirty. Stood around the corner, summoning our courage. Lenka pressed her hands against her chest. B.G. was leafing through an exercise book. We went in, single file. He smiled amiably. From the door, not approaching the desk, I said we wanted to talk about Fedya Alexandrov, and ask permission to call F. "Of course." He nodded and frowned. Irka turned round, perplexed. Anxious Lenka didn't understand. I shot out of the door. F. was coming towards me. "We came to talk with Boris Grigoryevich. With you, too, we hoped," loudly, as though they could have heard us. F. made a wry face, as she did at rehearsals when intonation is wrong. Then she nodded, and followed me. I joined the ranks without looking at Irka. We stood shoulder to shoulder, as if on parade, as though we'd gone out onto our stage and were standing under the raised curtain.

"The day before yesterday I went to the assembly hall to fetch the tray with the leftover gateau which everybody ate..." B.G. heard this epic beginning out. Those leftovers were utterly superfluous – there was no reason to bring them into this. "When I got there, they were rehearsing the American scene – Fedya, Lena Perova and ..." From the stage, I took them all in, looked at each of *them* in turn, *all of them*, everyone who had been looking at me, and I listed them, one after the other. "American?" B.G. checked, maintaining a serious face. It was all terribly stupid: my stupid impotence. She was sitting behind me. One second more and she would stand up, contemptuously. "It was smoky, they were all smoking." I saw how he got flustered. Something pathetic gradually surfaced on his face, a kind of pathetic smile. He looked startled but trusting. Irka tugged the hem of my dress. "I picked up the tray and left, but then I met Andrei Nikolayevich and he said it was a preview. He and..." – without turning around, I used her name and patronymic – "they watched, and then she fell ill because it's a hideous play..." "We want to ask you," I heard Irka's voice, "To sort it out." "But you didn't try to talk with Fedya yourselves?" Following Irka's prompt, B.G. took up the role of the just pedagogue. "I think it's useless for *us* to talk to Fedya. He won't listen to us," Lenka chimed in with the bright, confident voice of the head girl;

the latch swung open. I caught Irka's eye. Disdain. Irka despised me for *how* I spoke. "You, you – go on, you!" I begged with my eyes. Something snakelike flitted over her lips. "You see," she'd only just begun, but I already knew: she'll do it. "They want to perform this play on the Day of Theatre. There will be guests, and if they perform it, you teachers… for you…" She was saying: 'you teachers, for you,' but her words were aimed at him alone. F. stood up and walked towards the door. I saw *how* B.G. followed her with his gaze. Perhaps, in that moment, his whole life flashed before his eyes because the very next moment, when he looked at me, fear was already there – the terror of being exiled from school, a terror which we, his beloved children, had brought.

We were standing on the landing. "Why did you go on about smoking?" Irka scowled. "I don't know." And now I really didn't know. Something repulsive, like warm tights, was sticking to my hands. "But why did you bother… She only has to lift her finger…" Lenka muttered, throwing sidelong glances at us. Beads of sweat broke out on Lenka's face. "Maybe he wanted to express something of his own," Lenka rummaged for the word. "She never permits anything *personal*, not so much as a squeak." "You already squeaked once, you want to go again?" Lenka's beads of sweat began dripping. "But what can I do if that's how I feel, if I feel Russian?!" "Yeah!" said Irka. "You can say you delighted the whole Russian nation with your Russianness!" She wiped her hands on her pinafore.

We called them all out, one by one. Irka was explaining calmly: what happened, our logic, what decision we took, and how the conversation had gone. Irka had a precise memory, like a tape recorder. By the end of the day, we'd managed to talk with all 'ours.' The fact that F. was ill knocked everyone for six. Kostya said it wouldn't be a bad idea to lay into Fedya, give him a good beating. Nobody asked me why I'd brought up smoking. Mishka said, Fedya had really gone too far. Overall, everyone supported us. Irka was right. Nobody doubted that B.G. would deal with it justly. It reached Fedka's ears in a flash. B.G. called Fedka and Lenka. Barashkova saw them entering his office. She shuttled back and forth between us and them, and back again. Everyone knew about it, but they shared it dutifully. Barashkova said she's keeping her finger on the pulse. She didn't whine any more. The next day, B.G. watched the scene. Afterwards, he went straight to F's office. Barashkova swore he wasn't there long. F. kept quiet. During the lesson, she spoke about gerunds. On the way home, Irka said: seems it's blown over.

THE LANGUAGE
OF MOTHERLY HATRED

Lenka most likely told her mother herself. I can just imagine it: sitting in the corner, teeth chattering. "Smoking?!" Good Lord! Mother's panic was justified: final exams just around the corner. "No, no, not us! We didn't! They were lying." "But they could give you bad marks for behaviour, no college will take you!" Or maybe she didn't tell. Maybe one of the parents rang. Either way, Perova didn't come to school the next day.

I answered the doorbell in my dressing gown, towel round my head, after the bath. She entered: "I want to talk to your mother." Mum was already coming out of the living room to greet her. Raising her fur coat, Alla Georgiyevna sat on my sofa and announced she wanted to talk without me. I got up and went into another room. Alla Georgiyevna began speaking loudly and distinctly: my sister and I could hear her every word from our room. "I came to tell you that your daughter and two other girls," she didn't name them, "Went to Boris Grigoryevich to denounce my daughter. My daughter was defamed, they said she smoked. This could lead to bad marks for behaviour. All Institutes of Higher Education will be closed to her. I want to clear it with the school administration, of course: Boris Grigoryevich is a reasonable man. But since this may have happened as a result of your daughter's thoughtlessness, it would be better if she *herself* goes to Boris Grigoryevich and takes it back." "They'll beat the living daylights out of you," whispered my sister, with a shiver.

"This is a tragedy! For a girl to start life with a betrayal on her conscience. It's not too late to help them both, you see, your daughter and mine." Mum kept mum. "It's *easier* between the children, they get beaten, but my daughter and her friends…" I crept up to the door and leant towards the crack. Mum was sitting there, eyes lowered. Her cheeks were burning … "Of course, I'm against *such* methods myself, but sometimes it's precisely harsh measures which helps save them from worse calamities, instil the norms of decent behaviour into them." I stood up and went in to them. "You mean to say, I must have the living daylights beaten out of me?" I spoke with utter calm, as though, having found the right expression, I was translating simultaneously from the language of her maternal hatred. "I mean to say," her voice crescendoed with each syllable, "An intelligent girl must be aware." Something tripped me up, as though the key word had fallen out, and now, standing in front of them, I was losing the tempo of my simultaneous translation. Like polished pebbles, her words rolled around in my mouth. They were smooth and greasy, as though smothered with another's saliva. My Mum was nodding, her eyes still lowered. Shuddering from unfamiliar aversion, I swallowed this greasiness. Everything turned upside down, began swimming before my eyes: swimming in a synchronous line, a line with no gap; I did not forget a single word. Her words were a translation, but I knew the script. I recognized it straightaway.

"…You, you're a freak, not like other kids, this one just pisses, take off all your pissed-drenched stuff…" She spoke to me in the coarse language of my day nannies. But the other, tender language, of my night nurses – fear and anguish – unfurled above my head. I heard it rustling. "…You have no mother, no father, no sister, no brother. Here you stand alone in this wide world…" As they had before, they skilfully chose their moment to swoop down to rescue me.

"What I said about your daughter is true. I saw it myself, and no-one can make me take my words back." I looked at her, full of motherly hatred as she was, for now she was completely right: I was grassing on her daughter. Not then, but *now*. "You're a little shit. You're just jealous of Lena because she's from a different family, from a different…" She choked, choosing a word. Racing ahead of her lips, her native tongue was making a dash for freedom: foul language which was *my* native tongue, too. The words of her motherly hatred were landing in my heart because it was made to *their* measurements, it was their dear cradle. My infancy had fallen to it, not to F. I was looking at her patiently, not letting my eyes close, but something which I could not yet name was guffawing in me with the bestial laughter of a filthy whore… I watched as my mother got up and followed her. "Don't be afraid. I'll watch over you. They won't beat you when I'm around." My sister came to me and sat beside me on my bed.

SHOT

I'm an idiotic wooden puppet dangling between heaven and earth – boys below, girls behind. I am a hollow, wooden doll, with a wooden face. Must be, since I don't remember the blow. I only remember the hand which struck: "I forbid it! I forbid you to go to *her*! If I find out you were *there…*" *It* guffaws in me with bestial laughter while I grab my coat and tie my red scarf over the white one. Flat-snouted buses carry me through the night. Unflinchingly, 'til I see stars, to my dying breath. I will remember *their* lessons: can't wait 'til morning. Have to do it right now. Get there, warn her.

She should have been surprised but she wasn't. Neither by the late hour nor by my hospital-like appearance, in a gown and white headscarf. I sat down on the sofa and began, panting like Lenka's mother. Empty walls. Table covered with a white cloth. A cloth like a bedsheet in admissions. "Calm down," she takes my hand. I'm not panting any more. Just sit and tell her how it all happened, in order. With *real* words. Because she knows *their* language. She is silent. Gazing into the distance. Above the no man's land. I cried, of course, as I was running through the cold, running along the narrow path past the distant houses with their human inhabitants, rubbing my cheeks with my woollen mitts – the one they beat and the one they didn't beat – and now, in her admissions ward, they were covered with itching mange. I didn't have the strength to control my hands; they were drawn to scratch and scratch again. Fire in my cheeks. One hand wasn't enough. I ripped the second one from her hand. She sat before me, in the white hospitalesque light. Her face was mournful and pure. "Tomorrow my mother will go to B.G. and," nails were scraping the last remaining scabs from my cheeks. "She says, she forbids me to visit you."

It arrived. A dark explosion flashed in her eyes, lighting me up with a heavy glow. Not my mother, but I myself, out of my boundless, headlong love, had spilled the *whole* truth to her, but in her language, this truth was an insult. Not my mother, but I myself tore my hand from her concerned hand. "I want to stay here with you, I don't love anyone but you..." I was shouting. She hoisted me over the fire. A wave of her arm, and I was hurled into the flames. "You can't," she was looking into the fire with pensive pity. "Now we'll go together, I'll take you myself. I'll explain to her. Get up," she ordered, and I dared not disobey. What could I do against her resolute pity. She was leading me away from herself, to hand me over to the mother, the mother of *another's* child. The white hospital headscarf slipped towards the back of my head. I pulled it forwards, covering my head with fiery red, red like my scabbed cheeks, red like Marina's dead lips. A doctor, she was discharging me into the world, not fully cured. F. stirred the fire and flung open the door. We left the house, went along the path. We walked as we had done then, only now she walked beside me. My feet didn't slip. The path was too narrow to accommodate two. I walked along the dark strip, along the dark purple shadow of the flanking bushes.

Mother opened the door. She looked at us with complete calm, as if, after what had happened that day, it was F.'s duty to bring me home. As if F. was a nanny, whom she herself had hired for me, and now intended to fire, exchanging mercy for wrath. F. began softly and tenderly: "I've brought your daughter to you. There's something I need to explain." They sat opposite each other, across the empty table covered with a festive oilcloth – fruit bowls on a dark blue background: apples, pears, grapes. Empty garden. F. didn't order me, she gave me a look, and I stood up. My sister was sleeping. She spoke softly, I didn't dare eavesdrop.

The door opened. Now, after their quiet conversation, my mother's face wore a perplexed expression. "Maybe you'd like some compote?" Mum looked at me as though looking for support. I darted to the window ledge, grabbed the pan. F. said neither yes nor no. Mother poured compote into cups, ladling the heavenly dried fruits from the pan bottom: apples, pears, raisins – dried up and boiled down. Mum said that now she knows how to reply to Boris Grigoryevich, knows the proper answer. Putting on her coat in the porch, F. said it would be better if Mother didn't let me go to school the next day. That's exactly what she said – not to me: don't go, but to her: don't let her go, for several days. "Don't go tomorrow," Mum said, as though what I heard wasn't enough. I made it to my bed and fell asleep, dead to the world. I fell asleep fast, without even wondering: how will she, alone, in the middle of the night…?

The next evening the phone rang for the first time. Solemn Barashkova spilled out the latest news: Lenka's mother had come home and laid into Lenka, so Lenka was forced to admit they'd smoked, and her mum gave her a right old dressing down, and didn't let her go to school, went herself instead – straight to B.G. What about, nobody knows, but Lenka called Lariska, and Lariska passed it on, and lots of folk have decided to stop talking to you. What's more, B.G. came after class and said this story was going too far, parents are getting involved. He said he viewed the play and *he personally* sees nothing dreadful in it, even though there are several speeches which, had it all turned out differently, he would have *advised* excluding, cut, without altering the gist, it's normal practice in adult theatres, too… I was holding the receiver, squinting at the earpiece as though it were a telegraph machine. And the narrow, yellowy ribbon was streaming from it, pushing right into my eyes. There were other words on it, not Lenka's. Then, Lenka was chirping, Fedka got all agitated and said of course he was ready to cut, his father told him, the viewing before the premier is always like that. But B.G. *scowled* – really dreadfully – and says: the situation has turned this way so *now*, he has made up his mind: take it down, unconditionally. As for everything else – here Lenka said he probably meant smoking – all problems were resolved and wouldn't influence the marks. But when B.G. left, well, then *it* began!

Everyone was yelling the likes of you should be killed and if you dared show your face in school… So I mean, you'd better not. By the way, have you got pneumonia again or what?… (I kept quiet). At this point, by the way, Lenka went on in a mysterious whisper: I saw it myself, after, when B.G. went to his office, F. went in and came out *dreadfully* pale, and B.G. shoots out after her, trots along beside her, and she says to him: "The matter is settled, I heard you." "Fine, I'll come tomorrow." "Reeeaally?" I could tell she was *dreadfully* pleased. I came. English was first. We stood by the door. Everyone was silent, eyes averted. F. opened the door, saw me, and said: "Enter." She waited for them to go in, then closed the door. We were left alone in the corridor. "Get the hell out of here! Get out of my sight!" Her eyes held a distant, undiminishing blaze. I started walking. The door slammed like a shot. Now, after a quarter of a century has passed, I know what to call it, that shot to the back of my wooden head.

And then the phone rang for a second time and Irka said: At English, today, there was a conversation. Terrible! F.'s face… She said everything happens faster in our school. Well, with those, after they left school, but with us, well, we'd not even managed to leave. She spoke for a long time, all lesson. Too much to remember, Irka said, but along the lines of: we are her handiwork, but our handiwork is that we're left – Irka paused – in the rubbish dump… Then she started about you… Irka fell silent, waiting for my prompt. I kept quiet. In short, she's warning everyone: if anyone, with word or look or anything else, so much as dares to take it out on you, she promises that somebody that she'll find a way to massacre them. "*Massacre.* Remember this word. You can convey it to your parents. I don't care." So there you are, Irka said. Now you can come.

And then the phone rang for a third time and Irka said Fedya and Lenka went to B.G. and asked him to take them into his group. And Barashkova trotted after them coz she told Irka she doesn't generally approve of F.'s methods. But B.G. suggested they find someone from his group to volunteer to move to F.'s. But there wasn't anyone, coz everyone's known for ages that

F. has different standards, and they'd never lived in such an environment before. Yet they still swapped; B.G. agreed because F. came to him and asked him herself. *Somehow* found out they'd been asking, she said. So, Irka said, well, now, it'll reflect on the marks. That's when they all start to *shine*, you see. Curious. If they get fives in the last semester, will they get fives for the whole year, too? By the way, there was a parents' meeting on Saturday. Mum went. Came home and said: "B.G. came up to me, asking about your health. Then says: maybe you want to talk to me? Maybe you have some questions? I don't have any questions, I replied."

I'm lying down, face to the wall. The wall: dark ornaments with gold, dim like hair losing its sheen. Long nightie flows along the legs, long fingers stretching towards the cheeks. The wall is the hospital mirror. I can't walk away, can't climb the chair. So now that's how it will be, I always will be looking, admiring the swollen cheeks my hands are drawn towards, itching to scratch. Brown stains on the pillow. The ribbon chirps, comes out in shudders, strong as rope, can't rip it off. Voices, voices – more frightening than the telephone emptiness. I scratch, thinking: Good Lord, this has already happened! Someone who *it* massacred. Oh, Lord, now it's me; now *it is with me... I* did it. I chose this filth, to protect her. Cannot scream, screams terrify those who sleep. Wash your hands, put on a nightie, mustn't be so pale. Their words, that is them. They came again: they came again, fear and anguish, hammering at my gates, my eternal kindergarten hell. I raise the candle. The window is closed. Boys below, girls behind my back. I blow away the yellow. I need the light no more.

THE POWER AND THE GLORY

I went to school on Monday. *No-one dared*. Maybe among themselves, but not with me. I asked Kostya to come in the evening. I don't love you, I said. He stretched out his hand. "Don't you dare!" *He* doesn't dare touch my cheeks, scratched red raw. I can never love someone like him. Against the whole world. I am not lady Anne, I'm not Nastassia Filippovna. I am a freak. Nothing new.

On Tuesday, F. called Kostya and me to stay behind, warning a photographer would come tomorrow. B.G. had asked, the school should have our photographs. She's speaking indifferently. "Says he wants to make a special drama stand next to the war memorial museum. For the generations to come." She pronounced B.G.'s words with such force, as though we were already gone. The photographer came in the afternoon, they took us out of class, we were given an empty study. F. came with us, sat in the corner, not interfering. The photographer said: "Let's begin," and we stood up, as if about to go out on stage. Because we thought we would perform, and he would snap away in the appropriate places, like the foreigners. But he said: no need. "Just chose some poses. The most, well, dramatic. Key scenes." F. shrugged, barely noticeable; he didn't see. "Your beauty, with a rapier, bid me farewell," she listed rapidly. We got up, demonstrated them one after another. Frozen, wordless. She looked past us as though now, tongue-less we were no longer her creation. The photographer muttered and clicked: "Good, good, next." Then he thanked us, said he'd bring them in a couple of days, give them directly to B.G. F. brought them on Friday. Again, we stayed behind after class, and F. began pulling them from the envelope, all doubles, two of each.

She examined them carefully, then gave them to us. They did the rounds, connecting us for the last time, as it were: four scenes, photograph-twins. I pored over them, but not in the way you look at photos: I didn't see *how* I came out. Something else, unlike Richard or Anne, was looking out at me from these black and white pictures. I looked at them as though they were already hanging on the stand of our glorious devotion. I looked with the eyes of those other children, the children who will come after us. B.G. will tell them about us. He will begin by listing our victories and the words he utters will light up his blackboard with flaming letters. He will remember the best and forget the worst, as though mistaking us for his own youth and past happiness, just as Marina mistook her war. And one day, trying to defer an oral exam, they will cajole him, and he will say, solemnly, and without going into details: There was one scene not quite fitting for a school theatre, but all in all, everything was resolved peacefully; you could always strike a deal with *those* children.

I guessed it all, of course, how could I fail to guess, since, right then, I was the first of those new children, the ones who would come after us. I looked at us with a stranger's eyes but saw more than the new children could, since I stood in the middle: I was the translator, the one Irka had spoken of while discussing her forefathers and descendants. We were all translators: we knew the language our forefathers could not yet speak and our descendants had not yet begun to speak. We knew many words because we stood at the summit which we ascended thanks to F's labours, and from which our long downward path stretched ahead of us. It's just a saying: it's harder to ascend, but you fly downwards as though on wings, swallowing the years.

The new children will not suspect a lie; he can give them the correct explanation in the language which will become their own. He will find the words which will become a *good* explanation: she left because she found a new school closer to home, and they will believe in *that*, since, coming after us, they will be stronger than us. And then he will grow old, and due to Maman's charity, they will keep him on to take after-school class for the juniors. And then he will embark upon creating a *real* museum of our times long gone, and young trail-blazers –which our school will never lack – will begin collecting materials. They will send out letters, then, on the quiet, laugh at him and at us, just as we laughed – only one *epoch* before their laugher – at Marina's red glory, which she smeared with clown's makeup over her old and frightening lips. They will laugh as all children do, born by chance where the dead are laughed at, the dead glory of past times mocked. And the kingdom, and the power, and the glory... Dying kingdom.

Just two weeks later, F. informed B.G. that this year, due to ill health, she would not be able to prepare a full-scale Theatre Day, but if one of the other teachers wanted to... None of our English teachers dared.

I come to visit her day after day. She continues rehearsing that cycle of five sonnets with me, the longest cycle, as if nothing had happened. We work, not talking about anything else. We start anew each time, because *this* is completely different, more difficult and important than the *Twelfth Night* with its cross-dressing girls and funny mistaken identities. Again and again, as though demonstrating *what* can be done *after death*, too, she drives me back up to the summit, like a shepherd driving his flock over the pass at sunset. She stands, her shining eyes gazing beyond me, as though she sees beyond the pass, glimpsing a new herd coming towards her from beyond my worn-out, work-weary back. I am the last – the last survivor from all that perfidious brood which she drove and drove before her for all these years. Now I know why she chose me: due to the course of events for which I am probably not responsible, I passed her summit and was now descending headlong into my own, real, doomed life. But still, I was leaving more slowly than the rest. I walked falteringly, and, perhaps sensing this, she began driving me back. No, she did not try to save and preserve me. She no longer believed, she couldn't believe, that I would hold my own on the heights. She saw the fading flame in which I – who had failed the test – was burning out before her very eyes. But she had promised B.G. a new cycle, and so she must prepare it, and, most importantly, she knew she could rely on me, since I was already enveloped in the flames. Then, in our last school months, she relied on me in a special sense: in that short period, I was becoming the only translator between her life and real life. Obedient to her will, I could still ascend the summit of immortality – which she no longer believed in – one last time. For a brief instant, I could stand firm, although the virus of death already raged within me. And, gazing from her high vantage point, I could talk and cry about the unbending will of deadly time, not from hearsay. I could – in other words, I must – talk with *them* as the terminally ill with the terminally ill. They no longer believed her, but they must believe *me*. Word by word, those words which she put into my mouth at the end were becoming her and my testimony, since the emptiness from which she once returned was now awaiting me, jaws agape. I heard the boom of the earth my foot stood upon. I was burning in time, and, ever obedient to it, I was returning from her heights to the gluttonous earth to be swallowed when my turn came. I was the last one, the suitable one, for those who came after me did not yet know how to count the hours, did not know *how* the vainglorious events of disgusting night can swallow the brave day of enlightenment. The new, the sweetest offspring, not yet formed and not yet swallowed, were waiting for F.'s appurtenance, as it were, to begin their first brave day. My offspring because they were coming after me, and I was leaving them behind, and she was counting on their courage. She was brimming with power: who else but she had the right to count on a future? To them, ready to traverse the pass, she was a drover and witness of future glory. I will never dare ask, never dare put this question to her: did she know the number of broods coming towards her was finite and had already been allocated? Did she think that one day, from behind the worn-out, work-weary backs of her very last, the sweetest and most perfidious brood, others would come to her, and she would no longer be able to rely on their daytime courage? In my blood, I heard the pulse of life's pride. I was entering Time, where everything becomes sickness: youth and love, pleasure and joy, pride and bitterness, because everything – no matter what you take – either wins or moves on. I had not entered yet, but they should have listened to me *then*, since *fore-knowledge* came through my lips. It was stronger than the daytime reasoning, and reasoning – my poor, despairing healer – had resolved to leave me.

In March, it was B.G.'s fiftieth. We filled a card with our best wishes, in English of course, in Shakespearean language, with 'thees' and 'thous.' Kostya and Sasha Reshetin prepared a Whatman sheet so it looked like an ancient manuscript; they smeared it with pounded pencil lead and slightly singed the edges. The manuscript was rolled up and a wax seal melted onto the cord. When his birthday dawned, we invited B.G. into the rec hall, read out the greetings and then presented him with the manuscript. B.G. unrolled it and fell silent. Then he began crying, said he loves us *all*, will never forget any of us, and will never love any future students more than us. We grew light and joyful at his words: on the eve of parting, he was telling us the truth, and *all* our teachers would have joined him in this momentary truth. All except F.; she wasn't in the rec hall. Those words would not have passed her lips as she had already set her hopes on those who would come after us. She could love *all*, but only on the eve of meeting.

We performed the 'Twelfth' at the end of May, at the Prom. I read the new cycle to them then, too, for the first and last time. It was a completely different audience, unlike the usual Theatre Day public. This was the festive farewell audience. Parents had waited for the last day. They had waited for ten years to snatch us from the teachers' hands; the grown-up children belonged to them. The perplexed smiles of the teachers and triumphant smiles of the parents affirmed this. The parents sat solemnly in tight rows; the first row of teachers – usually Maman sat in the centre – seemed semi-see-through: the parents' smiles shone with earned and long-awaited triumph through the gaps between teachers' shoulders. We performed the 'Twelfth' under the flashes of the parents' cameras. It was my cue. I stood, waiting for the introduction. It didn't start for a long time, perhaps for a whole minute. For the last time, I stood on *her* summit. Pride came to a standstill in my blood, bitterness prevented me from opening my lips. There was nobody in front of my eyes, neither children nor parents. The boundless desert of my future life lay at my feet. Turning my eyes inward, my pride and bitterness joined at once, like two palms, in the most hushed meekness – and with the sound of their unification, the music began. Forlorn and sorrowful, I descended down the stony slope, not daring to look back towards the place where she stayed, and all the stones of the world pierced my bare feet... I chose that filth myself. When I fell silent, all was quiet. I came back, and saw B.G. He was sitting in the front row. Right in front of me. He was crying silently, not raising his hands to his face. He was crying as that lacy one had once cried, having come to a foreign land to hear *hers*. I alone could see his tears. But I, who could see, looked beyond. Witnesses don't cry. I was a witness: that very moment, F., who had been sitting in her usual place in the corner, stood up and went towards the door. I looked at her and knew she was walking away from me forever. Something got twisted out of shape, irreparably ruined, floundered as never before. The voice inside me was no longer there, no longer saying: 'You will be with her forever...' And then, when she left, I returned my eyes to his tears, because there, in his tears, my *own* life was beginning, a life I still hoped to live out.

Even now, when our common life is already over, I cannot imagine what would have become of us had I run after her then, and, having caught up with her, had climbed back up the stony slope and begged her not to leave me. Maybe she would have taken pity on me, as she did each time or, when, without waiting for her word, I turned away, renounced, gave up everything which caused her eastern brows to frown. Why, then, in my seventeenth year, was I unable to turn away from this common celebration? Its far-off, effervescent lights, like the electric lights of St. Elmo's fire, were crackling in the valley into which my feet were carrying me. The celebration promised to be warm, moist with love-struck warmth so full of temptation and untrustworthy truth that her departure, severing the umbilical cord, seemed undeserved and merciless: gave birth and left.

"Is your father here?" I'd once asked Fedka that, waiting for our shared tights to cool down. They were a rehearsal for another cooling down. His father had not been in the hall then, as we peeped through the velvety crack. No need for that now. It wasn't a torn veil, it was the heavy velvet drop curtain, flung wide open – from earth to the sky, and our parents' voices vibrated in this veil, invitingly lying on the earth itself. What would I have replied, should he have come to me and asked: is your *mother* here? Had she allowed me to persuade her, she would have spoilt everything; she never allowed herself to spoil anything.

We began our shared celebration. The parents outdid themselves: champagne, cakes from the famous 'Nord' bakers, lemonade… We feasted, danced and performed our festive repertoire. Each of us had prepared our own: couplets about school life which we sung to the tune of a romance. A.N. accompanied us on the piano. Lots of couplets, more than I can remember now. Good Lord, how they laughed! I remember their faces, contorted with laughter, as clearly as I remember my heart contorted with the grimace of gaiety.

I saw her once more, at the exam, when she was sitting in the panel and listened to our synopses with teacherly indifference We all excelled. She had nothing to worry about: her job was done. The rest was up to us. Having waited my turn, I stood up and went towards the desk where they were sitting: Maman, B.G., A.N., and she. I replied mechanically, almost by heart, without even a second's thought. I translated simultaneously, flying from tongue to tongue; B.G. barely managed to finish his sentences. She looked at me with a warm expression; I never did see the indifference in it. After the exam, we didn't see each other for seven years.

INCISIONS IN THE ONION

We all *got places*. The parents had done the right thing by enrolling us into this school back then. Sergei Ivanovich's memorable words, with which he forewarned us about taking a frivolous attitude to exams, came true in reverse. F. left our school. They said she'd found something closer, courses for adults, apparently. I found out about it third hand. I remember my surprise: surely she's not directing Shakespeare with adults? A quick mental calculation – a two-year course: Year Six level English, at best. Didn't occur to me they might perform in Russian. Marred by that story of ours, the Russian language smacked of disgrace, demise and dust, which I daren't disturb. We all made it up again after a few years. The details of the distant school story faded with time; time knows how to be merciful, for its own fleeting ends. We all procured our adult memory, which played with scraps of school memories, arranging them like a child's building blocks, arbitrarily. Meeting up, we would share our delight at successes, our commiseration at misfortunes. In those years, packed with personal and professional hopes which did or didn't materialise, we preferred not to look back at our collapsed little world. The leftover shards, strewn behind our backs, seemed a distant, almost alien, memory. But should the conversation stray in *that* direction, we would avert our eyes, lowering them, as though in secret, belated fright: don't chafe. There was another oddity, not so easily explained: to a greater or lesser degree, we all viewed the world around us with a certain superciliousness, as though, upon mature reasoning and sober calculation, we had entered into a contract with it, something akin to a wedding contract, into which we brought our noble birthright of the first-born – our collapsed little world of cruel Judaic arrogance and Hellenistic enlightenment. And the world, the other partner in this marriage contract, brought a simple but seductive life force, which we hoped to harness for our purposes. From time to time, however, the shaky foundations of this marriage – to continue my rather strained metaphor – were felt: not many of us learnt to talk with the betrothed in its language. Let me not be misunderstood: even though I mentioned our conversation might stray in *that* direction, I don't mean we *discussed* that story. For our eyes, always ready to look away and down, an indirect mention sufficed. That is how the members of an English family avert their eyes, privy to information about some distant but murky story regarding how one of the older daughters lost her honour, or the improper behaviour of a nephew.

I remember exactly why I came to Barashkova: for text books. I wanted to start giving private lessons. It was a lucrative business in those times, but not without risks – the law on private enterprise had come in. But I needed money to exchange flats: A.N. and I had separated by then. English textbooks were not sold openly. But Lenka, who had shot up the career ladder and was already Head of Studies at an English school, promised to bring me a dozen books from her library. She kept her promise, and now I was sitting drinking tea at her place, eyeing the plump parcel gleefully; I was grateful to her. The conversation wound around the female teachers Lenka supervised. "It's terrible," Lenka complained, finding a sympathetic ear in me. "I explain, explain, explain, but they don't get it." Lenka began speaking in English, giving examples of their lack of knowledge. I listened to the language made up of words and expressions I knew, but could only follow the general gist with some difficulty. The language gave way under the weight of Lenka's voice. I wanted to sigh her words out, not keep them. I'm ashamed to say, I sympathised with the teachers. "Do you test them?" I asked in Russian. "The Director insists: the DDPE methodologists show up after me," Lenka replied, at which point we both lowered our eyes. "By the way," Lenka paused, "Did you know, F. is teaching in a school somewhere near the Techno metro station?" She had ventured far beyond the bounds, and now she fell silent.

I sighed, overcoming the stuffiness. But the stuffiness of Lenka's English wouldn't let me go. "Which one? Do you know the number?" I asked, taken aback by the calmness of my own voice. Lenka paused. Thinking. Tempered by seven years of solitude, my ears were tormented by Lenka's muttering. She was going through the school numbers as if looking for an empty slot, as though I, a loser, had come to her for old time's sake, and she, endowed with worldly power, was sincerely trying to help me find my feet. "No, on one of the Red Army Streets… I can look in the general register tomorrow…" "Don't bother." The events of the last few years: divorce, forced to swap flats, English courses, they were beginning to make sense. They were falling into place. I laughed at the simplicity of the task: to find one in a dozen streets. "What, you mean you haven't seen her all these years?" Lenka took my laughter as permission to continue. I thanked her for the textbooks and got up.

Combing the Red Army district, block by block, I scrutinised the façades of the buildings, as though expecting to find something akin to our school – whitish façade, three- paned windows, concrete lintel over the porch. Nothing of the kind. I had already ruled out two, marked by unfamiliar numbers, but found no trace of plaques listing the subjects taught until, after having pored over an old, lumpy façade decorated with stony monograms, I stumbled upon what I was looking for. A plaque hanging to the right of the high entrance bore a strong resemblance to ours. The inscription was identical, word for word, except for the number – this number was in the two hundreds. I looked around, gave the high door a shove, and went in. The long stairway leading to the first floor was trammelled by narrow walls under a low-slung ceiling. I climbed, my breath slow and cautious, as though I could be caught and expelled at any moment. The hall turned out to be small and rather dark. A child-minder was sitting in a corner, in the yellow circle of a desk lamp. I went up, gulped, and pronounced the name and patronymic. The yellowish circle glowed with a perpetual, forlorn yellowness. She could have said: "No, not here," but, looking at me indifferently, the day minder spoke, gave the room number. "On the first floor. Go and wait there. The bell's in ten minutes." Once there, I leant against the pier opposite.

From here, from my pier, I could see a massive door crowned with little a glass window. Children's classroom voices trickled through the cracks in the door. I could make out the momentous voices of eternal retelling. I didn't hear her voice; perhaps she wasn't chiming in. Trusting the child-minder, I waited patiently. It rang right above my ear. I started, looked round: a metallic little cupola, the bell's sting was thrashing around inside. It fell silent. The children's voices rose to a crescendo behind the door, it burst open, and the little flock of Year Sixers spilled out towards me, running towards the stairs. They eyed me up, on the run, with fleeting interest, taking me for someone else's parent. They didn't greet parents in this school. I stood motionless. The corridor emptied. My eyes, fixed on the door, were losing hope; the child-minder had got mixed up, a day child-minder, a deaf fool. The door opened by itself. F. stepped into the corridor, keys in her hand. Her face was pale and tired. Her eyes slid along the wall. Reached the pier, and stopped. The polite surprise registering on her face pushed me into the wall. Without a word, she stepped aside and pushed the door again, inviting me in.

"How are you doing?" she asked glumly, as soon as we had sat down. Colleges, families, children – she was preparing to listen to this whole senile list. "Barashkova told me you are here." "You look well," she responded, gratefully, realising she was absolved. "You didn't take your bag, were you on your way to the canteen?" She looked at me attentively and nodded. "I have a rehearsal in about twenty minutes." She looked at her watch. "In fifteen." She didn't have a secretary to tell me the audience was over. Something rather cold appeared in her eyes: now I should ask about what she is rehearsing and then, having politely replied to my question, she could stand up and bid me farewell. "If I find out you have come to rehearsal hungry, I'll suspend you." I remembered how she had answered my mother's concern. Her concern about me. In this school, I was a parent. "There's no time for you to eat now. It's because of me. I came unannounced. Here," I opened my bag and took out a pasty. "But it's with onion, I bought it by the metro." She reached out her hand. I saw how it wavered, her reaching hand. The daylight lamps folded their wings under the ceiling. The windows, covered with yellowish curtains, were tall and narrow, not at all like ours. She took the pasty, unwrapped it, and took a bite. I sat in front of her, silent, like a dried out, empty shell: a piece of dry pasty without any filling. "Why didn't you visit?" she asked in a different voice, as if she only noticed me now, when I had returned from where one cannot dally. I kept quiet. We both knew the answer. I didn't need to reply. "I came to ask permission to come." She nodded, understanding. "If I'd come to you at home, you would have felt awkward about getting rid of me straight away, but here," I gave a weak smile, as you do after an illness. "I wouldn't have kicked you out," she said hesitantly. "Can I come?" "Yes," she replied, composed and business-like, and looked at her watch again. "In a couple of days, next week, I'll call you myself. They've just installed a phone in my place, but I'm still waiting for the number. And you shall come. Leave me your number." I wrote the number on a scrap of paper, stood up and left.

They rang a week later, when I had already lost hope. A rather simple female voice called me by name and introduced itself as her neighbour. "So. I'm ringing from a phone box," the voice was resentful. I had no time for either surprise or fright. "She gave me the number. No-one picked up, and I went round myself. The door was open, the ambulance had left it like that, left without locking it. And she couldn't get up, so she was lying like that with the open door…" "But where was she lying?" "On the bed, as they left her. Gave injections and left. They don't care. But then she lost consciousness. I dropped in by chance, saw the door was open, a scrap of paper with a number lying on the table. So I took it and said: shall I ring? No, she says, then she says: ring. She came herself, she says. Go and call, but not from here…" "I'm coming, I'll just nip into the shop, get some food for her – what can she eat?" "What, don't you know yourself? You have kids, raise them, raise them, then neither hide nor hair. Neighbours ringing round all over, I didn't even know she had… pish." She slammed the phone down.

I got there fast. The door wasn't locked. The neighbour, drawing her own conclusions, had correctly understood that as things stood, I may well not have a key. I went in, locked the door, shoved the bag in the corner, and then approached the door to her room. "Don't come in," I heard her quietest of voices, utterly helpless. "I don't want you to see me like this." "I've brought some things, I'll cook, so you can eat…" She kept quiet. I waited, my ear pressed against a crack in the door. "A piece of bread." I nodded, forgetting she couldn't see anything. In the kitchen, I quickly put on the kettle, took out the groceries and, looking round, found a pan for the bouillon. The kettle soon boiled. I made tea, sliced the bread, put a small dab of butter on a saucer. I approached the door and knocked. "No," she said inexorably. "Leave it all in the kitchen." "I can just open the door a crack and hand it you…" "No," she remained adamant. "I won't look, I'll just come in, leave it, won't raise my eyes." Silence. I opened the door carefully. Lowering my eyes like a priest whose one careless, impudent glance is punishable by death, I slowly came up and set it down. *While you bring popes from Paris…* It surfaced by itself, turning on my lips. I repeated and repeated it while creeping backwards to the door, not raising my eyes. The white blob of the bed. My eyes, covered by the Franciscan's hood, self-proclaimed monk. Now back in the corridor, pressing myself to the crack in the door, I said I'd put the bouillon to boil and would wait until… "Fine," she agreed meekly. "Take a stool and sit there so I can hear you." The cup clattered, barely audibly. I sat, swallowing my saliva with difficulty, as though the little piece of bread placed by her bed wouldn't go down her throat, and now, by swallowing, I was helping her swallow. "Your pasty was tasty. I smelt of onion at the rehearsal," she joked with her last strength. "I collapsed the same day you… after rehearsal… home…. And collapsed. Crawled to the bed, rang them. The phone was already connected. They came. Injections. And then – I don't remember…

Then they disappeared. I saw you all the time. Your hair was waving, like it did in Richard...The last thing I saw, dying..." She was lying alone in the scene of her death: "A horse! A horse! My kingdom for a horse!" I wasn't there. If they'd locked the door... If it hadn't been for the neighbour... "You won't die," I said quietly, afraid even a spasm in my wretched throat might disturb her. She hadn't eaten for a week. "No, of course I won't die. Especially if you feed me on pasties..." Something was thawing in me, filling up, as though I were really a piece of dry pasty and she, lying helplessly on the bed, could fill me, stuff me with a small, diced onion bulb, able to save me from death. "Good Lord!" I thought, "Good Lord, I went to the school, found her that very day..." "You came that very day." Her voice was rustling, growing warmer. "Your pasty was the last thing I..." The body was returning to me, my rejected body. I shuffled on the stool. "Take the key and go. I'll get up later and switch it off myself. Go." I didn't dare stay.

Actually, she didn't get up again. The stroke which she had survived alone affected her vestibular apparatus. For some time afterwards, she still hoped to return to work. The new school's administration waited for her patiently, her new pupils came to visit: initially she wouldn't let them cross the threshold. Then, overcoming her rising nausea, she tried to go down the stairs, go out for a walk. I was bringing in doctors, cajoling them with anything I could think of. One day, que sera, sera, we thought, and set off for an audience with a famous psychic, whom I hadn't managed to entice to a house call. The attempt amounted to nothing: it turned out that F. was immune to hypnosis. Then it was the physiotherapist's turn. He turned out to be quite a vulgar specimen, like a trainer: kept promising full recovery and, sniggering, promised to find her an 'old boy', too. She put up with it. Then we made it to the Polenov Institute, which, back then, boasted the only scanner in town able to take snapshots of brain impulses and locate the damaged regions. There was a six-month waiting list, but, having burst into the head of the department's office, all it took was thirty minutes of stirring speech, and the doctor began apologizing he couldn't hospitalize her here and now.

"Please forgive me, but it's simply impossible today. There is no place at all." He took her into the ward the next day, and, having performed the necessary electronic analysis, made his diagnosis. When I came to talk with him a week later, he spent a long time showing me the scans and diagrams, explaining that the affected region of the brain – the small vessel under the skull in the back of the head – could, in principle, be operated on, but the success rate was no higher than fifty percent, and the other fifty percent face the prospect of becoming a vegetable since some kind of special centres are located nearby and could be damaged. Eyes lowered, he was explaining that time – now hopelessly lost – was crucial; had he got her here under a drip immediately, after two or three hours… Hoping to bribe lost time, I assumed he was dropping a hint and promised him large sums of money. His consternation was genuine: "Why? Why do *all of you* take me for some monster, capable of extorting money in *such* cases? I would have done all I could, believe me, after what you told me… Let's go." He showed me a young woman in the next ward; after the operation, she could no longer recognise her own children. I transmitted all this to F, told her about the one who didn't recognise, and, after a brief discussion, we declined the operation. Without throwing in the towel, we made attempt after attempt, but all to no avail. Sometimes she would get better: the bluish shadows under her eyes would vanish, her cheeks would flush pale pink, her lips would clear of roughness. And then she could entertain visitors, who would flock to her from all sides, just as before. This entertaining generally ended in a relapse. She was getting worse right in front of their eyes, but, deceived by her calm voice, they still had no inkling. Sometimes she would get worse. Then she could see no-one but me, and even then, only with difficulty. On those occasions, I would sit on the little bench by her bed.

The world, which for me had shrunk to the confines of her room, was rapidly expanding, yet the sensation – that constant companion of my last years of school life – that what was to come was inevitable didn't slacken its grip. Of course, this growing sensation was first and foremost due to her illness, though at times, when she felt better, I was still hoping for salvation. Hope of recovery, a flippant hope I was unable to overcome even as I sat by her bedside, gave me strength. I believed in her victorious-ness. This belief had not diminished with the years, and now it let me laugh and joke, make her laugh, and care for her. From time to time, as though drawing back our velvet curtain a chink, we would peek outside, as though we were secretly observing new scenes which were played out by *present time,* at its Day of Theatre. The eastern despotism, under which she, maybe not fully consciously, had been preparing us to live, was rapidly fading into the past. The empire was crumbling. Its borders were being washed away like sand banks under the onslaught of time's high tide. Before our very eyes, the USSR was coming to an end – huge and mediocre, a great Zinnober. The fairies who had combed its hair for decades were leaving. Uncombed, unkempt locks were falling onto the broad forehead. The foreigners who for long years had observed the creations of the frauleins' hands were no longer enraptured. However, with the death of the empire, our world was coming to an end, too, our new age of Enlightenment. Our school world was a small island there, a little world which faded forever, lost in the mists of time. Her illness coincided with this period. The mean characteristics of the present – the arrival of which she had contained by her mere presence – were crossing *all* thresholds, unobstructed, altering human voices beyond recognition. From time to time, listening to the speeches flowing from the radio, she was tortured by the one dimensionality of the voices, calling them: plain. These uprooted voices sounded as though they had no past. She had no desire to converse with them. "*These,*" she would say in a weak voice, propped up on her pillows, "*will not heat the streets.*" Nevertheless, maybe due to her ever-present skill, she lent an ear to them, and in those moments, her face, wearied by years of pain, would become sharp and aloof. Black, gaping emptiness would appear in her eyes, as though she saw: like stiff scum from the bottom of the font, others were surfacing from below the flat voices. She did not survive to see them settle as insoluble sediments of devilry. Weak from her illness, she could not fight the filth of the advancing world, the first traces of which were tramped into her clean home on our feet. Her strength was only sufficient to turn away from the filthy world, to exorcise herself with the same harshness with which she had previously exorcized the defiled. "If it's freedom he wants, let him secure it himself, at his own expense." She always secured her own freedom by herself.

Sometimes I think someone could have been found, someone born in the expanse of the flailing Empire, who could have tried even without her. B.G. had thought about it when he tried to save the Day of Theatre, back then, in our remote past, when she was still so very close, standing beside us, on guard. But none of our English teachers found the courage. Yes, now I know: *that* time is lost, hopelessly.

The lives of my classmates played out differently, as human lives should. The cruel, everyday realities overwhelmed us all equally, without differentiating. But – and this I know for sure – many of us had the strength to resist. Under our teacher's demanding eyes, we had undergone a training. For monastic life, I would say now. It turns out that the antidote she was offering us on the tip of the dagger or sword while preparing us for life in the vast and cruel Empire can sometimes be effective even after the latter's collapse. We came to know a language our parents did not know and our children are unlikely to know, and that means no-one will require our translation services. Our descendants will get along just fine in their world without us, but no-one will give them an antidote. They will enter the big time defenceless. Sometimes I think all those who passed through her hands were indeed Zinnobers. After all, there is no getting away from it – we were praised for something which was not our handiwork. Now we are ageing: my classmates have families and children, and none of us are performing Shakespeare. But something I cannot name has remained. Something which does not cloud our eyes. The good and evil her hands tugged from us remained *our* good and evil. Only a few of us submitted to the *other*. By the way, it is not for me to judge. "You are good," that's what she was telling me, slightly mockingly.

She died ten years later. Her mother – death – bided her time before snatching her from me. Ten years of illness accommodated many events: living beyond the confines of her small flat, time went its own way. The world changed, sometimes for the better, sometimes for the worse. But these changes were not played out before our eyes. Our world, the world in which she and I lived after her 'death,' as she put it, was filled with other concerns, the minority of which came as the natural burdens of her illness, while the majority was devoted to our conversations, which blossomed as the years passed. She did what she wanted – created her own world, independent of time, which could have been perfect if not for her incurable illness. Closed within the space of her room, from time to time this world of hers would open via the TV screen. She observed external life and shared her observations with me. These observations were marked by harshness and visionary turns of phrase, the correctness of which I never had reason to doubt, even for a second. But more often than not, we talked about what was dear to us, and these Anglo-Russian conversations often led us into heights and depths from which we returned reluctantly. Our eyes were fixed on each other, we gazed at each other, getting used to the coming, aching emptiness.

The fact that I could no longer reply to her in English soon became clear. Initially busy with matters relating to her illness, I paid it no heed, perhaps secretly hoping everything would change. Then I blamed it on my Russian throat, incapable of stepping back from the seven years of life spent away from her. Then I made peace with it, as you reconcile yourself with time hopelessly lost. *Those who are more worthy, Lord, O Lord, they shall see Thy kingdom.*[34]

....

[34]   From *Those born in the deaf years* by A. Blok: 'Te, kto dostoyney, Bozhe, Bozhe, da uzryat tsarstviye Tvoye'.

I have reached the end. With meekness, all that remains to my lot, I filled page after page. Those who happen to read these writings may think that we, moral and physical wrecks, rested on the ruins of our little world as on laurels. I know you; I recognize you with a single glance. You cannot deceive me. You, who call love slavery and slavery love, you may never may enter her world, her perfect, doomed world. Ever.

Afterword:

Elena Chizhova's *Little Zinnobers* in the Context of English, Russian, and World Culture and History

It is fitting that a translation of Elena Chizhova's *Kroshki Tsakhes* (literally, The Children of Zaches), first published in 2000,[35] should allow the anglophone reader an opportunity to become better acquainted with a talented contemporary Russian writer who has a particular interest in English culture and history. Elena Chizhova was awarded several literary prizes in the early 2000s, but she rose to unprecedented national and international attention when she won the Russian Booker Prize for her novel *Vremia zhenshchin* (*The Time of Women*), cited as 'the best novel written in Russian in 2009' and translated into English in 2012.[36] The aim of this introduction is to give the English-speaking reader more information about Chizhova's life and work, while shedding light on certain literary and historical references within the text of *Little Zinnobers* which would be understandable to the Russian intelligentsia, especially in St Petersburg and Moscow, but not always clear to the anglophone reader.

....

[35] Elena Chizhova, 'Kroshki Tsakhes: roman' was first published in the St Petersburg journal *Zvezda*, No. 4 (2000), and made available online at 'Zhurnalnyi zal', <http://magazines.russ.ru/zvezda/2000/4/chizh-pr.html> [accessed 6 January 2017]. Since then, it has appeared in book form in various editions.

[36] Elena Chizhova, 'Vremia zhenshchin', *Zvezda*, No. 3 (2009); The *Time of Women*, translated by Simon Patterson and Nina Chordas (London: Glagoslav, 2012). For further information on this novel, see Ellen Barry, 'A Writer Invites Russia to Engage Its Painful Past', <www.nytimes.com/2010/03/06/world/europe/06author.html> [accessed 17 August 2017].

Elena Chizhova was born on 4 May 1957 in Leningrad (renamed St Petersburg in 1991), which constitutes the setting for many of her works. She began her career as a poet, writing her first poem when visited by inspiration at the age of twenty-one; a small selection of her poetry was first published in English translation in 1993.[37] Her poems treat themes which are usually called 'eternal' and subsequently feature in her prose: love and death, time and eternity, free will and predestination, loyalty and treachery, and the transcendent value of art. Her early command of poetic form, influenced by Pushkin, Lermontov, Akhmatova, Mandelstam, Brodsky, and other major Russian poets, can be sensed through the lyrical quality of her prose.

Chizhova's fascination with English literature and history, which is so evident in *Little Zinnobers,* began at the age of four, when she began to learn English. William Shakespeare (1564–1616) is by far the most significant English writer to whom she was introduced at school. The influence of Shakespeare's history plays is clearly demonstrated in Chizhova's verse play, *Tragediia Marii Stuart* (*The Tragedy of Mary, Queen of Scots,* 1992). Like the play *Maria Stuart* (*Mary Stuart,* 1800) by Friedrich Schiller (1759–1805), which was also influenced by Shakespeare's plays dealing with the Wars of the Roses, Chizhova imagines a meeting between Queen Elizabeth I of England (ruled 1558–1603) and her victim Mary, Queen of Scots (1542–1587).[38] In order to write this play, Chizhova consulted about forty memoirs and books on Tudor England in English and Russian in the Saltykov–Shchedrin Public Library in Leningrad/St Petersburg (known fondly as the 'Publichka'), which also features in *Little Zinnobers.*[39] Other English-language writers who have

....

[37]   Rosalind Marsh, 'New Developments in Russian Poetry: Elena Chizhova', *Essays in Poetics,* 18. 2 (1993), 88–110; Elena Chizhova, 'Kassandra' ('Cassandra'), in *An Anthology of Russian Women's Writing, 1777–1992,* trans. and ed. by Catriona Kelly (Oxford: Oxford University Press, 1994), p. 334.

[38]   Mary, Queen of Scots (8 December 1542–8 February 1587), also known as Mary Stuart or Mary I of Scotland, was Queen of Scotland from 14 December 1542 to 24 July 1567, and Queen consort of France from 10 July 1559 to 5 December 1560.

[39]   In 1993 I was glad to have the opportunity of inviting Elena to a tour round the south of England, sponsored by the Arts Council, under the title 'Voices of Russian Women'. At this time,

exerted philosophical and creative influences on her include John Donne (1572–1631), the famous metaphysical poet of sexuality and religion, the Elizabethan dramatist Christopher Marlowe (1564–1593), and the American poet, playwright, teacher and translator Thornton Wilder (1897–1975).

Chizhova's impulse to write prose arose from an accident that occurred on a ship in December 1998. This is Elena's own dramatic, tragi-comic account of the incident, which also reveals her intimate personal relationship with God:[40]

I was sailing in a small ship on the Black Sea. I was returning from Stambul [Istanbul] to Simferopol. At night a fire started. The Turks responded to our SOS signals by saying that we were no longer in their territorial waters, but in Ukrainian waters. The Ukrainians said that they would have flown out, but that they had no kerosene to fuel the fire-fighting helicopters. We were on fire for six hours. Then the crew managed to put out the fire. While we were on fire, I sat in my cabin and spoke to God. Or more precisely, I engaged in negotiations. I said that I had everything ready to begin writing prose. (Yes, previously I had written poems, but not prose.) And that I needed ten years. After that I would be ready to die. When I landed I really gave up work in business. And began to write. I wrote without days off, trying to be on time. During that time I wrote and published several novels. *Kroshki Tsakhes* [*Little Zinnobers*] was the first.

In the 1990s, after the collapse of the Soviet Union, Chizhova worked for several years as assistant to the director of a large furniture factory. In the 2000s, however, when she had started writing prose, she was able to give up this work and use her expertise in a more congenial manner as general editor

....

in preparation for her prose works, she also made a brief study visit to Oxford to continue her research into Russian and English history in the Bodleian Library.

[40] Email to author from Elena Chizhova, 4 January 2017.

of the journal *Vsemirnoe slovo* (a German version is published under the title *Lettre International*), which was concerned with cultural and historical links between Russia and various European countries.[41] She was responsible for producing special issues devoted to Russia and England, Russia and Germany, and other countries, including Poland, Sweden, Italy, and Spain. This demonstrates her extensive knowledge of international culture, which is also evident in her interviews and critical articles published in journals such as *Voprosy literatury* (Questions of Literature). In *Little Zinnobers* it is her familiarity with English and German literature that is most clearly illustrated.

This short autobiographical novel is a record of the anonymous narrator's love for an English teacher who introduced her to English literature and history, and also an unparalleled glimpse into the Soviet educational system of the 1960s and 1970s. As a former pupil and teacher in the Soviet system herself,[42] Chizhova is well placed to present school life from both sides. There is a tradition in Russian literature of writers evoking their own or a character's childhood, as in Leo Tolstoy's *Detstvo; Otrochestvo; Iunost'* (*Childhood; Boyhood; Youth*, 1852; 1854; 1857), Ivan Turgenev's *Pervaia liubov'* (*First Love*, 1860), Fyodor Dostoyevsky's *Podrostok* (*A Raw Youth*, or *The Adolescent*, 1875), and Boris Pasternak's *Detstvo Liuvers* (*The Childhood of Louvers*, 1922). However, school stories do not feature particularly prominently in Russia by comparison with the rich tradition in English literature by both men and women:[43] Thomas Hughes's *Tom Brown's Schooldays* (1857); James Hilton's *Goodbye, Mr Chips* (1934); Antonia White's *Frost in May* (1933);

....

[41]   *Vsemirnoe slovo* was published in Russia from 1996 to 2005; *Lettre International* is still being published in Germany.

[42]   After leaving school Chizhova obtained a higher degree (*Kandidat nauk*) in economics and spent some time researching and teaching in the Institute of Economics and Finance, while 'leading a double life' at night, researching world literature from the ancient Greek philosophers Plato and Aristotle onwards: <http://readrussia.org/writers/writer/elena-chizhova> [accessed 17 August 2017].

[43]   One interesting exception is N.G. Pomialovsky, *Ocherki bursy* (*Seminary Sketches*, 1862–1863), a harrowing account of the cruel education given to boys in training for the priesthood.

Muriel Spark's *The Prime of Miss Jean Brodie* (1961), to mention but a few.[44] Stories by Russian women writers featuring a schoolgirl, such as Nadezhda Khvoshchinskaia's *Pansionerka* (*The Boarding-School Girl*, 1861), or a teacher (Anastasiia Verbitskaia's *Istoriia odnoi zhizni* (*Story of a Life*, 1903)), generally emphasize the great value of education for women. Russian writers depicting schoolgirls are not burdened with the English writer's baggage of formulaic stories 'for the sake of the school' (Angela Brazil, 1868–1947), or the uncontrollable girls in the farces of St Trinian's. Elena Chizhova has acknowledged that one of her influences is the Austrian writer Robert Musil (1880–1942), and indeed his *Die Verwirrungen des Zöglings Törleß* (*The Confusions of Young Törless*, or *Young Törless*, 1906) is perhaps the work that is most reminiscent of Chizhova's novel, with its detailed analysis of adolescent psychology, including sadistic impulses. More closely related to the period depicted in Chizhova's novel is Solzhenitsyn's story 'Dlia pol☒zy dela' ('For the Good of the Cause'), published in the liberal journal *Novyi mir* in 1963, although this is generally considered one of the weakest of his stories. It is, however, his only story on a contemporary theme, based on a real incident in Riazan, a town 122 miles south-east of Moscow, where he was teaching mathematics after his return from exile.[45] Like Chizhova's novel, it evokes the bureaucracy and corruption of Soviet society through the eyes of young people — in Solzhenitsyn's case, through the experiences of students in a provincial technical college.

Little Zinnobers is a fascinating example of 'life writing' presented in fictional form. The narrator's story begins in a summer kindergarten on the Finnish Gulf, where children boarded. She convincingly evokes the feelings

....

[44] The same remark may also hold true of Irish, North American, and other anglophone fiction for both adults and children dealing with school experiences, although this is an enormous subject that deserves much fuller treatment than can be given here.

[45] Aleksandr Solzhenitsyn, 'Dlia pol'zy dela', *Novyi mir*, No. 7 (1963); Alexander Solzhenitsyn, *For the Good of the Cause*, trans. by D. Floyd and M. Hayward (London: Sphere, 1971). For more information, see Michael Scammell, *Solzhenitsyn: A Biography* (London: Hutchinson, 1984), pp. 471–472, 478–479.

of a little girl, suggesting that, apart from her enjoyment of walks by the sea, this was not a very happy time for her, as she wetted the bed and was scolded by the night nannies. She later claimed that her two constant companions were 'fear and anguish'. At the same time, her kindergarten teacher Nina Ivanovna, speaking enthusiastically but vaguely, tells the students [fairy] tales about the 'new happy time' to come — the communist future she confidently expects — providing the narrator with an early experience of the difference between theory and practice, reality and propaganda.[46]

Subsequently she goes to a very prestigious English school in Leningrad, whose teachers were chosen and monitored by the District Party Committee. Her best and most charismatic teacher, who introduced her to Shakespeare and other English writers, is only referred to by the initial 'F'. We subsequently learn that the narrator does not wish to name her because she takes the view expressed in Shakespeare's Sonnet 71, which asks the addressee to forget the poet's name: 'Do not so much as my poor name rehearse'. However, this may also be a protective act, as the teacher is evidently of non-Russian origin, a Tatar whose mother and grandmother came from a village near Kazan in the Tatar Autonomous Soviet Socialist Republic (TASSR, now known as Tatarstan), where she was brought up as a Muslim. The letter 'F' could also designate 'Fairy' (*feia* in Russian), as in the fairy tale on which Chizhova's novel is based.

E.T.A. Hoffmann and Chizhova's Novel

The title of Chizhova's novel and several references within the story allude to a bizarre and disturbing fairy story by E.T.A. Hoffmann (Ernst Theodor Amadeus Hoffmann, 1776–1822) entitled 'Klein Zaches, genannt Zinnober:

....

[46]   For an extended treatment of this theme in the 1970s, see the dissident work by Aleksandr Zinov'ev (1922–2006), *Ziiaiushchie vysoty*, first published in Lausanne in 1976; Alexander Zinoviev, *The Yawning Heights*, trans. by G. Clough (London: Bodley Head, 1979). The title is a play on the Soviet cliché '*siiaiushchie vysoty*' (the allegedly 'shining' or 'radiant heights' of communism). See also Chizhova's satirical use of the word 'shining' (p. 19).

Ein Märchen' ('Little Zaches, Great Zinnober: A Fairy Tale', 1819),[47] in which the basically good-hearted, but powerful and manipulative Fairy Rosabelverde puts the ugly dwarf Zaches under a spell that makes all who meet him see him as handsome, intelligent and superb at everything he does. The Fairy's motivation is that she, along with all the other fairies and magicians, has been banished from her homeland of Jinnistan because the new ruler is in favour of 'enlightenment' rather than the untrammelled 'freedom' which his father favoured. The dwarf gains praise he does not deserve that rightfully belongs to others, such as those who recite poetry or play the violin in his presence; indeed, artists are the only people who can see him as he really is. He adopts the proud name 'Zinnober', the German word for the powdered mineral 'cinnabar' — the common form of mercury sulphide that ranges from brick red to bright scarlet, a highly toxic substance which constitutes the historic source for the brilliant red or scarlet pigment in painting usually called 'vermilion'. Some doubt is, however, cast on Zinnober's abilities because this word can also mean 'nonsense, rubbish'. Nevertheless, the striking but dangerous dwarf rises so swiftly in his career that he becomes a minister and gains the love of the beautiful heroine Candida until the Fairy finally breaks her spell. Hoffmann himself was a Prussian state judge, and his tale has been recognized by critics as a political allegory on repression, arrogance, nepotism, hypocrisy, and received ideas in the early nineteenth century, such as Enlightenment rationalism.[48]

....

[47] This is not a Hoffmann story that has been paid much attention in Britain. The most accessible translation is Michael Haldane's online version, <http://www.michaelhaldane.com/kleinzaches. pdf> [accessed 10 August 2017]. For more information on the reception of Hoffmann in Russia, see <http://www.michaelhaldane.com/HoffmannDissertation.htm> [accessed 4 September 2017].

Hoffmann's story was published in many editions in pre-revolutionary Russia and by the major Soviet publishing house *Sovetskii pisatel'*, but for a modern Russian translation, see *Kroshka Tsakhes, po prozvaniiu Tsinnober*, trans. by A.A. Morozov (Moscow: Vita nova, 2014).

[48] See, for example, Val Scullion and Marion Treby, 'Repressive Politics and Satire in E.T.A. Hoffmann's Fairy-Tales, "Little Zaches Acclaimed as Zinnober" and "Master Flea"', *Journal of Politics and Law*, 6. 3 (2013), <http://dx.doi.org/10.5539/jpl.v6n3p133> [accessed 5 September 2017].

Hoffmann's Romantic, gothic tales[49] (a genre that is generally dated back to Horace Walpole's novel *The Castle of Otranto*, first published in 1764, which combines medieval elements with terror), aroused interest in Russia around 1819, the time of their first publication — earlier than in any other foreign country — and exerted influence on the fantastic stories and novels by Nikolai Gogol (1809–1852) and Fyodor Dostoyevsky (1821–1881), who, in their mature work, were idiosyncratic adherents of the Slavophile point of view (see below, p. 183).

The influence of Hoffmann on Russian writers is not difficult to understand, as fairy tales and fantasy are often genres through which uncomfortable truths can be conveyed to an intelligent audience living under a repressive government. Russia during the second part of the reign of Emperor Alexander I (ruled 1801–1825), and the following reign of Nicholas I (1825–1855), after the unsuccessful Decembrist revolt by liberal Russian noblemen in 1825, was as repressive as Prince Klemens von Metternich's Austria[50] and the Prussian state under King Friedrich Wilhelm III of Prussia (reigned 1797–1840), where Hoffmann lived and worked. Both were conservative rulers who had to deal with the difficult period of the Napoleonic Wars and the end of the Holy Roman Empire, and both introduced laws against dissidents, including writers and scholars. Hoffmann's satirical tales were censored, and he himself was threatened with legal action, which he only escaped because of his early death from syphilis and alcohol abuse. Like Hoffmann, both Gogol and Dostoyevsky resorted to fantasy and melodrama — including paranormal phenomena and the supernatural (ghosts, devils, doubles (doppelgängers), horror stories), crimes

....

[49]   In the second edition, Walpole applied the word 'gothic' to the novel in the subtitle 'A Gothic Story'. Walpole was particularly influenced by the Ghost in Shakespeare's *Hamlet*, the stories of succession and blood lines in *Macbeth* and *Richard II*, and the mixture of comedy and tragedy (the scenes with the 'rustics' and 'clowns') in *Twelfth Night*, *A Midsummer Night's Dream*, and other plays.

[50]   Metternich (1773–1859) was an important German diplomat and statesman, a traditional conservative who served as the Austrian Empire's Foreign Minister from 1809 and Chancellor from 1821 until the liberal revolutions of 1848 forced him to resign.

and scandals — in order to say something meaningful about bureaucracy and corruption in the oppressive Russia of their day.

Hoffmann's works continued to be influential in Russia before and after the Bolshevik Revolution of 1917, both for writers and cultural figures who were officially acceptable in the USSR, and for Soviet and Russian dissidents from the 1920s to the present. In 1921, a group of writers called *Serapionovy Brat'ia* (The Serapion Brothers) was formed in Petrograd, named after *Die Serapionsbrüder* (*The Serapion Brethren*), a literary and social circle formed in Berlin in 1818 by Hoffmann and some of his friends, and after which he named a four-volume collection of stories (1819, 1820, and 1821). In works first published in the 1920s and the 1960s, the prominent literary theorist Mikhail Bakhtin (1895–1975) developed the concepts of 'Menippean satire'[51] and 'carnival', characterizing Hoffmann as belonging to the comic, grotesque and self-parodying tradition, usually in prose, which combines realism and fantasy to shed light on contemporary life, as in the works of Cervantes, Diderot, Voltaire, and Dostoyevsky.[52] Subsequently, some critics have used this idea to refer to Bakhtin's contemporary Mikhail Bulgakov (1891–1940), and his great novel *The Master and Margarita* (see pp. 201, 222-223). Chizhova's novel can to some extent be regarded as belonging to this tradition.

....

[51] Named after the Greek cynic, parodist and polemicist Menippus (third century BC), whose works, now lost, influenced other classical writers such as the Roman scholar Marcus Terentius Varro (116 BC–27 BC), and the Greek satirist Lucian (125 AD–after 180 AD), who often poked fun at traditional stories about the gods. Lucian influenced both Shakespeare and Marlowe.

[52] M.M. Bakhtin, *Tvorchestvo Fransua Rable i narodnaia kul'tura srednevekov'ia i Renessansa*, first published in 1965; Mikhail Bakhtin, *Rabelais and His World*, trans. Hélène Izwolsky (Cambridge, MA: M.I.T. Press, 1968). See also Bakhtin, *Problemy tvorchestva Dostoevskogo* (*Problems of Dostoevsky's Art*), which was first published in 1929, then revised and expanded for an edition of 1963 under the title *Problemy poetiki Dostoevskogo* (*Problems of Dostoevsky's Poetics*). The first edition does not refer to Menippean satire and the carnivalesque, but devotes a chapter to Dostoyevsky's relation to the adventure novel. On Bakhtin's view of Menippean satire, see M.M. Bakhtin, *Problems of Dostoevsky's Poetics*, ed. and trans. by Caryl Emerson (Minneapolis: University of Minnesota Press, 1984), pp. 112-121. This concept was later applied productively to Bulgakov's *The Master and Margarita*: see Lesley Milne, *The Master and Margarita: a comedy of victory* (University of Birmingham, 1977).

Hoffmann's tales have also exerted a powerful influence on the modernist film and theatre directors Sergei Eisenstein (1898–1948), Vsevolod Meyerhold (1874–1940), and Alexander Tairov (1885–1950),[53] and on Russian animated film (see p. 74). In the late Soviet period, Hoffmann's work had a particularly significant impact on the dissident writer and critic Andrei Siniavsky (1925–1997), who published fiction under the pseudonym 'Abram Terts [Tertz]'. His novella 'Kroshka Tsores' (published 1980 in Paris; translated as 'Little Jinx', as the Yiddish word '*tsores*' means 'trouble' or 'woe') specifically uses and inverts Hoffmann's 'Little Zaches', depicting an unfortunate boy who does not wish to do evil, but inadvertently causes the death of his five half-brothers. As in Chizhova's novel, Siniavsky's protagonist is partly autobiographical, a writer alienated from Soviet society. It is highly likely that Chizhova was familiar with the works of all these cultural figures who played a prominent part in the history of St Petersburg and Moscow.

Like Siniavsky/Tertz, Chizhova also plays on the title of Hoffmann's story, but, unlike Siniavsky, uses the plural '*kroshki*' ('offspring, children'), emphasizing the many characters in her novel who are subject to manipulation, rather than just one. In Chizhova's novel, Hoffmann's parable of mass delusion is used both to refer to the schoolchildren, whose good English is due to F., not themselves, and to the Soviet Union of the 1970s, which is not as wonderful as propaganda might have led people to believe. Hoffmann's relevance to questions of identity and the position of the artist in Soviet society under Brezhnev can also be demonstrated by a decision made in 1974 by the great film director Andrei Tarkovsky (1932–1986) to compose a screenplay about Hoffmann's life entitled 'Gofmaniana' ('Hoffmanniana'). Tarkovsky submitted it first to Tallinnfil'm (Estonia) and then to Goskino (the State Committee for Cinematography). It received approval, and the screenplay was published in 1976, although after Tarkovsky's emigration in 1982 he abandoned the project.[54]

....

[53]   Dassia N. Posner, *The Director's Prism: E.T.A. Hoffmann and the Russian Theatrical Avant-Garde* (Evanston, IL: Northwestern University Press, 2016).

[54]   Although Tarkovsky's films are not explicitly mentioned in *Little Zinnobers*, intellectuals

In the post-Soviet era, 'Little Zaches' came to public attention shortly before the first publication of Chizhova's novel, when it was used to parody the newly appointed Vladimir Putin on the popular television show *Kukly* (*Puppets*), the Russian version of the satirical British television series *Spitting Image* (1984–1996), which had been shown on the privately owned station NTV since 1994. It was particularly associated with the well-known satirist, scriptwriter and radio host Victor Shenderovich (b. 1958). In the episode of 23 January 2000, the oligarch and business magnate Boris Berezovsky (1946–2013), the one-time protector of both Yeltsin and Putin, was cast as Fairy Rozabelverde, and the newly-born Putin as a 'political dwarf'. Although *Kukly* appears to be quite a mild satire from a western point of view, it was detested by both Yeltsin and Putin and eventually proved so contentious that it was taken off the air in 2002,[55] after the independent NTV had already been forcibly brought under state control.

Hoffmann's tales, which are not particularly well known in Britain, may be more familiar today in both Russia and Britain through Jacques Offenbach's famous (unfinished) *opéra fantastique Les Contes de Hoffmann* (*The Tales of Hoffmann*, 1880), first performed in 1881, a year after the death of its composer Jacques (born Jacob) Offenbach, the son of a Jewish synagogue cantor. In this opera the poet Hoffmann appears (in fictionalized form) as the protagonist. The prologue is set in the Luther Tavern in Nuremberg, where students sing a famous drinking song while waiting for the poet Hoffmann. When he finally arrives, he attempts to entertain them with the legend of 'Little Zaches' (Kleinzach, the dwarf) by singing (in French) the aria 'Chanson de Kleinzach' ('Song of Little Zaches'): 'Il était une fois

---

of the calibre of F. and Chizhova's narrator could not have failed to be familiar with his work. Interestingly, Tarkovsky also directed *Hamlet* at the Moscow Lenkom Theatre in 1977, and Mussorgsky's *Boris Godunov* in Covent Garden (London) in 1983. He considered *Hamlet* to be 'one of the greatest works of genius in the whole of art'. See the Shakespeare Institute Library, <https://silibrary1.wordpress.com/tag/andrei-tarkovsky/> [accessed 10 April 2018].

55 'Klein Tsakhes, po prozvaniiu Zinnober', <https://ru./wikipedia.org/wiki/> [accessed 5 September 2017]. The episode can be seen on YouTube: <https://www.youtube.com/watch?v=eZJx9bgwdv0> [accessed 5 September 2017].

à la cour d'Eisenach' ('Once upon a time at the court of Eisenach'). This song is clearly based on the short story 'Little Zaches, Great Zinnober', but Hoffmann is unable to finish it because he is distracted by his love for the opera singer Stella.

Hoffmann's name may also be familiar from ballets based on his stories, notably Pyotr Tchaikovsky's *Shchelkunchik* (*The Nutcracker*), subtitled 'Balet-feeriia' (A Ballet Based on a Fairy Tale), (first performed in St Petersburg's Mariinsky Theatre in 1892),[56] and Léo Delibes's *Coppélia* (premiered in Paris in 1870).[57] Modern-day productions are traditionally derived from the revivals staged by the French-Russian dancer and choreographer Marius Petipa (1818–1910) for the Imperial Ballet of St Petersburg in the late nineteenth century. Both these ballets are particularly popular with children and young people and are often performed at Christmas. These references suggest another theme of Chizhova's novel which is typical of Russian culture in general: the close connection and interrelationship between different branches of the arts, history and politics.

Another theme announced early in the novel is the role of language, culture and ethnicity, particularly the problems facing non-native speakers of Russian in the former Soviet Union. The narrator suggests that F.'s mother, who obtained a humble job as a janitor, cannot be described as an 'immigrant' because both Leningrad and her 'distant, non-Russian village' belonged to the same empire. Nevertheless, her life was an immigrant's life to some extent, because her imperfect Russian prevented her from getting a better job. F. and her mother lived in considerable poverty in a half-underground communal

----

[56] The libretto is adapted from E.T.A. Hoffmann's story 'Nussknacker und Mausekönig' ('The Nutcracker and the Mouse King', 1816), by way of Alexandre Dumas, *père*'s retelling of the story, 'Histoire d'un casse-noisette' ('Story of a Nutcracker', 1844). It was given its premiere at the Mariinsky Theatre in St Petersburg in 1892, on a double-bill with Tchaikovsky's last opera *Iolanta*. In 1973, an animated film of *The Nutcracker* was released, directed by Boris Stepantsev, partly based on Tchaikovsky's ballet, but mainly on Hoffmann's story.

[57] The libretto and original *mise-en-scène* by the French choreographer Charles Louis Étienne Nuitter were based upon two macabre stories by E.T.A. Hoffmann: 'Der Sandmann' ('The Sandman', 1816) and 'Die Puppe' ('The Doll', 1819).

flat, where she had to be her mother's 'ears' and take responsibility for her in an environment that was sometimes hostile. When F. discovers English literature in 1940, at the age of six, through a Russian translation of Chaucer's *Canterbury Tales* (written between 1387 and 1400),[58] this is compared to Columbus's discovery of the 'New World' of the Americas. Reading such works out loud helps her and her mother to survive the terrible 872-day siege of Leningrad (from 8 September 1941 to 18 January 1943).

Shakespeare in Russia

Throughout the novel, F. trains the children to recite poems and act scenes from Shakespeare and other Russian and foreign writers which are relevant to her own life, but contain adult themes that they sometimes struggle to understand. Like Shakespeare himself, Russian writers influenced by him often used their fiction or translations to say something true about their own history and society, or human life in general, which could not be said explicitly in a society where censorship and repression were rife.

Shakespeare, the most important English writer cited in Chizhova's novel, has been known in Russia since the eighteenth century, if not before.[59] Alexander Sumarokov (1717–1777), a poet and statesman known as the founder of the Russian classical theatre and the first translator of *Hamlet* (in 1748), expressed an equivocal view of Shakespeare in his *Epistle on Verse Composition* (1748), regarding him as an 'inspired barbarian [...] in whose work there is much that is bad and exceedingly good'.[60] Empress Catherine II,

....

[58]   Extracts from Chaucer's *Canterbury Tales* first appeared in Russian translation in 1859 and 1875 (although it has been suggested that 'The Knight's Tale' was known to Pushkin earlier, perhaps through a French translation).

[59]   Works dealing with Shakespeare and Russian literature or Shakespeare in Russia are too numerous to mention here, but see, for example, *Russian Essays on Shakespeare and His Contemporaries*, ed. by Alexandr Parfenov and Joseph G. Price (Newark: University of Delaware Press, 1998).

[60]   A.P. Sumarokov, 'Epistola II (o stikhotvorstve)', in *Russkaia poeziia XVIII veka* (Moscow, Khudozhestvennaia literatura, 1972), p. 663; cited in Andrew Dickson, 'As they like it: Shakespeare

known as Catherine the Great (reigned 1762–1796), who read Shakespeare in French, even produced an adaptation of *The Merry Wives of Windsor* under the title *Vot kakovo imet' korzinu i bel'e* (*A Pretty Basketful of Linen*, 1786) — a unique occasion when Shakespeare has been translated by a head of state.[61]

From the nineteenth century onwards, Russians have even at times seemed to regard Shakespeare as their own, Russian writer, and the introverted, disturbed Prince Hamlet as a particularly Russian character akin to the *lishnii chelovek* ('the superfluous man [or person]' typical of Russian literature). This term itself was popularized by a novella by the famous writer Ivan Turgenev (1818–1883), *Dnevnik lishnego cheloveka* (*The Diary of a Superfluous Man*, 1850), and was applied afterwards to characters from earlier novels. It has been used to refer to a character (usually a hero or anti-hero) who often has brains and talents, sometimes a high social position, but no way of exercising them adequately in the repressive society of nineteenth-century Russia. Instead, he may sink into boredom, cynicism, disregard for other people and rejection of social and moral values, sometimes indulging in gambling, drinking, romantic intrigues, and duels.

This literary hero is exemplified first and foremost by the eponymous protagonist of Pushkin's classic 'novel in verse' *Evgenii Onegin* (*Eugene Onegin*, 1825–1832).[62] Onegin in turn has acted as the model for many later 'superfluous men' who evolved from the 'Byronic hero' (who first appeared in Lord Byron's semi-autobiographical epic narrative poem *Childe Harold's*

in Russia', <https://www.calvertjournal.com/features/show/2321/Shakespeare> [accessed 21 July 2017].

[61] More oddly, Catherine also adapted Shakespeare's little-known tragedy *Timon of Athens* (1605–1606), which in the Soviet period was presented as an attack on unfettered capitalism. During the second half of her reign, when she retreated into repression after the French Revolution, *Hamlet* was banned, presumably because it depicts the murder of a king, his queen, and highly-placed aristocrats, and concludes with a successful foreign invasion.

[62] There are numerous translations of *Evgenii Onegin* into English, but none that can be recommended uncritically.

Pilgrimage (1812–1818), well known to Pushkin). These included Grigory Pechorin in Mikhail Lermontov's *Geroi nashego vremeni* (*A Hero of Our Time,* written in 1839, published in 1840, revised in 1841), and numerous characters in the works of the 'Westernizers' (or 'Westernists') Turgenev and Chekhov. The term 'Westernizers' (*zapadniki* in Russian) was first applied to intellectuals of the 1840s and 1850s who believed that western ideas such as industrialization and liberal government needed to be implemented throughout Russia to make it a more successful country. They emphasized the values that Russia shared with Western Europe, whereas the 'Slavophiles' (*slavianofily*) stressed Russia's unique destiny and argued that the West should adopt Russian cultural values rather than the other way around. The conflict between these two Russian types and the ideas they represent has survived the Bolshevik Revolution of 1917 and the fall of the Soviet Union in 1991, and has endured, in different forms, up to the present day. In Chizhova's novel, the young Fedya (or Fedka), who has been abandoned by his parents and brought up by his grandparents, could be regarded as a 1970s version of a *'lishnii chelovek'.*

In the nineteenth century, the first significant Russian writer to acknowledge Shakespeare's influence was Alexander Pushkin (1799–1837),[63] the father of modern Russian literature, who was probably familiar with Shakespeare and English literature in general through French translations (Russians seem to have had access to French translations of Shakespeare plays from as early as 1745–1748). The most striking example of Shakespearean influence on Pushkin's work is his major history play *Boris Godunov* (1825), which drew extensively on Shakespeare's *Hamlet* as well as the history plays, most notably *Henry IV, Part Two* and *Richard III.*[64]

....

[63]   See Catherine O'Neil, *With Shakespeare's Eyes: Pushkin's Creative Appropriation of Shakespeare* (Newark: University of Delaware Press, 2003).

[64]   For a brief, though still authoritative discussion of the many Shakespearean influences on *Boris Godunov,* see A.D.P. Briggs, *Alexander Pushkin: A Critical Study* (Bristol: Bristol Classical Press, 1991), pp. 160–164.

Shakespeare, Pushkin, and Russian History

The Wars of the Roses, which form part of the subtext of Chizhova's novel, were fought between supporters of two rival branches of the royal House of Plantagenet — the House of Lancaster (signified by a red rose) and the House of York (the white rose). They are usually dated to the sporadic fighting that took place during the fifteenth century, especially in the period 1455–1487. Eventually, after the death of the pious, but mentally infirm Henry VI (reigned 1422 to 1461, and from 1470 to 1471), the last Lancastrian ruler of England in a reign dominated by civil war, England became more peaceable as the reign of Henry VII became more stable. Henry VII (reigned 1485–1509), otherwise known as Henry Tudor, a Lancastrian prince of Welsh ancestry, had little claim to the throne, but won it in battle from Richard III at the Battle of Bosworth Field, fought on 22 August 1485 (*Richard III*, v. 4, a scene cited in Chizhova's novel). Henry VII ultimately managed to defeat all opposition and unite the two houses of York and Lancaster under the emblem of the Tudor rose. Subsequently the Tudor dynasty was consolidated during the reigns of the well-known and even more powerful Henry VIII (reigned 1509–1547), and Elizabeth I, Shakespeare's first royal patron.

A parallel can be drawn between this period of English history and the period of medieval Russian history depicted in Pushkin's *Boris Godunov*: the years 1598–1605, part of the turbulent era known as *Smutnoe vremia* ('the Time of Troubles', 1598–1613), which culminated in the establishment of the Romanov dynasty (1613–1917). As Caryl Emerson has suggested in relation to Pushkin's play, doubles and pretenders are inevitable in any system in which power remains in the hands of one person.[65] I would add, following Shakespeare and Pushkin, that there is always a danger of mistakes of birth,

....

[65]   Caryl Emerson, 'Pretenders in History: Four Plays for Undoing Pushkin's *Boris Godunov*', *Slavic Review*, 44. 2 (1985), 257–279 (p. 257). The 'False Dmitrii' in Pushkin's *Boris Godunov* and his successors are comparable to the two Pretenders in England during the reign of Henry VII: Perkin Warbeck (*c.* 1474–1499) and Lambert Simnel (*c.* 1477–*c.* 1525).

mental illness, or tyranny if authoritarian rule is left in one person's hands. For many Russians, however, the lessons to be learnt from the Wars of the Roses and the 'Time of Troubles' are the dangers of a period of anarchy and the need for a strong ruler.

Historians disagree about whether the Wars of the Roses were caused by the structural problems of feudalism or Henry VI's personal ineffectiveness as king. Comparisons could be drawn between this period and the latter half of Yeltsin's reign, when the Russian President was becoming increasingly sick, drunken, and incapable, leading to the rule of an initially little known, then powerful, immovable leader. However, since there are no exact historical parallels, every reader can interpret Shakespeare, and Chizhova's view of his plays, in his or her own way. Like all Shakespeare's kings, queens, and historical characters, the real historical figures on whom they were based are now presented by modern scholars as very different from their fictional counterparts, although Shakespeare's (and Pushkin's) depictions may well have exerted more long-term influence on their audience than serious historical analysis.

Drunken Merriment

Another parallel between Shakespeare and Pushkin is the famous comic tavern scenes that feature in their work. In both parts of Shakespeare's *Henry IV*, Prince Hal, the Prince of Wales and future hero Henry V, misspends his youth, carousing with his friend Sir John Falstaff and his 'followers' or 'irregular humorists' Bardolph, Pistol, Justice Shallow and others, presided over by the quick-witted Mistress Quickly, hostess of the Boar's Head, Eastcheap. These scenes, and their comic predecessors in *The Merry Wives of Windsor*, which are also acted by a group of children in *Little Zinnobers*, are paralleled in Pushkin's *Boris Godunov* by another farcical inn scene, later reproduced in the opera of the same name by Modest Mussorgsky (1839–1881), composed between 1868 and 1873 in St Petersburg. In an inn near the border of the Polish-Lithuanian Commonwealth, the runaway novice monk Grigory Otrepyev and his companions, the wandering friars Varlaam and Misail, enjoy drinking until officers representing Godunov's government chase them away. Grigory escapes over the border and subsequently enters Russia as the False Dmitry I, at the head of a Polish army.

One of the sympathetic English teachers in *Little Zinnobers*, Andrei Nikolayevich, is described by the narrator as 'a magnificent Falstaff, the best I ever saw'. The discrepancy between Shakespeare's and Pushkin's approach to drunken behaviour might be at least partially explained by the fact that Pushkin himself enjoyed quite a riotous youth, and died in a duel at a much younger age than Shakespeare, who died, presumably of natural causes, at the age of fifty-two. In this respect, Pushkin and Lermontov (1814–1841), who both died in duels at a very young age, are closer to the enigmatic Christopher (Kit) Marlowe, a university-educated outsider and dissident, perhaps a government spy, considered by Puritan critics to be a Catholic or an atheist.[66] Marlowe was the author of the controversial plays on troubled rulers, Jews, and metaphysical quests: *Tamurlaine the Great, Part 1* (*c.* 1587), Part 2 (*c.* 1587-1588); *The Jew of Malta* (c. 1589); *The Tragical History of Doctor Faustus* (*c.* 1589, or *c.* 1593);[67] *Edward II* (*c.* 1592), and other plays and poetry on classical and historical themes. He was murdered in mysterious circumstances, possibly during a brawl over an unpaid bill, in a house in Deptford, south-east London, in 1593, at the age of twenty-nine.

Coincidentally or not, Deptford, the former London dockland (previously associated with Elizabeth I and the adventurer Francis Drake), was the part of London where the young Tsar Peter I (Peter the Great, 1672–1725; sole

---

[66] A warrant was issued for Marlowe's arrest on 18 May 1593, for which no reason was given, although it was thought to be connected to allegations of blasphemy — a manuscript believed to have been written by Marlowe was said to contain 'vile heretical conceipts'.

[67] There is no agreement among critics when Marlowe's play *Doctor Faustus* was written and performed, although it exists in two versions. It was an Elizabethan tragedy based on German stories about the title character Faust that was first performed some time between 1588 and Marlowe's death in 1593.

ruler, 1682–1725) came in 1698 on his 'Grand Embassy', his diplomatic tour of Western Europe (1697–1698), during the reign of William III and Mary II. He stayed there for three months while studying shipbuilding at the royal dockyard, and famously got drunk with his companions, seriously damaging the interior of Sayes Court, the house belonging to the diarist and gardener John Evelyn (1620–1706), and breaking down his fine holly hedge.

The Tsar allegedly came to England anonymously (although he was about six foot seven inches, the tallest man in Europe, so anonymity was difficult). At the same time, he had a somewhat disturbing fascination for little people and even celebrated an elaborate 'dwarves' wedding' for the royal dwarf Iakim Volkov,[68] which, once again, establishes a subtle connection with 'Little Zaches' and *Little Zinnobers*. As was the vogue in the early eighteenth century, Peter the Great harboured a partiality for oddities and curiosities; a passion that led to the establishment of his Kunstkamera (the first museum in Russia, completed in 1727), a cabinet of strange objects dedicated to preserving 'natural and human curiosities and rarities', such as deformed human and animal skeletons. Apparently, Peter collected deformities in order to curb people's belief in monsters. Today the Kunstkamera Building, situated on the Universitetskaia Embankment in St Petersburg opposite the Winter Palace, hosts the Peter the Great Museum of Anthropology and Ethnography, well-known to inhabitants of Leningrad/St Petersburg and tourists alike.

Peter the Great's reign was a period of contradictions: in 1703, Peter founded St Petersburg to give his navy access to the sea, at the cost of the lives of tens of thousands of serfs; in 1718 he had his son Aleksei Petrovich tortured to death for opposition to him; but ultimately he established a strong, more westernized state and empire.[69] Perhaps the point being made by Chizhova is that, if young people survive alcohol abuse and the

....

[68] Lindsey Hughes, *Peter the Great: A Biography* (New Haven: Yale University Press, 2002), pp. 90–92.

[69] See, for example, Evgenii V. Anisimov, *The Reforms of Peter the Great: progress through coercion in Russia*, trans. with an Introduction by John T. Alexander (New York: M.E.Sharpe, 1993).

mayhem, even death, it may cause, they may later grow up to achieve great things. Likewise, she suggests that artists may use their experience of drunken merriment in creative ways: the tavern scenes in *Henry IV* can be compared with similar fictional scenes in works by Pushkin, Lermontov, Hoffmann, and many other Russian and foreign writers, artists and composers, based on the real lives of these artists (see the references to Blok and Yesenin below). One cannot, however, but regret the early deaths from alcohol abuse of significant writers and artists in Russia, England — indeed, any country.

The Faust Theme

Roistering inn scenes like those in Shakespeare's *Henry IV* occur in the prologue and epilogue of Offenbach's opera *The Tales of Hoffmann*, reflecting Hoffmann's own dissolute youth in East Prussia, and in other works based on the German legend of *Faust*,[70] in which a poet or scholar searching for the meaning of life sells his soul to the Devil. Possibly through an English translation, it influenced Christopher Marlowe's controversial play *Doctor Faustus* (*c.* 1589, or, *c.* 1593), the first work of the early modern period of English literature to deal with the demonic realm, and a source for Chizhova's novel.[71] Other famous works on this theme are the great German drama *Faust* (1790, 1808, 1828-1829) by Johann Wolfgang von Goethe (1749–1832); Hector Berlioz's opera *La damnation de Faust* (first performed in Paris in 1846); and Charles Gounod's opera *Faust* (1859). These works are well known in Russia and Ukraine as sources of Bulgakov's 'novel about the devil', *The Master and Margarita* (written 1928–1940).[72] These and other

....

[70]   This classic German legend first appeared in the fifteenth century, based on the historical Johann Georg Faust (*c.* 1480–1540).

[71]   *Doctor Faustus* also deals with other themes touched upon in Chizhova's novel: sex and love, beauty, evil, sin, despair, pride, repentance, destiny and predestination. Another fictional character who makes a pact with the Devil is Ibsen's Peer Gynt, discussed below, pp. 224, 226.

[72]   Bulgakov's novel was first published in Russia in a censored version in the journal *Moskva* in

works treating the Faust theme, demons, or the Devil, can also be seen as influences on Chizhova's novel.[73]

Love and Art

Another aspect of the *Faust* theme treated in the novel is the relationship between love and art. In the Prologue of Offenbach's opera *Tales of Hoffmann*, Councillor Lindorf (an incarnation of the Devil) coaxes the poet Hoffmann into telling the audience about his former loves, so the poet regales tavern drinkers with tales of the three great loves of his life, Olympia, Giulietta and Antonia – an automaton, a courtesan, and an invalid — three different manifestations of love's dangerous, seductive power. As we will see, this theme is also suggested in *Little Zinnobers* through references to *Romeo and Juliet*, *Twelfth Night*, *Macbeth*, a folk ballad about Queen Eleanor, and Nastasia Filippovna in Dostoyevsky's *The Idiot*.

Chizhova sometimes implies that art and love may come into conflict. In the Prologue to the opera *Tales of Hoffmann*, Hoffmann's Muse expects him to devote his life entirely to her, by writing poetry (as Chizhova's narrator does in her roles as poet, writer, and 'witness' of her age), and forgetting his lovers, present and past. In the Epilogue of the opera, when Hoffmann is no longer infatuated with the opera singer Stella, the Muse's wish is ultimately fulfilled (as it is in *Little Zinnobers* too).

·····

1967–1968; the first full publication of the novel in 1973 became a literary sensation; it was also staged by the director Yuri Liubimov at Moscow's Taganka Theatre in the 1970s.

[73] There have been many treatments of this theme over the last 400 years. In Russia, they include Turgenev's *Faust* (1856); references to a petty devil and demons in Dostoyevsky's *Brat'ia Karamazov* (*The Brothers Karamazov*, 1879–1889*)* and *Besy* (*The Devils*, 1871–1872); Valerii Briusov's *Ognennyi angel* (*The Fiery Angel*, 1907–1908), and especially, Bulgakov's *Master and Margarita*. See also *Russian Literature and its Demons*, ed. by Pamela Davidson (London: Berghahn, 2000; 2010). This theme has also inspired music by Mussorgsky, Prokof'ev, Schnittke, and others.

Literature and Censorship

Pushkin's *Boris Godunov* was written under the surveillance of the tsarist secret police, but not approved for performance by the censor until 1866, twenty nine years after the poet's death. Even then, the 1831 version was not performed until 1870, in St Petersburg's Mariinsky Theatre, and, astonishingly, the original, uncensored play written by Pushkin in 1825 was not produced until the twenty-first century, when on 12 April 2007 it was staged in Princeton, USA, but only in an English translation.[74] In Russia and the former USSR, Pushkin's *Boris Godunov* has often been used to comment on the unscrupulous nature of Russian and Soviet leaders, especially during the presidency of Boris Yeltsin (1991–2000), who was sometimes nicknamed 'Tsar Boris'. The phrase 'the Time of Troubles' has, moreover, been employed by some Russian writers and mentioned in private conversations since the Gorbachev era to describe the difficult circumstances of Russian history, especially in the 1990s until the accession of Vladimir Putin in 2000, or even in more recent times.[75] Thus the fate of Pushkin's play (not to mention Mussorgsky's better-known opera of the same name, partially based on Pushkin's text) demonstrates not only how interpretations of Shakespeare and Pushkin have for centuries been adapted to changes in Russian history and politics, but also how major Russian writers (and composers) have constantly been subject to censorship and repression. This subtext in Chizhova's novel highlights the strange fate of many of the greatest works of Russian literature that have been constrained by censorship and the power of the secret police.

Other more recent examples mentioned in *Little Zinnobers* are famous works by two winners of the Nobel Prize for Literature: Boris Pasternak's

....

[74] *The Uncensored Boris Godunov: The Case for Pushkin's Original Comedy*, ed. by Chester Dunning, Caryl Emerson, and others, with Annotated Text and Translation (Madison: Wisconsin University Press, 2006).

[75] See Rosalind Marsh, *History and Literature in Contemporary Russia* (Oxford: St Antony's/ Macmillan, 1995), p. 213.

Doktor Zhivago (*Doctor Zhivago*, first published in Russian in Italy, 1957; published posthumously in Russia, 1988), and Alexander Solzhenitsyn's *Arkhipelag GULag* (*The Gulag Archipelago*, first published abroad in 1973; subsequently published in Russia in an author-approved abridged version in 1989–1990 before Solzhenitsyn returned to Russia in 1994). We should, moreover, remember that 'Shakespeare's plays were censored too'.[76] Shakespeare's career bridged the reigns of Elizabeth I (who died in 1603) and James I (ruled 1603–1625), and he was obliged to work hard to remain a favourite of both monarchs (unlike Marlowe). Nevertheless, throughout English history Shakespeare has been censored for many reasons, including dissent or political rebellions, religious controversies, sexual frankness, or crude language,[77] and similar factors have led to the censorship of Shakespeare in Russia and many other countries too.

If Pushkin's *Boris Godunov* is only a latent intertext in Chizhova's novel, Pushkin's one historical novel in prose, *Kapitanskaia dochka* (*The Captain's Daughter*, 1836) is directly mentioned as one of the less controversial works of Russian literature that could be taught in Soviet schools. This novel, which depicts the most extensive peasant uprising in Russian history (1773–1774), treats the very modern theme of a ruler (Catherine the Great) who is subjected to terror, then uses terror against her enemy (the Don Cossack Emelian Pugachev (*c.*1742–1775), who claimed to be Catherine II's husband Peter III, actually assassinated in 1762). Both sides are equally violent and equally culpable.[78]

....

[76]   Title of a letter in the *Financial Times*, 8 April 2016, <https://www.ft.com/content/84a8c31a-f766-11e5-803c-d27c7117d132> [accessed 17 August 2017]. See also Caitlin Griffin, 'Censoring Shakespeare', <http://teachingshakespeareblog.folger.edu/2013/09/24/censorship-sh> [accessed 3 September 2017].

[77]   Richard Dutton, 'Shakespeare and Marlowe: Censorship and Construction', *The Yearbook of English Studies*, 23, Early Shakespeare Special Number (1993), 1–29.

[78]   For a modern interpretation of the horror and impact of war on the civilian population, see the work by Svetlana Alexievich, winner of the 2015 Nobel Prize for Literature, *The Unwomanly Face of War*, trans. by Richard Pevear and Larissa Volokhonsky (London: Penguin Classics, 2017).

Pushkin's novel, influenced not only by Shakespeare, but also by Lord Byron (1788–1814), the series of historical novels by Sir Walter Scott (1771–1832) originally known as the 'Waverley novels',[79] and an 1818 volume of Nikolai Karamzin's monumental twelve-volume *Istoriia gosudarstva Rossiiskogo* (*History of the Russian State*, 1816–1826), the Russian version of Raphael Holingshed's *Chronicles*, the source of Shakespeare's history plays,[80] depicts a typically stereotyped Romantic heroine. In *Little Zinnobers* Chizhova once again emphasizes the disparity between truth and illusion, contrasting the clichéd description of the 'shining eyes' of Pushkin's heroine Masha, as she falls romantically in love with the handsome young Lieutenant Grinyov, with the 'shining eyes' from starvation of people in the siege of Leningrad. In an extended metaphor, they are also compared to Columbus and the later Spanish conquistadors, greedy for gold, who, in turn, are reminiscent of profiteers and cannibals in the siege, hungry for gold and plump human bodies.

The first language into which Shakespeare was translated was German, and some Shakespeare plays in German toured Europe in the seventeenth century. Subsequently, under the influence of Romanticism, German translations of Shakespeare became widespread in Russia in the nineteenth century. Shakespeare's plays were sometimes translated into German by great writers: for example, Schiller himself translated *Macbeth* (first performed in Weimar, 1800; first printed in 1801), as well as writing his own play on a British historical theme, *Maria Stuart* (which, as mentioned above, was one of the influences on Chizhova's early work). Subsequently, Goethe adapted *Romeo and Juliet* for the Weimar stage in 1812. The translations of Shakespeare by August Wilhelm

....

[79] T.J. Binyon, *Pushkin: A Biography* (London: HarperCollins, 2002), p. 598 suggests that *Kapitanskaia dochka* bears most similarity to Scott's *Rob Roy* (1818) and *The Bride of Lammermoor* (1819).

[80] Many critics believe that Shakespeare used the revised second edition of Holinshed's *Chronicles of England, Scotland, and Ireland* (published in 1587) as the source for most of his history plays, the plot of *Macbeth*, and for portions of *King Lear*.

Schlegel (1767–1845) are generally considered some of the best in any language.[81]

These and other translations gave Russian writers who travelled to Western Europe unprecedented opportunities to become familiar with Shakespeare. In particular, Turgenev was a well-known 'Westernizer' who wrote several stories on Shakespearean themes, such as 'Gamlet Shchigrovskogo uezda' ('Hamlet of the Shchigrov District') in *Zapiski okhotnika* (*A Sportsman's Sketches*, 1852), and 'Stepnoi Korol' Lir' ('King Lear of the Steppes', 1870). Perhaps his best-known reference to Shakespeare, however, is the famous lecture entitled 'Gamlet i Don-Kikhot' ('Hamlet and Don Quixote') that he gave in 1860 at a public reading in St Petersburg in aid of writers and scholars suffering financial hardship.[30] In his essay Turgenev states that both these significant characters in Russian literature date back to works published at the beginning of the seventeenth century — Shakespeare's *Hamlet*, and *Don Quixote* by Miguel de Cervantes (1547–1616) — and argues that man is torn between the self-centred scepticism of Hamlet and the idealistic generosity of Don Quixote.[82] These two character types figure in many of Turgenev's own novels; and Dostoyevsky, who was present at the lecture after returning from exile in Siberia, attempted in *Idiot* (*The Idiot*, first published serially in 1858–1859), to depict a tragic hero, Prince Myshkin, who, as we will see later, resembles Don Quixote in many respects.

Pushkin and Dostoyevsky are the main classical Russian writers mentioned in the novel who were allowed to be taught in Russian literature classes in the 1970s, but not Tolstoy, who was famously hostile to Shakespeare.[83] Dostoyevsky did not always find acceptance in the USSR

....

[81]   Schlegel laid claim to Shakespeare on behalf of his German readers, saying that he was 'ganz unser' ('entirely ours').

[82]   I.S. Turgenev, 'Gamlet i Don-Kikhot', available at <http://svr-lit.ru/svr-lit/articles/turgenev-gamlet-i-don-kihot.htm> [accessed 7 April 2018]; 'Hamlet and Don Quixote', trans. by Moishe Spiegel, *Chicago Review*, 17. 4 (1965), 92–109. Cervantes's *Don Quixote* was first published in 1605 and 1615.

[83]   Lev Tolstoi, 'O Shekspire i o drame' ('Shakespeare and the Drama'), <http://tolstoylit.ru/

either, but he was 'rehabilitated' in 1956 as an anti-capitalist writer,[84] and in the mid-1960s *Prestuplenie i nakazanie* (*Crime and Punishment*, 1866) was finally included on the Soviet school syllabus.

Dostoyevsky, who is praised in Chizhova's novel by F. and several foreign teachers visiting the school, is known to have been influenced by *Macbeth*'s themes of murder and guilt, treated extensively in *Crime and Punishment*. This is demonstrated by the famous sleepwalking scene from *Macbeth* acted by the children (v. 1), in which Lady Macbeth constantly appears to wash her hands, muttering 'Out, damned spot! Out, I say! [...] Hell is murky [...] Yet who would have thought the old man to have had so much blood in him? [...] What's done cannot be undone'. She subsequently refers to other rivals murdered by her husband: the ghost of Banquo, who appeared to Macbeth in the middle of a feast, and Lady Macduff and her children: 'The Thane of Fyfe had a wife? Where is she now?', before committing suicide offstage. Thus Chizhova presents Lady Macbeth as 'a queen dying in sin', but troubled by guilt, like Eleanor of Aquitaine in the English folk ballad discussed below (pp. 204-205). Likewise, in *Henry IV, Part Two*, the once powerful, but now sick and dying King Henry feels the need for understanding, atonement, expiation through suffering, and reconciliation with the younger generation (his wayward son Prince Hal). Chizhova's novel depicts a similar reconciliation and the transfer of power from generation to generation: from F. to the narrator, until F. in the conclusion acknowledges her earlier role as Fairy Rozabelverde.

The Dostoyevsky novel which F. especially wants the children to act a scene from is *The Idiot*, in which the author set himself the task of depicting a 'positively good and beautiful man'[85] in a corrupt, egoistic, materialistic

....

tolstoy/publicistika/publicistika-23.htm> [accessed 18 September 2017].

[84]   Temira Pachmuss, 'Soviet Studies of Dostoevsky, 1935-1956', *Slavic Review*, 21 (1962), 709-721.

[85]   Dostoyevsky letter quoted in Richard Peace, *Dostoyevsky: An Examination of the Major Novels* (Cambridge: Cambridge University Press, 1971), pp. 59–63.

society. In particular, she wants the children to re-enact the scene towards the end of Part One, in which the 'demonic', doomed, destructive woman Nastasia Filippovna throws 100,000 roubles into the fire to demonstrate that she refuses to marry for money. There is a love triangle between Nastasia, the 'fallen woman', the passionate merchant Rogozhin who eventually murders her, and the pure-hearted Prince Myshkin, a Christ-like figure. Myshkin is presented as a variation on the fool in many Shakespeare plays who 'tells truth to power', such as Touchstone in *As You Like It* (1599–1600), Feste in *Twelfth Night* (1601), and, most notably, the unnamed Fool in *King Lear* (1605–1606). He is also one of the most striking examples of the ubiquitous 'holy fool' (*iurodivyi*) in Russian literature, along with the fool in both Pushkin's *Boris Godunov* and the second, 1874 version of Mussorgsky's opera, which adds a concluding lament by the fool that serves as a warning to the people of Russia of the 'Time of Troubles' to come. Could the fact that Myshkin eventually goes mad be a hint that F., to some extent, regards herself as marginalized and doomed in Soviet society?[86] The character regarded as sick or 'mad' in Russian, Soviet and post-Soviet literature is often the individualist, the dissident, or the rebel.

To emphasize the parallels between Shakespeare's plays, Dostoyevsky's novel and Chizhova's, the text is permeated by references to 'idiots' and 'idiotic' people and events. Since F.'s plan to act a scene from *The Idiot* fails to materialize, this could perhaps be seen as a partially optimistic conclusion. Or is it the conformists who are 'sick' or 'mad', whereas F. and the narrator are female 'holy fools', who, like Cassandra, their precursor in Greek mythology — the subject of one of Chizhova's poems — always tell the truth, but are never listened to?

....

[86]   For further discussion of the importance of 'madness' in Russian culture, see Angela Brintlinger and Ilya Vinitsky (eds), *Madness and the Mad in Russian Culture* (Toronto: University of Toronto Press, 2007). In the 1970s, Soviet dissidents were often confined in mental hospitals.

Shakespeare in the Soviet Era

In the Soviet era, particularly under Stalin, translations of Shakespeare and other foreign writers were often used as a method of commenting indirectly on aspects of Soviet society that writers could not mention directly in fiction. The best translator of Shakespeare's plays was Boris Pasternak (1890–1960), who used his translation work, especially his major translations of *Gamlet, Kniaz' datskii* (*Hamlet, Prince of Denmark*, 1941) and *Korol' Lir* (*King Lear*, 1949), both as a means of survival when his own poems could no longer be published, and a way of communicating at least some of his ideas within Russia and beyond the 'iron curtain'. Moreover, Pasternak's poem entitled 'Gamlet' ('Hamlet', written in 1946), the first and most famous 'Zhivago poem' in the last chapter of *Doctor Zhivago*,[87] became a dissident statement of social and moral opposition to the regime. It portrays an actor playing Hamlet who actually *becomes* Hamlet in a play that Pasternak himself interpreted as a 'tragedy of duty and self-denial'.[88] It was recited at Pasternak's funeral by 'a young and very anguished voice',[89] and later by the actor Vladimir Vysotsky (1938–1980), at the beginning of an influential production of *Hamlet* directed by Yuri Liubimov on the stage of Moscow's Taganka theatre from 1971, running in repertory until Vysotsky's early death (217 performances in all).

Similarly, the famous black-and-white film *Gamlet* (*Hamlet*), directed by Grigory Kozintsev and Iosif Shapiro using Pasternak's translation and a score by Dmitry Shostakovich, which was first shown in Russia in 1964, the last year of Khrushchev's rule, was able to comment in an Aesopian manner on

....

[87]   Boris Pasternak, *Stikhotvoreniia i poemy*, ed. by L.A. Ozerov (Moscow-Leningrad, 1965), pp. 690–691.

[88]   Pasternak, 'Zametki o Shekspire' ('Notes to Shakespeare's Tragedies'), first published in 1944; rewritten in 1956, in *Sochinenia*, 4 vols (Ann Arbor: University of Michigan Press, 1958–61), ed. by Gleb Struve and Boris A. Filippov, 3 (1961), p. 195.

[89]   Olga Ivinskaya, *A Captive of Time: My Years with Pasternak, trans. by Max Hayward (London: Collins and Harvill, 1978), p. 331.*

Soviet politics and society in the 1960s. The protagonist was the celebrated actor Innokenty Smoktunovsky (1925–1994), whose son F. taught in an earlier, allegedly happier time — presumably the early 1960s, when Khrushchev's destalinization policy allowed more truthful, historically accurate literary works to be published, notably Solzhenitsyn's *Odin den' Ivana Denisovicha* (*One Day in the Life of Ivan Denisovich*), published unexpectedly in November 1962 in the liberal journal *Novyi mir*. It is generally agreed that Kozintsev emphasized the public and political aspect of *Hamlet*, in contrast to Laurence Olivier's film of 1948 which focused on Hamlet's psychological conflict. Kozintsev stated: 'Olivier cut the theme of government, which I find extremely interesting. I will not yield a single point from this line'.[90] Chizhova emphasizes that F. far prefers Innokenty Smoktunovsky's subtle, introverted performance in the role of Hamlet, ridden with inner turmoil, to the star of the new generation, the poet, actor and husky-voiced singer-songwriter Vladimir Vysotsky, who played an uninhibited, modern 'Hamlet with a guitar' at the Taganka. Both these references would be familiar to a Russian intellectual audience — indeed they were emblems of freedom and protest for the oppressed Russian population of the 1960s and 1970s. However, for an English audience of the older generation they can be seen as roughly similar to the legendary difference between the interpretations of John Gielgud (who played Prince Hamlet as a sensitive, indecisive intellectual in six different productions over fifteen years from 1934) and Laurence Olivier (whose Hamlet was an extrovert and man of action in the film of 1948, based on a shorter text).

Another famous theatre director mentioned in the novel is Georgy Tovstonogov (1915–1989), born in Georgia, who travelled to Russia to become a theatre director, the head of the St Petersburg Bolshoi Academic Theatre of Drama (formerly called the Gorky Theatre), which now bears his name. He was the first director to return Dostoyevsky to the Soviet theatre by his

....

[90]   Grigori Kozintsev, *Shakespeare, Time and Conscience*, trans. by Joyce Vining (London: Dennis Dobson, 1967), p. 287.

productions of Dostoyevsky's *Oskorblënnye i unizhënnye* (*The Insulted and Humiliated*, 1861), staged in 1956 in Leningrad's Leninsky Komsomol Theater, and *The Idiot* (1957) in the Gorky Theatre. Another of his productions was Gogol's *Revizor* (*The Government Inspector*, originally published in 1836; staged in 1972), a timeless satire on political bureaucracy and corruption, and human stupidity and greed. He also directed *Henry IV, Part One* (1969), but avoided *Henry IV, Part Two*, which is much darker, dealing with Henry's old age and death, and the transfer of power to his son, Henry V. In the 1950s and 1960s, when 'Stalin's heirs' were still struggling to inherit his power,[91] this might have been too controversial a subject to present.

Another important Russian/Soviet translator of Shakespeare cited in *Little Zinnobers* is the Jewish writer Samuil Marshak (1887–1964). His translation of Shakespeare's Sonnets written in the last decade of Stalin's rule (1948), when new lyrical poetry was practically banned in the Soviet Union, allowed him to evoke and transmit eternal human emotions, enjoying a popularity unprecedented for translated verse.[92] Sometimes Marshak added to his translations, bringing them closer to the reality of Soviet society. In Sonnet 74, for example, Shakespeare simply says '[…] When that fell arrest/ Without all bail shall carry me away', referring to his eventual death, whereas the Marshak translation states: 'When I am put under arrest/ Without ransom, bail, or adjournment', alluding more clearly to the arrest he feared as a Jew and a member of the Soviet 'Jewish Anti-Fascist Committee'. This

---

[91]   'Nasledniki Stalina' ('Stalin's Heirs') was a famous poem by Yevtushenko published in *Pravda* in 1961, in which he stated that although Stalin was dead, Stalinism and its legacy were still alive. He directly addressed the Soviet government, begging them to make sure that Stalin would 'never rise again'. This poem was not republished until the Gorbachev era.

[92]   *Sonety Shekspira v perevodakh S. Marshaka* (Moscow: Sovetskii pisatel', 1949). Marshak was also famous for translating Robert Burns ('Rabbie Burns', 1759–1796), the Scottish poet of freedom who is perhaps known as well, if not better, in Russia than in England. This is suggested in Chizhova's novel by the reference to a 'Robert Burns Club for International Friendship'. The largest selection of Marshak's translations from Burns appeared in 1963 in two volumes with an introduction by R. Rait-Kovaleva and a postscript by M. Morozov. The collection consists of two parts, 'Songs and Ballads' and 'Epigrams', containing a total of 171 poems, about a quarter of the number of poems Burns wrote.

organization had been set up by Stalin in 1942 to combat Nazi Germany, but many of its members, including eminent poets and scientists, were arrested on trumped-up charges of spying, tortured, and executed by firing squad in 1952 after a secret mock trial, as part of the persecution of Jews in the last years of Stalin's rule. The mass executions of 12 August 1952 became known as 'Noch' kaznënnykh poetov' ('the Night of the Murdered Poets'). The reasons for this policy are still unclear, but it has been suggested that Stalin and elements of the KGB were worried about their influence and connections with the West, especially after the establishment of the state of Israel in 1948. They were officially rehabilitated in 1988, during the Gorbachev era.

In Chizhova's novel too, Shakespeare's sonnets and plays function as an alternative aesthetic and morality to those prevalent in Soviet society, which F. is alienated from. In Sonnet 29, 'When in disgrace with Fortune and men's eyes/I all alone beweep my outcast state', the poet most obviously turns away from an unfeeling society that hounds him.[93] The only consolations for the poet, as for both F. and the narrator of Chizhova's novel, are art and love. The sonnets referring to time, age and death (especially Nos 71 and 74, cited in English in the text) call upon the addressee to preserve the poet's memory after death, as the narrator does as a 'witness' to the life of her beloved F. The well-known scenes from *Richard III* (1592–1593), *Romeo and Juliet* (1595), *Henry IV, Part One* (1596–1597), *Henry IV, Part Two* (1597–1598), *The Merry Wives of Windsor* (1597), *Hamlet* (1599–1601), *Twelfth Night* (1601), *Macbeth* (1606),[94] and other Shakespeare plays that

....

[93]   Poems by Pushkin and Lermontov that refer to society as '*chern*" ('the mob') express a similar sentiment, and the reference to Thackeray's *Vanity Fair* (1847–1848) in Chizhova's novel also implies satire of a selfish, greedy, hypocritical society.

[94]   I have based the approximate dates of composition of Shakespeare's plays on the work of E.K. Chambers in 'The Problem of Chronology', published in his book *William Shakespeare: A Study of Facts and Problems,* Vol. 1 (Oxford: Clarendon Press, 1930). This is the main source for most modern chronologies, available at <https://archive.org/details/williamshakespea017475mbp> [accessed 7 April 2018]. Quotations from the plays are taken from William Shakespeare, *The Tudor Edition of The Complete Works,* The Players Edition (London and Glasgow: Collins, 1970), ed. with an introduction and glossary by Peter Alexander. According to Alexander's chronology, p. xv, the Shakespeare plays mentioned in Chizhova's novel all belong to the first three periods

F. chooses for the children to act on 'Theatre Day' are relevant to some of the themes of the novel. The shyness and embarrassment of young love are depicted in *Romeo and Juliet*; bureaucracy, dogmatism and sycophancy are epitomized by Malvolio in *Twelfth Night*; betrayal is a prominent theme at the end of *Henry IV, Part Two* (Prince Hal's rejection and banishment of the 'fat knight' Sir John Falstaff, the companion of his misspent youth, with the cruel and self-righteous words 'I know thee not, old man' (v. 4)); and the presentation of the ordinary inhabitants of Elsinore as good-hearted, simple people exploited by corrupt rulers in the graveyard scene of *Hamlet* (v. 1). One scene that is particularly unusual for a school to perform is the seduction of Lady Anne by Richard III, who has murdered her husband Edward and her father-in-law King Henry VI (*Richard III*, I. 2). Since Richard III is sometimes used as an analogy to Stalin, this could be seen as an allusion to the charismatic attraction of power and evil, and especially the Russians' desire for a 'strong hand' to rule them.[95]

Shakespearean Servants, 'Clowns' and 'Fools'

Chizhova also touches on the theme of class, referring to classical drama's depiction of clever servants who play tricks on their masters: for example, the narrator agrees (reluctantly) to swap her role as the noble Olivia in Shakespeare's *Twelfth Night* with the role of Maria, her smart, cunning maid. Although many of Shakespeare's servants are loyal to their masters or mistresses, they can sometimes be treacherous, like the Nurse in *Romeo and Juliet*. Literature and opera are full of smart servants: Sancho Panza in Cervantes's *Don Quixote*; many characters in Molière's plays, such

of Shakespeare's life and work.

[95] In Solzhenitsyn's novel *V kruge pervom* (*The First Circle*, first published in 87 chapters in the West in 1968), his Stalin compares the fickle allies who willingly surrendered to the victor with Lady Anne in *Richard III*. On analogies between Stalin and Shakespeare's *Richard III*, see Rosalind Marsh, *Images of Dictatorship: Stalin in Literature* (London and New York: Routledge, 1989; repr. 2017), pp. 142, 166, 206.

as Dorine in *Tartuffe, ou L'Imposteur* (*Tartuffe, or The Impostor*, or, *The Hypocrite*, first performed in 1664), who unmasks the hypocritical villain; Figaro in operas by Mozart (*The Marriage of Figaro*, 1786), and Rossini (*The Barber of Seville*, 1816), both based on Pierre Beaumarchais's French comedy *Le Barbier de Séville* (1775); Leporello in Mozart's *Don Giovanni* (1787), and others. They often play tricks on villains or fools, in order to demonstrate their vices and show them up in their true colours, as Maria does to the bureaucrat Malvolio in *Twelfth Night*, encouraging him to appear before his beloved mistress Olivia cross-gartered and in yellow stockings (*Twelfth Night*, II. 5. 143–58).

This tradition also gave rise to Woland's retinue (the Devil's disciples) in *Master and Margarita*, including the enormous black cat Begemot, whose name means 'hippopotamus' in Russian, but also 'Behemoth', or the biblical Beast (Job 40. 15–24 and Revelation 13. 11), who can even become transformed into a human being. Another of Woland's followers is the enigmatic Koroviov-Fagot, perhaps at least partially based on Hoffmann's Kapellmeister Kreisler, the moody and over-sensitive composer who features in three of Hoffmann's novels, his story 'The Golden Pot', and some of his journalism. Servants or 'rustics' in classical drama, including the frequenters of taverns, not only represent characters with whom average members of the audience could identify; they also add indispensable comic elements to a basically tragic plot. Similarly, Elena Chizhova includes both tragic and comic elements in *Little Zinnobers*.

'Rustics' or 'clowns' date back at least to Greek and Roman comedy. In Shakespeare's plays, lower-class or comic characters are able to comment on their social betters, as do the 'two clowns' (ordinary working men) who converse in the graveyard scene of *Hamlet* (v. 1). Falstaff is not only a provoker of mirth, as in *Merry Wives* and *Henry IV, Part One*, or just a rogue and a scoundrel, but is also able to tell inconvenient truths (for example, Falstaff's speeches rejecting macho virtues of 'courage' and 'honour', and his attempts to escape or profit from war), or can become

ELENA CHIZHOVA

touching and human, as at the end of *Henry IV, Part Two*, when he is rejected by Prince Hal (v. 5). Female servants may also add an element of earthy, realistic sexuality to contrast with romantic (often unbelievable) love.

Another significant figure of this type is the fool, common both in Shakespeare's plays and Russian literature. The courtly fool, or jester, in England dates back to appearances in the courts of medieval aristocracy during the twelfth century. By the time of Queen Elizabeth I's reign, courtly fools were a common feature of English society, and have been regarded as being of one of two types: natural or artificial. 'Natural' fools included physically or mentally disadvantaged or exotic people used to amuse royal or noble masters — indeed, they were often seen as 'pets' and much loved, like Peter the Great's 'blackamoor' (see pp. 208-209) and dwarves — but could also be used to make the villains show themselves up in their true colours. This phenomenon fits in with Hoffmann's 'little Zaches' and references to 'exotic' Tatars, Jews, or mixed-race people in *Little Zinnobers*. The intellectual fools, portrayed by Shakespeare as outsiders with a ready wit and gift for intellectual repartee, have a satirical potential, and are able to tell their masters, or other powerful people, provocative, unconventional truths which other sycophants ignore or conceal. Both F. and the narrator can be regarded as subversive 'fools' of this type.[96]

In Russia, as we have seen, the main character epitomizing such qualities is the '*iurodivyi*', or 'holy fool', who can be seen as dating back to Christ himself, to St Paul's identification of himself and other Christians as 'fools for Christ's sake' (1 Corinthians: 4. 9–14), and in Russian history, to the autobiography of the Old Believer and martyr Archpriest Avvakum (1620/21–1682), a first-person narrative written in the late seventeenth century, in which the narrator constantly mocks himself as a stupid person. Avvakum's autobiography was widely read in the Soviet period, and most

[96] The female 'holy fool' is far from common in Russian literature, but one literary precursor is Svetlana Vasilenko's 'Durochka' ('Little Fool'), first published in *Novyi mir*, No. 11 (1998).

probably influenced Chizhova, whose narrator frequently berates herself for stupidity and lack of understanding.

Literature and Music

Chizhova suggests that in Russia, literature and music are closely linked. In the Soviet Union, recitals of poetry were sometimes accompanied by music, which is uncommon in England. This is why the narrator's recital of Shakespeare sonnets to the music of the eighteenth-century composer Christoph von Gluck (1714–1787) so impresses an Englishwoman (described as the 'lacy lady') that she weeps with emotion.[97] On other occasions, the narrator recites to the accompaniment of the Romantic composer Jules Massenet (1842–1912), a French composer best known as the composer of the operas *Manon* (1884), based on the famous novel of the Abbé Prévost, and *Werther* (1892), based on Goethe's novella *Die Leiden des jungen Werthers* (*The Sorrows of Young Werther*, first published in 1774), both of which concern the fate of two young people. Another favourite with F. is Sergei Rachmaninov (1873–1943), who emigrated with his family after the Bolshevik Revolution, first to Finland, then to the USA.

This theme also evokes other occasions when Shakespeare has been set to music by Russian composers, and the close connections between music and literature, history and politics in Russia. The opera *Boris Godunov*, for example, has been set to music by Mussorgsky, Rimsky-Korsakov, and Shostakovich; Pasternak originally studied musical composition from 1904 to 1910 under the influence of the composer Scriabin; and Tchaikovsky composed works based on Shakespeare or Pushkin, such as the 'Overture-Fantasy' *Romeo and Juliet* (first performed 1870), and the opera *Evgenii Onegin* (1879). The composer who suffered most from political interference

....

[97]   Hoffmann never met Gluck, but his very first story, 'Ritter Gluck' (1809) concerns the ghost of Gluck, who communicates to a musician through the encoded nature of music itself.

was Shostakovich, who wrote the controversial opera *Lady Macbeth of Mtsensk* (first performed in 1934, but condemned in *Pravda* in 1936). Later he composed the Seventh symphony, regarded as a patriotic work, which was performed in the besieged city of Leningrad; and in the Khrushchev era he set Yevtushenko's poem 'Babii Yar' (1961), with its famous condemnation of the mass murder of Ukrainian Jews by the Nazis in 1941, in his Thirteenth Symphony (1962).

Other Anglophone Literature in the Soviet Era

The surprising knowledge of English literature in the Soviet Union because of the availability of excellent translations is also demonstrated by the pupils' acting of 'Queen Eleanor's Confession', an English folk ballad about Eleanor of Aquitaine translated by Marshak,[98] which is not particularly well known in England itself. The real Eleanor of Aquitaine (1122–1204) was Queen consort of France (1137–1152) and England (1154–1189), and Duchess of Aquitaine in her own right. As a member of the 'House of Poitiers' in south-western France, she was one of the wealthiest and most powerful women in western Europe during the High Middle Ages. She was married to the Plantagenet English King Henry II (1133–1189), and was also important in English history as the mother of King Richard I ('The Lionheart'; reigned 1189–1199), and King John ('Lackland'; reigned 1199–1216).

In the ballad, however, Eleanor is dying and penitent. She secretly summons two Catholic friars from France to a deathbed confession (roles played by her husband King Henry II and his henchman the Earl Marshal, disguised as friars). She confesses that she has had an affair with the Earl Marshal and prefers her son by him to her son by her husband. The King cannot kill the

[98] 'Queen Eleanor's Confession', or 'Queen Elanor's Confession' is an English folk ballad that can be dated back to 1723. It is Ballad No. 156 in *The English and Scottish Popular Ballads*, ed. by Francis James Child (Boston and New York: Houghton Mifflin, 1904). For the Russian translation, see 'Koroleva Elinor', in *Angliiskie i shotlandskie ballady v perevodakh S. Marshaka* (Moscow: Nauka, 1973), pp. 72–75.

Earl Marshal because earlier he promised not to touch him. This story, which hints at treachery in high places, appears to be apocryphal, but it does show how powerful women in history have often been treated worse than powerful men in popular culture, as is the case of many of the 'she-wolves of England',[99] Marie Antoinette in relation to Louis XVI of France, and Catherine the Great in comparison with her precursor Peter the Great of Russia.

F. criticizes the narrator's performance of Queen Eleanor with an enigmatic phrase: 'In England,' she looks at me with disdain, 'They fall more quietly...'. This phrase could have multiple possible interpretations, but the narrator interprets it as meaning that a western queen would have had more dignity and integrity than an eastern woman, who would have prostrated herself like a slave. F's rebuke reflects the traditional Russian view of the polite, reticent English, which may not be as true in the twenty-first century as it was in the time of John Evelyn and Peter the Great.

Through this ballad and other cultural representations of significant historical figures in English history (especially Shakespeare's history plays), Chizhova may also be suggesting that the deposition and execution of kings, and the occurrence of revolutions, rebellions, and civil wars were as common in England as in Russia, just not so recent. After the bloody medieval Wars of the Roses, two queens were executed in sixteenth-century England: Lady Jane Grey, often known as the Nine Days Queen, was *de facto* Queen of England and Ireland from 10 July until her execution by order of Mary I on 19 July 1553; and Mary, Queen of Scots, who was executed by order of Elizabeth I in 1587. Seventeenth-century England was particularly unstable and violent: the English Civil War (1642–1651) led to the execution of King Charles I in 1649 and the establishment of the Commonwealth of England, Scotland, and Ireland by the republican Lord Protector Oliver Cromwell (ruled 16 December

....

[99]   The term 'she-wolf of France' was first used by Shakespeare to refer to the redoubtable Queen Margaret (Margaret of Anjou, the wife of Henry VI) in *Henry VI, Part Three* (1591), I. 4. 111–12. See also Helen Castor, *She-Wolves: the Women Who Ruled England Before Elizabeth* (London: Faber & Faber, 2011), made into a television series on BBC 4 (2012–2017).

1653–3 September 1658), and his son Richard Cromwell, second Lord Protector, in office from 3 September 1658 to 25 May 1659 (only 264 days). The period of the Republic culminated in the Restoration of the Stuart monarchy under Charles II in 1660, when reprisals were taken against Protestant supporters of the Commonwealth.

Subsequently, the transition from the personal power of the Stuart kings to the more constitutional role of the Hanovers occurred in the eighteenth century, after the so-called 'Glorious Revolution' of 1688 (actually an invasion of Britain by the Dutch Prince William of Orange, supported by some influential British political and religious figures), which led to the deposition of the Catholic King James II and the establishment of the Protestant dual monarchy under William and Mary (1689–1702). The Hanoverian kings and queens also had to combat Jacobite rebellions in 1715 and 1745 before their thrones were secure. Looking back from the twenty-first century, however, it is possible to interpret all these vicissitudes as part of the lengthy process of moving to a constitutional monarchy in Britain, which began when King John was forced by the barons to sign the *Magna Carta* in 1213.

In Russia, by contrast, the two revolutions of February and October 1917, the execution of Nicholas II and his family in 1918, the cruel Civil War that lasted from November 1917 until at least October 1922, the brutality and divisiveness caused by Lenin and Stalin, World War II and its aftermath, and the 'new revolution', or collapse of the Soviet Union in 1991, are much more recent, causing lasting trauma in the minds of Russian and former Soviet people.[100]

Themes and Characters in Chizhova's Novel

F.'s teaching of English and the theatrical performances she organizes are clearly the most important aspect of the school — so much so that she eventually remarks, not arrogantly but truthfully, 'The English school is me'.

....

[100] Svetlana Alexievich, *Second-hand Time: The Last of the Soviets*, trans. by Bela Shayevich (London: Fitzcarraldo Editions, 2016).

The pupils obviously enjoy the experience; their amateur attempts to 'make do and mend' in order to improve costumes and props will be familiar to anyone who, like the author of these lines, also acted Shakespearean scenes at school. Delegations of party functionaries, sometimes accompanied by foreigners, often visit School No.1, giving F. and her pupils an opportunity to show off their knowledge of English. On such occasions the school, where students are obliged to clean the floors themselves — either because the school is poor, or to teach the pupils a useful lesson about the value of manual labour — turns into 'a blissful little show island of window-dressing'.

'Window-dressing' or 'masquerade' has been a common trope in Russian literature, reflecting the reality of Russian history, or its prevalent myths. It recalls the *Potëmkinskie derevni* ('Potemkin villages'), used metaphorically to mean any construction (literal or figurative) built solely to deceive others into thinking that a situation is better than it really is. The term comes from stories of a fake portable village allegedly built by Catherine the Great's lover Count Grigory Potyomkin to impress her during her journey to Crimea in 1787. Some historians, however, regard this story as a myth, or, at least, just an attempt to deceive foreign ambassadors travelling with the Empress.[101] This interpretation, however, can be seen as analogous to the school's attempt to pull the wool over the eyes of foreign visitors.[102] In the former Soviet Union, attempts to deceive well-meaning, but gullible left-leaning foreigners such as George Bernard Shaw, H.G. Wells, André Malraux and Lion Feuchtwanger about the real problems of the Soviet Union have become legendary.[103] Chizhova hints at this through the story of the American teacher Stanley,

....

[101] Norman Davies, *Europe: A History* (London: Pimlico, 1997), p. 658; Simon Sebag Montefiore, *Catherine the Great and Potemkin: The Imperial Love Affair* (London: Orion, 2010).

[102] Similarly, in the original 87-chapter version of *V kruge pervom* (*The First* Circle, 1968), Solzhenitsyn reworks a camp anecdote that imagines an elaborate attempt by the Soviet authorities to deceive Eleanor Roosevelt on a goodwill visit after the war by showing her an apparently model Soviet prison (in Chapter 54, 'The Buddha's Smile'); and in Chapter 87, 'Meat', he satirizes a French journalist who is fooled by the Stalinist secret police's use of vans labelled 'Miaso' ('Meat') or 'Khleb' ('Bread') to transport prisoners.

[103] See Arthur Koestler and others, *The God That Failed* (London: Harper, 1949).

who speaks excellent Russian and loves Dostoyevsky. He exclaims euphorically when taken round places in Leningrad allegedly associated with his favourite characters in *Crime and Punishment*: the murderer Raskolnikov, the drunken Marmeladov and his daughter Sonya, the prostitute with the golden heart: 'Oh, Russia hasn't changed at all, essentially!'. However, when the allegedly unchanging Russia in the guise of the Soviet Union deports him for importing forbidden books, he shifts his allegiance to communist China.

Another interesting subtext of the novel is that productions of Shakespeare in Russia and the Soviet Union have sometimes proved to be a haven for talented Black actors and writers, such as the prominent African-American actor Ira Aldridge (1807–1867), unable to perform in his homeland, who became a great star in Russia. He studied at Glasgow University and was welcomed in London and Dublin, but was eventually hounded out of England by racists. He played not only roles intended for Black and mixed-race actors, including Othello and Shylock, but also Macbeth, King Lear and Richard III. He was ultimately decorated by Alexander II (1818–1881), the 'Tsar-Liberator' who emancipated the serfs, and is the only actor of African-American descent honoured with a bronze plaque at the Shakespeare Memorial Theatre in Stratford-upon-Avon.

Reference to Pushkin also recalls the fact that Pushkin's own maternal great-grandfather Abram Gannibal (*c.* 1696–1781) was born in Africa, then brought to Russia to work for Peter the Great, where he rose from slavery to become a general. Pushkin began to write this astonishing story in his unfinished work *Arap Petra Velikogo* (*The Blackamoor of Peter the Great*, 1827). Thus Pushkin is not only the greatest Russian poet who has often managed to unite a divided nation,[104] but also the greatest Russian Black, or mixed-race poet (a point which successive Russian governments have been reluctant to recognize).

....

[104]   On the 1999 celebrations of 200 years since Pushkin's birth, see Marsh, *Literature, History and Identity*, pp. 109–110.

One sexually and racially daring work taught in the special Leningrad school in the 1970s is *The Path of Thunder* (1948) by the South-African born Jamaican writer Peter Abrahams (1919–2017), which explores the tragic fate of the teacher Lanny, a mixed-race Cape coloured man who falls in love with Sarie, a white woman, in apartheid-era South Africa.[105] Other interesting characters in a novel advocating equality and diversity are two generations of Jews, and the tough, but soft-hearted prostitute Fieta (perhaps partly inspired by Dostoyevsky's Sonya Marmeladova). Chizhova's reference to this novel suggests her special sensitivity towards people of mixed race or divided allegiance, and her understanding of the problems that can be caused by education, as well as its advantages. This work also inspired the ballet *Tropoiu groma* (*The Path of Thunder*), first performed at the Kirov Theatre (now called the Mariinsky Theatre) in Leningrad in 1958, with libretto by Yuri Slonimsky, music by the Azerbaijani composer Gara Garayev, and choreography by Konstantin Sergeyev, which won the prestigious Lenin Prize in 1967. The implication of these allusions to significant Black writers and artists is that lip service was paid to internationalism in the Soviet era, when acceptance of Black people was used as anti-American propaganda, as in the film *Tsirk* (*The Circus*), a popular musical comedy of 1936 directed by Grigory Aleksandrov and Isidor Simkov at the Mosfilm studios. The famous Soviet film star Liubov' Orlova plays an American circus artist who, after giving birth to a black baby, finds refuge, love and happiness in the USSR. In the late and post-Soviet periods, however, the position of ethnic and racial minorities deteriorated with the revival of Russian nationalism.

Gender and Sexual Orientation

Another aspect of the children's acting is that disguise, cross-dressing, and the changing of roles come easily to them: for example, Fedka as Romeo wears

....

[105] The novel was translated as *Tropoiu groma* (Moscow: Inostrannaia literatura, 1949).

the narrator's prized blue Czech tights. The relaxed acceptance and tolerance of changing roles and identities so prevalent in the theatre are also evident through the veiled references to opera and ballet: in Delibes's *Coppélia*, for example, the role of Franz was often played by a female dancer. Although Chizhova does not refer directly to Russian cultural figures famous for their homosexuality or bisexuality (Gogol, Tchaikovsky, Gippius), she does mention two of the greatest homosexual (or bisexual) writers England has ever known: Shakespeare and Marlowe. Moreover, although Chizhova does not accentuate this fact, it would be generally known to Russian intellectuals that the protagonists of Marlowe's *Edward II* and Shakespeare's *Richard II* are usually presented as homosexual kings surrounded by male 'favourites'. Historians also debate the question of whether the 'weak', disturbed, but pious king Henry VI, and Shakespeare's patron, James I of England and VI of Scotland, were homosexual. In a Russia where 'propaganda of homosexuality' is banned in an increasingly severe and violent manner, Chizhova does not deal explicitly with such issues, but the tolerant view emerges that these questions are secondary to talent, art and love.

Themes and Characters in the Novel

The sensitive psychological portrait of F. is the main focus of the novel. As Chizhova stated in an interview of 2014, her teacher emerges as a person of 'a different level of consciousness [...] free from stereotypes and conventions, not defined by external circumstances', but closely connected to world culture. To the narrator she seems like a creature from another planet.[106] She is an inevitable outsider in the Soviet education system, which tried to mould young people in collective and national values.[107] She is, however, not a perfect human

....

[106] E. Chizhova, 'Umenie nachinat' so zvuka'...Besedu vela E. Pogorelaia', *Voprosy literatury*, No. 3 (2011), <http://magazines.russ.ru/voplit/2011/3/ch17.html> [accessed 2 October 2017].

[107] James Muckle, 'The Educational Experience of the Soviet Young Person', in *Soviet Education: The Gifted and the Handicapped*, ed. by James Riordan (London: Routledge, 1988), pp. 1–28; Catriona Kelly, *Children's World: Growing Up in Russia, 1890-1991* (New Haven, CT and London:

being, but a woman who can sometimes be harsh, even cruel, because her personality has in some ways been distorted by post-traumatic stress caused by her wartime experiences, her continuing contact with Soviet society, and disillusionment with the behaviour of some of her pupils, past and present, which she regards as treachery and ingratitude. She also faces the common human need to contend with experiences of frailty, loss, pain and suffering. The narrator also draws brief portraits of the other teachers, with acuity, but also a touch of satire: the glamorous, ageing headmistress known as 'Maman' who is eager to obtain benefits from the party authorities; the English teachers, Russian and foreign, who befriend F.; and Marina, the out-of-hours teacher, who constantly talks about the Great Patriotic War (Russian terminology for World War II), when her fiancé, a Soviet lieutenant, was killed.

Slavists will ruefully recognize the comments made by foreign teachers of Russian about the difficulties they experienced in the 1970s: either their spoken Russian was poor because they were unable to spend much time in the USSR, or, if their Russian was good (usually because they were bilingual or married to a Russian émigré), their timetable does not allow them enough hours to teach the Russian language adequately. There are also convincing portraits of the other schoolchildren: the lively Fedka, the narrator's rival for good English parts; the gentle Kostya, who claims to love her; and her best friend, the decisive Irka, who plans to leave the country after graduation (presumably because she is Jewish). This is a reference to the change of official policy in the 1970s, allowing many Soviet Jews to emigrate to Israel and other countries.

Insights into Soviet History, Society and Literature

Most serious historical fiction not only sheds light on the past, but also on the present, the time when the work was first written or published. Chizhova's *Little Zinnobers* is no exception, providing insights into several decades of

---

Yale University Press, 2007), pp. 124–127, 543.

Soviet history, from the 1940s to the post-Soviet period of the 1990s and early 2000s. Chizhova conveys different views of the Great Patriotic War: Marina's romantic view of the 'bright past', when she still had marital prospects, and the nostalgic meetings of veterans that she organizes are contrasted with the narrator's father's realistic account of the horrific experience of killing another human being with a knife, and the starvation and cannibalism during the siege of Leningrad. We also learn that Leningrad University after the war had lost most of its celebrated non-Communist lecturers and professors from the old University of St Petersburg, although some good scholars still remained.

Chizhova also affords glimpses of the Khrushchev era (1956–1964), with its destalinization policy and partial cultural liberalization (known as periodic 'thaws'); the 'romantic' time when Komsomol volunteers (young Communists) went off to sow maize in the 'Virgin Lands' (1953–1963); and Khrushchev's other pet scientific projects, such as the development of 'Big Chemistry' (initiated in 1958), and the excitement of space travel. There is also a reference to the Sixth World Festival of Youth and Students (1957), the first time when young people in Moscow had the chance to meet a large number of foreigners of their own age.

The novel contains allusions to various problematic aspects of Soviet society in the Brezhnev era (1964–1982), often called 'the era of stagnation', which have proved to be deeply rooted and longstanding in post-Soviet Russia. In particular, we learn that hospitals and maternity wards are unhealthy, and that there is a widespread use of influence to secure students' entrance into a university or institute. Chizhova also provides insights into the economic reality of the Soviet Union in the Brezhnev period:[108] the teachers live in very small flats; the lack of consumer goods is suggested by

----

[108]   Leonid Ilyich Brezhnev (1906–1982), born in Ukraine, was a Soviet politician who led the USSR from 1964 to 1982 as the General Secretary of the Central Committee of the Communist Party of the Soviet Union (CPSU). His eighteen-year term of office was second only to that of Stalin (1878–1953), whose dictatorship lasted from the mid-1920s until his death in 1953.

the rarity of fresh fruit such as oranges; suitable tights to be worn in the plays have to be brought by parents from Czechoslovakia; and beautiful women's dresses and boots come from former Yugoslavia. We also gain insights into the stratification of the supposedly classless Soviet society in the Brezhnev era. The narrator, despite her acting talent, is not allowed to go on a tour of the south of England because only 'children of working-class families' are included: she comments ironically, 'Politics, it turned out, began at birth'. Of course, 'working-class families' were often interpreted in the USSR as meaning those whose parents were members of the Communist Party, and of Russian ethnic origin.

The reality of the tense relations between Russia and the West during the Cold War (1947–1991)[109] is conveyed by the difficulties experienced by two visiting foreign teachers of Russian in the 1970s (of German and American origin respectively). Stanley, a teacher from the USA, is expelled from the Soviet Union for importing forbidden books, after his colleague, the Russian teacher B.G., has been obliged to collaborate with the KGB to 'shadow' him and inform against him. Those of us who travelled to Russia at that time will remember Yevtushenko's famous poem *'Khotiat li russkie voiny?'* ('Do the Russians want a war?'), which was commonly recited to visiting foreigners. It still remains a warning against what some commentators call a 'new Cold War' in the twenty-first century.[110]

Chizhova also affords some insight into literary life and the writers favoured by different social groups in the Brezhnev era. These discussions hint at a perennial Russian theme: 'the intelligentsia and the *narod* (the people)', which has been treated by Turgenev, Tolstoy, Blok, Pasternak, and many other twentieth-century Russian writers. When a Russian teacher asks the pupils to prepare five minutes of poetry by a poet not on the school

....

[109] Historians do not fully agree on the dates, but they often refer to the period between 1947, the year when the Truman Doctrine was announced (a foreign policy of the USA pledging to aid nations threatened by Soviet expansionism), and 1991, the year the USSR collapsed.

[110] See, for example, Edward Lucas, *The New Cold War* (London: Bloomsbury, 2008).

programme, the 'higher' group whose parents belong to the 'intelligentsia'[111] suggest the great poets Mandelstam, Pasternak, Akhmatova and Gumilyov. Although the first three famously suffered in the Stalin era, but were 'rehabilitated' during the Gorbachev era, Nikolai Gumilyov (1886–1921), Anna Akhmatova's first husband, is perhaps the most daring choice, as he was one of the first major writers to be arrested and shot after the Revolution by the Cheka, Lenin's secret police[112] — in 1921, for alleged participation in a monarchist plot. He and his co-conspirators in the so-called 'Tagantsev case' were not politically 'rehabilitated' until 1992, in the post-Soviet era.

The students from the 'middle' group whose parents are from a technical background propose the peasant poet Sergei Yesenin (1895–1925) — a very popular choice. Yesenin died in mysterious circumstances in the Hotel Angleterre in St Petersburg, either by committing suicide after he had written his last poem, 'Goodbye, my friend, goodbye', in his own blood (as was the official verdict), or, as various sensationalist books and films published in the post-Soviet era suggest, was murdered by the Soviet secret police (the OGPU). It seems that Yesenin was disillusioned by the aftermath of the October Revolution; some commentators believe that he was led to take his own life by cronies and sycophants who encouraged him to drink heavily and take drugs, but others refute this interpretation. Whatever the true story of his death, Yesenin is yet another prominent Russian poet who died very

....

[111]   On the origins and development of the Russian intelligentsia, who have often been in opposition to the government of their day, see Isaiah Berlin, 'A Remarkable Decade', in *Russian Thinkers*, 2nd ed. (Harmondsworth: Penguin, 1981), ed. by Henry Hardy and Aileen Kelly, pp.114–209.

[112]   Lenin, Leninism, and the Civil War were not reinterpreted in Russia until 1989-1991, relatively late in the Gorbachev era: see Marsh, *History and Literature*, pp. 110–151. Older people in Petersburg might know Gumilyov's poetry through references in the poetry of Mandelstam and the line '*Ia k smerti gotov*' ('I am ready to die') in Akhmatova's *Poema bez geroia* (*Poem without a Hero*), her great poem about the city of Petersburg/Leningrad composed between 1940 and 1965, but only published in full posthumously. Young people in Russia today might be more likely to know Gumilyov's poetry through the songs of the Russian rock group 'Little Tragedies', founded in Kursk in 1994. Their own name is reminiscent of Pushkin's *Malen'kie tragedii* (*Little Tragedies*, 1830).

young, like Pushkin and Lermontov, and whose legend persists. Yesenin's work was not published again in Russia until 1966, after Khrushchev's fall.

Yesenin had a short but passionate relationship with the Paris-based American celebrity dancer Isadora Duncan, although they only spoke a few words of each other's language (they married on 2 May 1922, toured round Europe and the USA, but in May 1923 Yesenin returned to Moscow). This episode continues Chizhova's theme of language and 'deafness', the lack of translation, communication and comprehension between East and West. Another of Yesenin's wives, the actress Zinaida Raikh [Reich], later married the celebrated modernist theatre director Meyerhold, and, like her husband, was tortured to death by Stalin's secret police (the NKVD).

The other poets suggested by the 'middle group' are more conventional socialist realist poets: inferior, but 'safer' names such as Yulia Drunina (1924–1991), and Konstantin Vanshenkin (1925–2012). Although they were both poets and lyricists from Moscow, regarded as conventional Soviet writers best known for their patriotic poems and songs about World War II, their lives too were by no means simple. Drunina, who was a nurse and combat medic during the war, known for her lyrics and poetry about women at war, committed suicide in 1991, allegedly because of disillusionment at the collapse of the Soviet Union. Vanshenkin was born Konstantin Weinschenker (thus presumably of Jewish origin), changed his name for political reasons, then served in the Soviet army from 1942 to 1946 in the airborne troops of the Second Ukrainian Front and the Third Ukrainian Front.

We also learn that Solzhenitsyn's *Arkhipelag GULag* (*The Gulag Archipelago*), his monumental three-volume account of the Soviet prison camp system under Lenin and Stalin (originally banned in the USSR), was being read on a foreign radio station in the 1970s. When foreigners ask the pupils what they think of Solzhenitsyn, F. tries to avoid confrontation and protect her students, suggesting that they simply answer truthfully: 'We haven't read that work by Solzhenitsyn'. As was common among Soviet intellectuals in the 1960s and 1970s, attitudes to Solzhenitsyn's work are presented in *Little Zinnobers* as indicative of the morality and political sympathies of Soviet people, real and fictional: the narrator says of another favourite English teacher, 'An intelligent man and a Jew, how could he not have been on Solzhenitsyn's side?'[113] At the time of the first publication of Solzhenitsyn's novella *One Day in the Life of Ivan Denisovich* in 1962, there was a saying that circulated in Moscow: 'Tell me what you think of *One Day* and I will tell you who you are.'[114]

Little Zinnobers also contains echoes of other major historical and political discussions of the 1970s. One important issue is whether Stalin's industrialization of the country and victory in the war are sufficient compensation for the evil he did — a question that still remains unresolved in Putin's Russia. Another hotly debated issue was the question of whether Soviet Jews should adapt to Soviet politics and society or emigrate to Israel, the USA, or elsewhere. There is an argument between Lenka Blank, the head girl, who is Jewish but changes her name to her mother's more Russian-sounding name, Barashkova ('ram') because she 'feels Russian' — the dilemma of many Soviet Jews — and Irka Eisner, who prioritizes her Jewishness. The position of ethnic and racial minorities in the Russian Federation and the former USSR is still a continuing, unresolved problem.

Another interesting debate which arose in Russia in the early 1960s and continued in the 1970s is the controversy between Fedka and F. about the

....

[113] Chizhova's statement is, however, highly ambiguous: although *Arkhipelag GULag* refers to many Jewish people who died in Stalin's purges, many of the Communist Old Bolsheviks who repressed others in the 1930s and 1940s were also Jewish. See Solzhenitsyn's ambiguous and provocative book, *Dvesti let vmeste, 1795–1955* (*Two Hundred Years Together, 1795–1955*), 2 vols (Moscow: Russkii put', 2001, 2002), written as a comprehensive history of Jews in the Russian Empire, the Soviet Union and modern Russia between the years 1795 and 1995, especially with regard to government attitudes toward Jews. This controversial book is still only partially translated into English in *The Solzhenitsyn Reader: New and Essential Writings, 1947–2005*, ed. by Edward E. Ericson, Jr, and Daniel J. Mahoney (Wilmington, DE: ISI Books, 2009). For a concise account of the discussions on this subject, see <https://en.wikipedia.org/wiki/Two_Hundred_Years_Together> [accessed 25 September 2017].

[114] *Solzhenitsyn: A Documentary* Record, ed. by Leopold Labedz, enl. ed. (Bloomington: Indiana University Press, 1973), p. 79.

value of contemporary, topical or fashionable writers in comparison with the great writers of universal significance (Chaucer, Shakespeare, Pushkin, Dostoyevsky, and others), who will be read for centuries to come. Fedka and his supporters passionately defend the 'young poets' and prose writers of different political persuasions who rose to fame in the 1960s, such as the Westernizer and urbanite Vasily Aksyonov (1933–2017), the Russophile *derevenshchik* ('village prose writer') Vasily Belov (1932–2012), and the best-known poets, Yevgeny Yevtushenko (1933–2017) and Andrei Voznesensky (1933–2010), who filled football stadiums with their poetry recitals during the second Khrushchev 'thaw' of the early 1960s — a phenomenon that has not been repeated, either in Russia or the West (such crowds generally only gather for pop concerts or sporting occasions). Sadly, all the 'young poets' and 'young prose writers' mentioned in *Little Zinnobers* have now died. Only time will tell if they are still being read in Russia and elsewhere in a hundred, two hundred, or a thousand years.

At the end of the novel the narrator states openly that F. was trying to prepare her pupils for life in an 'eastern despotism', and that Shakespeare was the only antidote against the poison of the world around them. As in other anti-Stalin works published in the post-Soviet period, such as Liudmila Ulitskaia's *Zelenyi shatër* (*The Big Green Tent*, 2011), depiction of the Brezhnev era is being used to shed light on the current state of Russian society at the time of publication.[115]

Style and Translation

Little Zinnobers is not easy to translate because, although the plot is relatively simple, the novel is written in a 'stream of consciousness' narrative mode, with Soviet slang, Russian, English, and Tatar terms, expressions and proverbs,

....

[115] For a British journalist's impressions of Russia in early 2000, when Chizhova's novel was first published, see Shaun Walker, *The Long Hangover: Putin's New Russia and the Ghosts of the Past* (Oxford: Oxford University Press, 2018), pp. 12–17.

and multiple Aesopian references. Moreover, Elena Chizhova's prose, like her poetry, is rich in rhetorical devices, metaphors, similes, repetition, rhythm, rhyme, and sound effects. Her use of alliteration is particularly striking: for example, the sun is '*zhivitel'nym i zhestokim*' ('life-giving and cruel'); she thinks '*s gorech'iu ili gordost'iu*' ('with bitterness or pride'). Chizhova's poetic prose is difficult to translate without sacrificing the meaning, but the translator Carol Ermakova has been particularly successful in translating certain phrases containing both alliteration and assonance: for example, '*russkii iazyk otdaval pozorom, peplom i prakhom, kotoryi ia ne smela shevelit*'' [literally, 'the Russian language smacked of shame, dust and ashes which I did not dare to move'] is rendered as 'the Russian language smacked of disgrace, demise and dust, which I daren't disturb'. Chizhova also possesses the dramatic gift of conveying dialogue and conflict between people, and the storyteller's ability to build up and maintain tension, foreshadowing later events by hinting at difficulties ahead.

Chizhova makes skilful use of images of light and dark, sun and moon, animals, plants, and insects, buds and flowers, food, colours, fabrics, and images taken from Greek or Roman mythology. The most frequently mentioned colours are red and white, as in the phrase 'the little white and red flowers of our pinafores, shirts and ties', evoking not only the uniforms of Young Communist Pioneers[116] and the rival combatant in the Russian Civil War, but also the Wars of the Roses, which, as we have seen, is a subtext running throughout the novel. The headmistress Maman is described as 'a dark velvet rose' — one such rose is called 'Black Magic', which takes us back again to Macbeth, Faust and Bulgakov. As far as mythology is concerned, the unemployed theatre director sees himself as a 'fallen Jupiter', and the narrator plays the role of Thetis, a Greek nymph who tried to make her son immortal by burning off his mortality by day and feeding him ambrosia by night. In other interpretations, however, Thetis was the great goddess worshipped in

---

[116] The Young Pioneers, named after Vladimir Lenin, were a mass Communist youth organization for children aged 10–15 that existed in the Soviet Union between 1922 and 1991.

ancient Greece as the creator of the universe; or the mother of Achilles who bore some responsibility for the outbreak of the Trojan War.

As a former poet, Chizhova likes to play on ambiguous Russian words with several possible meanings: for example, *ten'* ('shade, shadow', or 'tail', 'spook'); *svet* ('light', 'world', or 'society'); *glukhoi* ('deaf', or 'obscure, dark'); *pioner* ('an explorer', 'trailblazer', or 'colonist', such as an adventurer or pirate who discovers the 'new world', like Columbus, Drake, or Raleigh), but it can also mean a member of a children's organization run by a Communist party. The words 'enlightened' and 'Enlightenment' are repeated several times, usually reflecting the teachers' desire to educate the children in the norms of Soviet society, but also suggesting the mistaken views of the new ruler in 'Little Zaches', who prefers 'enlightenment' to freedom. Another frequently used word is *golos* ('voice', or 'vote'), as emotions are judged according to a character's language, accent or tone of voice, rather than appearance, because many of the adults in the novel are used to dissimulation (and the children are learning fast). The word *glaza* ('eyes') is also mentioned very often, emphasizing the powers of observation traditionally considered characteristic of children and artists, the eyes as indicators of emotion in the absence of words, and the constant surveillance of the state. It also conjures up Hoffmann's malevolent Sandman, who is said to steal the eyes of children who would not go to bed and feed them to his own children who lived in the moon.

As in many works of modern Russian literature, notably Bulgakov's *Master and Margarita,* and novels by Solzhenitsyn such as *The First Circle* and *Cancer Ward* (both first published in the West in 1968), chapter headings in *Little Zinnobers* are often significant or symbolic. Some refer to biblical or liturgical themes, such as 'Zavet' ('Testament', or 'Covenant'), 'Izgnanie iz raia' ('Banished from Paradise'), and 'Sila i slava' ('The Power and the Glory'), and are echoed in the text by references to devils, angels, monks, religious observances, and biblical stories, such as the story of Martha and Mary of Bethany. St Luke relates that Mary chose listening to the teachings of Jesus over helping her sister prepare food, and Jesus responded that she was right (Luke 10. 38–42). Chizhova alters this story to suggest that in Russia (as in most parts of the world), women have to do the domestic work first before they can engage in creative or spiritual activities.

Other biblical and liturgical terms in the novel are used by Soviet people, who perhaps did not even know where they originated, since it was very difficult to find a copy of the New Testament in a modern Russian translation, and the Russian Orthodox Church often had to operate underground from the 1950s to the 1970s, after Khrushchev's virulent anti-religious campaign (1958-1964). The dinner lady Auntie Galya and her kitchen helpers, for example, compare the child actors to 'birds of the air' — a veiled reference to the biblical verse:

> Look at the birds of the air, for they neither sow nor reap nor gather into barns; yet your heavenly Father feeds them. Are you not of more value than they?
> Which of you by worrying can add one cubit to his stature?
>
> Matthew 6. 26–27 (New King James Bible)

The implication is that the talented children should concentrate on their acting and not bother about food or drink; Auntie Galya and her kitchen staff will try to help the nervous actors by becoming their 'bread sponsors' (an ironic play on an English word used in Russian for a situation more associated with the capitalist and post-Soviet worlds).

'The lion lies down with the lamb' is another biblical phrase used to evoke the plight of the naïve American Stanley who is being watched by the Soviet secret police and their 'shadows'. This is a common misquotation of Isaiah 11. 6: 'the wolf dwelling with the lamb while the leopard lies down with the kid [...] and the young lion'. It is a phrase that has morphed from its biblical origins: as with a phrase like 'Pride goeth before a fall', it is the abbreviation that has survived the test of time: the lion shall lie down with the lamb. Other biblical sayings in the novel include Christ's terrible cry on the cross: 'O Lord, why hast Thou forsaken me?' (Matthew 27. 47; Mark 15. 24). The narrator also refers to Christian rituals that continued in the Soviet period: for example, she sows seeds in peat pots so that they will spring to life by Easter Sunday, to mark the resurrection of Christ. Likewise, she alludes to Muslim rituals in Tatarstan, where believers have to purify themselves before prayer; and women, in particular, must engage in Namaz washing (purification during menstruation).

Another chapter heading takes us into the realm of supernatural and paranormal phenomena. It alludes to the supernatural beings known as *oborotni* ('werewolves', or 'shape-shifters'), mythological or folkloric human beings with the alleged ability to shapeshift into a wolf during the full moon, which F. compares to the children who, she believes, are doomed to betray her.[117] The werewolf myth may be particularly connected with children and young people because they are more subject to development and transformation. Elsewhere in the novel the out-of-hours teacher Marina Ivanovna, with her blood-red lipstick and romantic view of World War II, is compared by the children, rather cruelly, to a vampire sucking life out of the 'bright past', or an unrealistic socialist realist heroine who ignores the horror and complexity of the last war.

In contemporary Russian literature, as some critics have claimed, the prevalence of magical realism is a result either of the repression of the traumatic memories of the Soviet period, or, alternatively, because of the collapse of a great empire. Yefim Etkind, for example, has argued that 'The work of post-Soviet authors has engendered a host of strange beings, vampires, werewolves, subhumans, and superhumans.'[118] In *Little Zinnobers*, pursuing the supernatural theme, the narrator also compares herself to

....

[117]   On the importance of supernatural themes and characters in Russian literature, see Muireann Maguire, *Stalin's Ghosts: Gothic Themes in Early Soviet Literature* (Bern: Peter Lang, 2012).

[118]   Mark Lipovetsky and Efim Etkind, 'The Salamander's Return: The Soviet Catastrophe and the Post-Soviet Novel', *Russian Studies in Literature*, No. 46 (2010), 6–48 (p. 11).

a 'ghost', and wears a black cape like a witch; another child, the prankster Sashka Guchkov, is depicted as running as fast as 'a devil on a broomstick'; while other children act scenes of 'the three witches' in *Macbeth* who represent fate, or doom, for the tragic hero. Yet although Chizhova implies in her own play *Mary, Queen of Scots*, and in her references to Shakespeare's *Macbeth, Richard III*, and Dostoyevsky's *Crime and Punishment* in *Little Zinnobers*, that fictional tyrants or murderers are racked by guilt and the ghosts of their former victims, it is not clear whether she believes that this is also the case with the rulers of Russian history (notably Stalin).

At times, Chizhova creates a sense of foreboding and fate, like Hoffmann in his tales. The theme of destiny, or possible doom, for both F. and the narrator, could be evoked from the lines in *Romeo and Juliet*, V. 3. 90: 'One writ with me in sour misfortune's book' (or, in the alliterative translation by Pasternak: '*My v knige roka na odnoi stroke*').[119] In the novel, however, we learn only that F. sees herself and her pupils as 'doomed' to adapt to Soviet society, forgetting the lessons of Shakespeare, Pushkin and other great writers; and towards the end of the novel, F. herself directly refers to the 'devilry' of the post-Soviet period.

Chizhova's novel also alludes, more subtly, to striking images in certain well-known literary texts, but changes the context: for example, the phrase *mirok* ('the little world') used to refer to the school is reminiscent of the dying John of Gaunt's speech about England to his vain, superficial nephew Richard II:

This happy breed of men, this little world [...]
This blessed plot, this earth, this realm, this England [...]
(Shakespeare, *Richard II*, ɪɪ. 1)

....

[119]   'Romeo i Dzhul'etta', tragediia Uil'iama Shekspira, perevod Borisa Pasternaka, 1942, <http://www.romeo-juliet-club.ru/shakespeare/romeojuliet_pasternak1.html> [accessed 5 October 2017].

The narrator also refers to a moonbeam that illuminates the school stage as a '*lunnaia dorozhka*' ('moonpath'), which recalls the 'moonpath' in Bulgakov's *Master and Margarita*, the path leading up to the 'realm of light' which Pilate ascends to meet the philosopher Yeshua (Bulgakov's incarnation of Jesus), whom he had sentenced to death. The moon is often associated with the feminine, or with the subconscious area of the personality (as in the werewolf image, or the sleepwalking Lady Macbeth), and, in Gnostic philosophy, with purification. Since in Bulgakov's novel, according to Woland, Bulgakov's devil, 'to each shall be given according to his belief', Pilate's longing to meet Yeshua again is fulfilled.[120] The references to *Master i Margarita* suggest that for Chizhova, as for Bulgakov, values such as art, love, family affection, morality and religion are more important than politics.

The Italian phrase '*Che sera, sera*' ('What will be, will (or shall) be') was first cited in England as a heraldic motif in the sixteenth century, but its most likely source in *Little Zinnobers* is Marlowe's *Doctor Faustus*, suggesting the impossibility of predicting the future. At the beginning of the play, Doctor Faustus dismisses the study of Divinity:

'If we say that we have no sin we deceive ourselves,
    and there's no truth in us.'
Why then, belike we must sin and so consequently die.
Ay, we must die an everlasting death.
What doctrine call you this, *Che sera sera*.
'What will be shall be?' Divinity, adieu.

(Marlowe, *Doctor Faustus*, I. 1)

....

[120]   For further discussion, see Andrew Barratt, *Between Two Worlds: A Critical Introduction to 'The Master and Margarita'* (Oxford: Clarendon Press, 1987); J.A.E. Curtis, *Bulgakov's Last Decade: The Writer as Hero* (Cambridge: Cambridge University Press, 1987); *Master and Margarita: A Critical Companion*, ed. by Laura D. Weeks (Evanston, IL: Northwestern University Press, 1996).

'*Que sera, sera*' is also the title of a famous song written by Jay Livingston and Ray Evans sung by Doris Day in Alfred Hitchcock's 1956 remake of his 1934 film *The Man Who Knew Too Much*,[121] and which later became the signature song of the American sitcom 'The Doris Day Show' (1968–1973). The three verses of the song progress through the life of the narrator – from childhood, through young adulthood and falling in love, to parenthood – and each asks 'What will I be?' or 'What lies ahead?'. The answer in each case is the same resigned, fatalistic line, '*Que sera, sera*'.

Other chapter titles in *Little Zinnobers* consist of literary references, such as the title 'Vystrel' ('The Shot'), referring to the last, fatalistic story in Lermontov's *Hero of Our Time*. The onion that the narrator gives F. in the last chapter is reminiscent of the onion in Henrik Ibsen's *Peer Gynt* (first published 1867, but not performed until 1882), which the protagonist peels off, layer by layer, until the core of his personality is revealed. In both a chapter title and a section within the text, Chizhova cites the famous lines of the great Symbolist poet Alexander Blok (1880–1921), written on 8 September 1914 and dedicated to his fellow poet Zinaida Gippius (1869–1945) (to whom he once proposed in 1918):

Rozhdënnye v goda glukhie
Puti ne pomniat svoego.
My — deti strashnykh let Rossii
Zabyt' ne v silakh nichego.

(Those born in obscure times [literally, years]
Do not remember their way.
We, children of Russia's frightful years
Cannot forget a thing.)[122]

....

[121]   Apparently, the original Italian 'che' (what) was changed to Spanish 'que' in the film, because more people in the USA spoke Spanish than Italian.

[122]   Translated in *From the Ends to the Beginning. A Biligual Anthology of Russian Verse*, <http://

The line 'Those born in obscure times' refers to the outbreak of the First World War in 1914 and Blok's foreboding of the terrible future carnage. Chizhova may also be playing on the fact that the word '*glukhoi*' is an ambiguous word which also means 'deaf', suggesting that Russians in 1914 were oblivious to the problems to come. Zinaida Gippius (1869–1945), a famous poet, prose writer, critic, editor and religious thinker, managed to emigrate after the Bolshevik Revolution with her husband Dmitry Merezhkovsky, and even to support German forces attacking Stalin in World War II, whereas her friend Blok initially accepted the Revolution and remained in Russia, where he soon became bitterly disillusioned, finding comfort only in alcohol and brothels before his tragic death from endocarditis in 1921.

Chizhova also employs images of dolls, clowns and puppets to emphasize the dichotomy between reality and illusion, and to suggest that Soviet people (like the majority of characters in Hoffmann's 'Little Zaches') are being manipulated, for good or ill. While dolls can be harmless toys for children, they have also traditionally been used in spiritual, magic and religious rituals in many cultures. Through the equivocal image of the doll, Chizhova sometimes plays on the popularity of the Russian ballet: for example, Marie Stahlbaum in Hoffmann's 'The Nutcracker and the Mouse King' (usually called Clara in the ballet *The Nutcracker*) longs to return to the utopian 'kingdom of the dolls'; whereas *Coppélia* (sometimes subtitled *The Girl With The Enamel Eyes*) is a comic ballet telling the disturbing tale of a beautiful life-sized doll, Olympia, which comes to life under its Svengali-type figure Dr Coppélius. A similar effect was created by Meyerhold's famous production of Gogol's *The Government Inspector* in 1926, in which the last act was played by dolls resembling sinister figures in Hoffmann's *Tales*, or the Devil. The doll image also evokes the famous 'Russian doll', the nested matryoshka doll set, first made in 1890,[123] which was originally a representation of motherhood

....
max.mmlc.northwestern.edu/mdenner/Demo/texts/born_obscure_years.html> [accessed 12 October 2017].
[123] The first Russian nested doll set was made by Vasily Zvyozdochkin from a design by Sergei

and different female generations, but later often used to portray fairy-tale figures, writers or artists, or Soviet and Russian leaders.[124] Stripping off the different layers of these dolls recalls the onion metaphor in Chizhova's conclusion and Ibsen's *Peer Gynt*, discussed above (p. 224).

Clowns, whose role is to create humour, but are seen by some as sinister figures, evoke the perennial popularity of the Russian circus, along with Bakhtin's idea of 'carnival', a literary mode that subverts and liberates the dominant social and cultural forms through humour and chaos. The image of the puppet suggests the Petrushka puppet theatre in Russian and Soviet history (the Russian version of Punch and Judy), which dates back to Byzantine times. This was often used to illuminate both family and gender politics, but could also be used for political satire. All these non-verbal forms of communication are well known by Russians themselves and particularly popular with foreign visitors to Russia.[125]

The main image used throughout the novel, however, is drama and the theatre, which contrasts with the mundane reality of everyday life in the Soviet and post-Soviet periods. 'Masks' and 'masquerade' are common images in Russian literature,[126] as in Lermontov's play *Maskarada* (*Masquerade*,

....

Maliutin, who was a folk crafts painter at Abramtsevo, near Sergiev Posad, outside Moscow. The original sets were of Russian peasant women in a *sarafan* (traditional dress). The figures inside may be of either gender; the smallest, innermost doll is typically a baby turned from a single piece of wood. The dolls often follow a theme, but the themes may vary, from fairy-tale characters to Soviet and Russian leaders. These may be historical, as in significant tsars; or contemporary, as in Gorbachev and the post-Soviet leaders.

[124]   Matryoshka dolls of Soviet and Russian leaders became particularly common in the Gorbachev era (and were known as 'Gorby dolls'). This trend has continued under the post-Soviet leaders Yeltsin, Medvedev, and Putin, but is probably more popular with tourists than with Russians themselves.

[125]   For further discussion, see *Birgit Beumers, Pop Culture Russia!: Media, Arts, and Lifestyle* (Santa Barbara, CA: ABC-CLIO, 2005); Catriona Kelly, *Petrushka: The Russian Carnival Puppet Theatre* (Cambridge: Cambridge University Press, 1990).

[126]   Similar images are used in Alexander Blok's play *Balaganchik* (*The Fairground Booth*, or *The Puppet Show*, 1906); the setting of Act 3 of both the opera *The Tales of Hoffmann* and the ballet *Coppélia* is a masked ball in Venice. See also descriptions of the famous modernist productions of Shakespeare, Gogol's *Revizor*, Blok's *Balaganchik*, and the never-staged version of *Boris Godunov* by the acclaimed avant-garde director Vsevolod Meyerhold, who, as we have

written in 1832 and first performed posthumously in 1852, although the censorship was not finally lifted until 1862). Lermontov's play suffered from the tsarist censorship, as it was based on a real murder of an aristocratic wife by her husband, and implied criticism of the masquerade balls staged by the aristocratic Engelhardt family. Although Lermontov's play is sometimes compared to *Othello*, and Shakespeare's Romeo and Juliet first meet at a masked ball, the clearest analogy with Shakespeare in Chizhova's novel is the melancholy Jaques's famous speech in *As You Like It* (1599–1600): 'All the world's a stage,/And all the men and women merely players' (II. 7. 139–40). The image of the actor also recalls the many impostors or pretenders to the throne in England, Scotland, and Russia, evoked through rival claims to the succession in some of Shakespeare's tragedies and history plays, notably *Henry VI, Part Two* (1591), *Richard II* (1595), *Julius Caesar* (1599), *Richard III*, *Henry VI, Part Two*, and *Macbeth*, among others.

Conclusions

Although it might appear at first sight that *Little Zinnobers* is 'a drama from school life', as a subtitle on the cover of an edition of 2010 suggests,[127] the 'little world' of the school also has much wider implications for society as a whole. The novel is an attempt to evoke and reconsider the last years of the Soviet regime before the USSR, described as a 'huge and mediocre, a great Zinnober', finally collapsed. Moreover, at the end of the novel there is a suggestion that the post-Soviet period, which has given people something new, may also be a tragedy because it has taken too much away from them. The new era has removed not only the negative aspects of the past, which people themselves are glad to part with, but also certain positive features that they may regret for the rest of their

....

seen, became a prominent victim of Stalin's Great Purge (he was cleared of all charges in 1955).

[127]   Elena Chizhova, *Kroshki Tsakhes* (Moscow: AST, Astrel', 2010).

lives.[128] This insight is relevant not only to contemporary Russia, but to anyone moving from childhood to adulthood or adapting to rapid social change. *Little Zinnobers* is also a love story of universal relevance, if not a conventional one focusing on sexual love. The narrator refers to the different kinds of love in Greek, implying that the relationship between her and F. was a form of *agape* (spiritual love) or *philia* (deep friendship, or the love between parents and children). At the end she comes to see F. as some kind of non-biological 'mother' — a relationship between women of different generations also highlighted in other novels by prominent female authors of the post-Soviet period.[129]

As we have seen, Chizhova refers to a number of Russian and foreign writers and artists who were multi-talented 'Renaissance men'. This point is emphasized when the pupils suggest reciting poems by Petrarch (1304–1374), the Italian poet, scholar and humanist in Renaissance Italy, whose rediscovery of Cicero's letters is often credited with initiating the fourteenth-century Renaissance. Shakespeare was a poet, dramatist and actor; Rachmaninov was a virtuoso pianist, composer, and conductor. Jacques Offenbach (1819–1880) was a German-born French composer, cellist and impresario of the Romantic period born into a Jewish family in Cologne — a city which kept changing its identity in the nineteenth century. Offenbach's opera *The Tales of Hoffmann* is written in French but set in Germany and Italy in the early nineteenth century.

E.T.A. Hoffmann himself was also a fascinating 'Renaissance man': a Romantic Prussian writer of fairy tales and gothic horror stories, a composer and music critic, a draftsman and caricaturist, a jurist and political figure, who was born in Königsberg (now Kaliningrad, an isolated 'semi-exclave' between Poland and Lithuania on the Baltic Sea, which still

....

[128] Email discussion with the author, 20 June 2017. By the end of 2000, 75 per cent of Russians said that they regretted the collapse of the Soviet Union.

[129] See Rosalind Marsh, 'New mothers for a new era? Images of mothers and daughters in post-Soviet prose', *Modern Language Review*, Vol. 107, No. 4 (October 2012), pp. 1191–1219.

remains part of the Russian Federation). At different times he lived in areas belonging to both the western and the eastern parts of Germany, Austria, and Poland. Before the age of nationalism towards the end of the nineteenth century, nation-states did not exist; there were empires and, for the wealthy, grand tours of Europe, and for some, journeys to the 'new world' or the colonies.

It is interesting that the French librettists of Offenbach's *Tales of Hoffmann* credit the myth of 'Little Zaches' to the town of Eisenach in Thuringia, the eastern part of Germany, near the former border of East Germany — not the mythical 'Jinnistan' of the original tale. Once again, we see the irrelevance of geography in Chizhova's world, which prioritizes the telling and retelling of myths and stories over the supposed region or country of their origin. The stories, myths and legends mentioned in her novel, such as *Romeo and Juliet* and *Faust*, are told and retold in many different languages, genres and historical periods; works are produced in different versions, sometimes only published or staged posthumously, created and re-created in different art forms (painting, music, poetry, prose, drama, opera, dance, film, and popular culture), translated, re-translated and reinterpreted in many diverse cultures. Great works of art, such as Shakespeare's plays, which have now been translated into over ninety languages, belong to the world, not just to England.

Before the twentieth century, in particular, many Russian and European artists travelled, lived and worked in different countries, collaborated with foreigners, or were inspired by foreign literature and music. Chizhova's novel conjures up in the reader's mind works of art which demonstrate cooperation between artists of different countries, for example operas and ballets based on Hoffmann's tales, or plays by Pushkin and Shakespeare set to music by Mussorgsky, Rimsky-Korsakov, Tchaikovsky, Verdi, and others. Moreover, for many artists national and ethnic affiliation was often multiple and ambiguous: the composer Gluck, for example, who was born in the Upper Palatinate (now part of Germany), raised in Bohemia, and welcomed in the Habsburg court in Vienna, composed French and Italian operas and probably spoke Czech rather than German. Regions, cities and people frequently changed their identities in the nineteenth century, with the partitions of Poland, Napoleon's victories and defeats, and the unification of Italy and Germany. These changes became even starker in the twentieth century, with many revolutions and two world wars, the fall of the Berlin Wall in 1989, and the collapse of the USSR in 1991.

Chizhova rejects narrow Russian nationalism, emphasizing the importance of her Tatar heroine by referring to a number of famous writers and composers of Tatar origin, including Dostoyevsky, Rachmaninov, and Yevtushenko, to emphasize how multilingual and multitalented people were in the former Russian Empire and Soviet Union (and still are in the present-day Russian Federation). The implication is that accidents of geography, history and politics can be ignored by true artists of talent or genius. Chizhova also suggests that ethnic and racial identities — of Russians, Jews, Tatars, Ukrainians, Georgians, Kazakhs, and others — were largely irrelevant in the multi-ethnic Soviet Union of the 1970s, although, as is evident from some of the conflicts in her novel, antagonisms were seething under the surface, only to re-emerge, sometimes in ugly forms, towards the end of the 1980s and in the post-Soviet era. Although it was the Crimean Tatars who were subject to mass deportation under Stalin in 1944 (a policy declared illegal in 1989), the Volga Tatars (of which F. is presumably a member) would have felt sympathy for them, and the fate of the Crimean Tatars remains a difficult contemporary problem after Putin's annexation of Crimea in 2014.

Whatever the political difficulties they experienced, Chizhova draws no distinction between Russian and foreign writers and artists; or between authors and composers who stayed in Russia or emigrated after the Bolshevik Revolution of 1917: for example, Alexander Blok, who remained in Russia after the Revolution, affords a contrast to Zinaida Gippius, his friend, and the addressee of his poem 'Those born in obscure times', who chose to emigrate. Similarly, Chizhova does not distinguish between Westernizers and

Slavophiles, Reds or Whites, Soviet or anti-Soviet people, victims of Leninism (Gumilyov) or Stalinism (Mandelstam, Akhmatova), or those who suffered in the post-Stalin period too (Pasternak, Solzhenitsyn). For Chizhova, art is universal and international, depending only on talent or genius.

Nevertheless, Shakespeare productions by Russian companies still have political undertones, as in the Cheek by Jowl production of *Measure for Measure* directed by Declan Donnellan, which was staged in Russia and Britain in 2013–2015. Shakespeare's play depicts a 'good' duke who abandons his people, and an evil duke, Angelo, who tries to rape the nun Isabella. Pushkin was clearly aware of the potential of Shakespeare's 'problem play' about despotism, order, and justice, since he wrote *Andzhelo* (*Angelo*, 1833), a narrative poem on the same subject, which he valued highly.[130]

Hoffmann too continues to possess enduring relevance to contemporary Russia, but also to create new controversy. One prominent example is a stop motion-animated feature film 'Gofmaniada' ('Hoffmaniada'), using puppets rather than computer animation, the most ambitious project undertaken by the Moscow animated film studio Soyuzmul'tfil'm since the collapse of the USSR.[131] This eagerly awaited film, based on a concept by Mikhail Shemiakin [Chemiakin] (b. 1943), the famous non-conformist painter, sculptor and theatre designer,[132] is based on three of Hoffmann's most interesting tales about reality, illusion, and art: 'Little Zaches', 'The Sandman', and 'Der goldne Topf. Ein Märchen aus der neuen Zeit' ('The Golden Pot: A Modern Fairytale',

....

[130]   Binyon, *Pushkin*, p. 424.

[131]   See <https://en.wikipedia.org/wiki/Hoffmaniada> [accessed 15 April 2018].

[132]   Shemiakin helped to produce a notorious exhibition at the Hermitage Museum in Leningrad in 1964, after which the director of the museum and all the participants were forced to resign. Subsequently he formed the unofficial art group 'St Petersburg', but was compelled to undertake psychological treatment and exiled from the USSR in 1971. In 2001 he returned to Russia and was commissioned to create a monument on a somewhat Hoffmann-like theme, 'Children Are the Victims of Adult Vices', now to be seen in a park near the Kremlin. He has also created sculptures of Peter the Great in St Petersburg and Deptford, London (see p. 186). He loves Hoffmann's tales, and has directed two ballets for the Mariinsky Theatre in St Petersburg: an innovative new version of *The Nutcracker* (2001), and a second ballet based on the same story, 'Volshebnyi orekh' ('The Magic Nut').

1814),[133] which Hoffmann himself considered his best story. The main character is Hoffmann himself, and the film emphasizes the contrast between the power of the artist's imagination and his job as a humble government official. The film is directed by Stanislav Sokolov (b. 1947),[134] who also wrote the screenplay with the playwright Victor Slavkin (1935–2014), while the art design (including over 150 hand-made puppets) was created by Shemiakin, who reportedly withdrew from the project in 2016. The first thirteen minutes of this film appeared on Russian television in November 2005 under the title 'Veronika', but since then there have been serious difficulties with state funding.[135] A longer preview version of the film, including Part Two, 'Gofman i tainy chasovshchika' (Hoffmann and the Secrets of the Watchmaker), was shown in a closed venue at the Berlin Film Festival in February 2018 and at the Suzdal Festival of Animated Film in March, so there is some hope that the film may be on general release soon.

Chizhova's novel refers to some of the greatest writers, artists, composers and thinkers who, along with significant historical and political figures, have suffered censorship, persecution, arrest, torture, or execution throughout human history. Oppression has caused some creative people to commit suicide or die young, or sometimes to live as drunken or drug-addicted outsiders, regarded as aliens and blasphemers, while others have remained passive, either as conformists or non-conformists (sometimes both, at the same or different times). Nevertheless, although individuals live in history, for Chizhova art and love transcend sex, sexual orientation, gender, age, class, race, ethnicity, politics, even religion (but not necessarily God or morality).

....

[133] See E.T.A. Hoffmann, *The Golden Pot and Other Tales,* trans. and ed. by Ritchie Robertson (New York: Oxford University Press, 1992).

[134] Sokolov was also associated with the Russian–British series *Shekspir: Animatsionnye istorii* (*Shakespeare: The Animated Tales*), which appeared on BBC2 and S4C in 1992–1994, and proved very popular in Russia.

[135] The first 30 minutes of the film were published on the Internet on 27 October 2015 by the Ministry of Culture in an attempt to find financial partners: see <https://www.youtube.com/watch?v=QPFouuDqh_8> [accessed 22 April 2018].

Her work is not didactic, but promotes diversity, tolerance and ecumenism, like Liudmila Ulitskaia's novel *Daniel' Shtain, Perevodchik* (*Daniel Stein, Interpreter*, 2006) — ideas which are extremely necessary in the troubled twenty-first century.

Some of the subjects mentioned in *Little Zinnobers* are developed at greater length in Chizhova's later novels, which have moved from 'life writing' to fiction combining reality and fantasy which treats moral social, historical and religious themes, usually with female protagonists. By the time of writing of this essay (2018), she has published nine novels. The most famous, as mentioned above, is *The Time of Women*, which, set in the 1950s and 1960s, depicts three elderly women with the pre-revolutionary names Evdokiia, Glikeriia, and Ariadna who adopt the role of *babushki* ('grandmothers'), bringing up the mute daughter of an unmarried mother, a neighbour in a communal flat. They combat the enforced patriotism of Soviet society by the power of memory, telling her their own experiences of the history of Leningrad, including the Revolution, the early days of the Soviet Union, and the starvation and suffering of the siege. For a while they manage to resist Soviet bureaucracy and prevent the girl from being sent to a children's home, but they ultimately prove unable to save her. Significantly, inhabitants of Moscow have been able to see Chizhova's truthful evocation of Soviet history through the adaptation of *The Time of Women* by the young director Yegor Peregudov (b. 1983), which has played from April 2011 to (at least) April 2018 in the famous Sovremennik ('Contemporary') Theatre.

Chizhova's major emphasis on religion and morality is illustrated in another of her novels that was nominated for the Booker Prize, *Lavra* (*The Monastery*),[136] set in the Brezhnev period, which depicted a priest's wife searching for the meaning of life, but disillusioned with the official Orthodox Church. Chizhova's interest in ethnic minorities and people of mixed race received fuller expression in her third and most controversial

....

[136] First published in St Petersburg: *Zvezda*, No. 7, 8 (2002); republished in book form (St Petersburg: Zvezda, 2003).

novel nominated for the prize, which she entitled *Polukrovka* (The Mixed-Race Girl, 2005), but was later given a more anodyne title, *Prestupnitsa* (The Criminal), a work that evokes the problems of a Jewish girl in St Petersburg who is refused entry to university and subsequently resorts to petty crime.

As Yelena Furman correctly stated in relation to Chizhova's *The Time of Women, Chizhova's early novels,* like much contemporary Russian literature, explore 'the effects of the Soviet legacy on the country's inhabitants'.[137] More recently, however, she has developed themes that were only implicit in her earlier works. Her novel *Terrakotovaia starukha* (The Old Terracotta Woman, 2011) exposes the unconstrained materialism of post-Soviet society through her heroine Tatiana (reminiscent of Tatiana, the heroine of Pushkin's and Tchaikovsky's *Evgenii Onegin*), who looks at life through the prism of Russian literature. In her latest work to date, however, Chizhova has experimented with a different, non-realistic genre of counter-factual history: her novel *Kitaist* (The Chinese Specialist, 2017) is an anti-utopian work which imagines that German troops in World War II occupied the Soviet Union up to the Ural mountains. Such speculative fiction is a genre popular with other anglophone and post-Soviet authors too: for example, Len Deighton's *SS-GB* (1978), Robert Harris's *Fatherland* (2012), and works by the Russian writers Viacheslav Pietsukh (b. 1946), Vladimir Sharov (b. 1952), Vladimir Sorokin (b. 1955), Tatiana Tolstaia (b. 1951), and others.[138]

Chizhova's work is distinguished by emotional and intellectual honesty, literary craftsmanship, and a strong morality based on genuine Russian Orthodox faith. She said in an interview of 2011 that the author she feels most affinity with is the Turkish writer Orhan Pamuk (born in 1952), who

---

[137] See Yelena Furman, 'Soviet Scars: Elena Chizhova's "The Time of Women"', *LA Review of Books,* 20 May 2012. <https://lareviewofbooks.org/article/soviet-scars-yelena-furmans-the-time-of-women/> [accessed 22 September 2017].

[138] Rosalind Marsh, *Literature, History and Identity,* Chapter 7, especially pp. 271–282.

won the Nobel Prize for Literature in 2006.[139] Like Chizhova, he is a writer from an autocratic state who is prepared to investigate the true history of his country,[140] sometimes at the risk of criminal charges. Like her, he regards the art of the novelist as understanding 'the other'; he is interested in the relationship between East and West, and is opposed to present nationalism and past genocide (the Ottoman government's systematic extermination of 1.5 million Armenian citizens within the Ottoman Empire and its successor state, the Republic of Turkey, from 24 April 1915 to 1917, which is still denied by the Turkish government).

Elena Chizhova's views on sexual, ethnic and racial politics bring her close to what used to be called the 'liberal', or 'Westernist' trend in contemporary Russian literature, and represent an expression of what is often designated as 'universal human values' (perhaps naïvely or ironically, in today's diverse and deeply troubled world).[141] Chizhova's novel *Little Zinnobers*, like her other works, can be seen as a subtle attack on lying, dictatorship and violence, and a veiled plea for freedom of speech, freedom of expression and freedom of conscience. Similarly, Chizhova is opposed to national, ethnic and religious conflict: at the end of the novel the narrator meditates on the historical roots of Christianity, based on the Judaic and Greek traditions, and its coexistence with Islam. The respect in which she is held by her fellow writers has been demonstrated by her election as director of the PEN Club in St Petersburg. Her first novel *Little Zinnobers* should appeal not only to anglophone scholars and the general reader interested in Russia or Russian literature, but to people in any country who owe at

....

[139] Chizhova, 'Umenie nachinat' so zvuka'. See also her article with a title taken from a quotation by Pamuk: E. Chizhova, 'Orkhan Pamuk, 'Allakhu prinadlezhit i Vostok, i Zapad...' ['Both East and West belong to Allah...'], *Voprosy literatury*, No. 3 (2010).

[140] See, for example, Orhan Pamuk, *Kar* (2002); *Snow*, trans. by Maureen Freely (New York: Knopf, 2004). His latest novel is *The Red-Haired Woman* (2017).

[141] For a thought-provoking philosophical discussion of the failings of liberalism and humanism, see John Gray, 'Un-liberty: Some problems with the new cult of hyper-liberalism', *Times Literary Supplement*, 30 March 2018, pp. 3–5.

least some of their success to an inspirational teacher or coach. Chizhova is one of the most interesting and accomplished writers in contemporary Russia, and it is hoped that this second English translation will bring her work to a wider audience. Now that relations between Russia and the West have rapidly deteriorated (March–April 2018), personal and cultural contacts between Russia and the anglophone world are more necessary and significant than ever.

Professor Rosalind Marsh
University of Bath/Wolfson College, Oxford

The Time Of Women

by Elena Chizhova

Life is not easy in the Soviet Union at mid-20th century, especially for a factory worker who becomes an unwed mother. But Antonina is lucky to get a room in a communal apartment that she and her little girl share with three old women. Glikeria is the daughter of former serfs. Ariadna comes from a wealthy family and speaks French. Yevdokia is illiterate and bitter. All have lost their families, all are deeply traditional, and all become "grannies" to little Suzanna. Only they secretly name her Sofia. And just as secretly they impart to her the history of her country as they experienced it: the Revolution, the early days of the Soviet Union, the blockade and starvation of World War II.

The little girl responds by drawing beautiful pictures, but she is mute. If the authorities find out she will be taken from her home and sent to an institution. When Antonina falls desperately ill, the grannies are faced with the reality of losing the little girl they love – unless a stepfather can be found before it is too late. And for that, they need a miracle.

Buy it > www.glagoslav.com

A Brown Man in Russia
Lessons Learned on the Trans-Siberian
by Vijay Menon

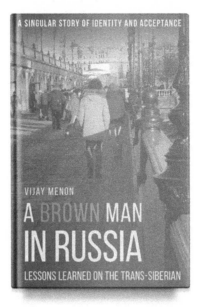

A Brown Man in Russia describes the fantastical travels of a young, colored American traveler as he backpacks across Russia in the middle of winter via the Trans-Siberian. The book is a hybrid between the curmudgeonly travelogues of Paul Theroux and the philosophical works of Robert Pirsig. Styled in the vein of Hofstadter, the author lays out a series of absurd, but true stories followed by a deeper rumination on what they mean and why they matter. Each chapter presents a vivid anecdote from the perspective of the fumbling traveler and concludes with a deeper lesson to be gleaned. For those who recognize the discordant nature of our world in a time ripe for demagoguery and for those who want to make it better, the book is an all too welcome antidote. It explores the current global climate of despair over differences and outputs a very different message – one of hope and shared understanding. At times surreal, at times inappropriate, at times hilarious, and at times deeply human, A Brown Man in Russia is a reminder to those who feel marginalized, hopeless, or endlessly divided that harmony is achievable even in the most unlikely of places.

Buy it > www.glagoslav.com

Leo Tolstoy – Flight from Paradise
by Pavel Basinsky

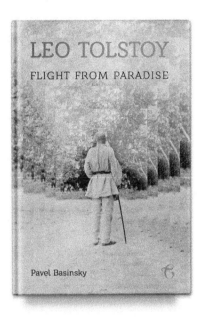

Over a hundred years ago, something truly outrageous occurred at Yasnaya Polyana. Count Leo Tolstoy, a famous author aged eighty-two at the time, took off, destination unknown. Since then, the circumstances surrounding the writer's whereabouts during his final days and his eventual death have given rise to many myths and legends. In this book, popular Russian writer and reporter Pavel Basinsky delves into the archives and presents his interpretation of the situation prior to Leo Tolstoy's mysterious disappearance. Basinsky follows Leo Tolstoy throughout his life, right up to his final moments. Reconstructing the story from historical documents, he creates a visionary account of the events that led to the Tolstoys' family drama.

Flight from Paradise will be of particular interest to international researchers studying Leo Tolstoy's life and works, and is highly recommended to a broader audience worldwide.

Buy it > www.glagoslav.com

TIME OF THE OCTOPUS

by Anatoly Kucherena

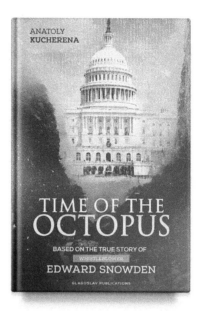

A frightening, prophetic vision of our world...

In Moscow's Sheremetyevo airport, fugitive US intelligence officer Joshua Kold is held in limbo, unable to leave the airport's transit area. He is on the run, after blowing the lid off the terrifying reach of covert American global surveillance operations. Will the Russian authorities grant him asylum, or will they hand him over the clutches of the global octopus eager for revenge for his betrayal?

As this gripping psychological and political thriller unfolds, a Moscow lawyer takes Kold to a secret bunker and grills him intently on just why he did it. Upon Kold's answers hang not only his own fate, but much, much more as the true extent of this chilling 1984 world unfolds.

Anatoly Kucherena is the famous Russian lawyer who took on the case of the American whistleblower Edward Snowden whose revelations about US intelligence operations sent shockwaves around the world in 2013. Time of the Octopus is a fiction, but it is based on Kucherena's own interviews with Snowden at Sheremetyevo, and provides the basis for Oliver Stone's major Hollywood movie 'Snowden' starring Joseph Gordon-Levitt, one of the movie events of 2016...

Buy it > www.glagoslav.com

Death of the Snake Catcher

by Ak Welsapar

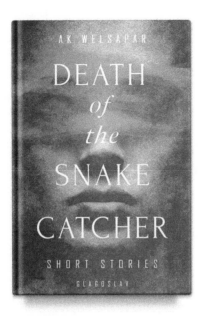

This book features people from one of the most closed countries of today's world, where the passage of time resembles the passage of a caravan through the waterless desert. This world has been recreated by a true-born son of that mysterious country, a Turkmen who, at the will of fate, has now been living for a quarter of a century in snowy Scandinavia. Is that not why two different worlds come together in *Ryazan horseradish and Tula gingerbread*, to come apart in *Love in Lilac*, in which a student from the non-free world falls in love with a girl from the West?

In the story *Death of the Snake Catcher*, an old snake catcher meets one on one with a giant cobra in the heart of the desert. In the dialogue between them the author unveils the age-old interdependence of Man and untamed nature, where the fear and mistrust of the strong and the hopes and apprehensions of the weak change places but co-exist as ever. *Egyptian night of fear*, in which a boy goes to an Eastern bazaar and falls into the clutches of depraved forces, is created in the writer's characteristic style of magical realism, while the novella Altynai celebrates first love, radiant and sad, pure as virgin snow.

Buy it > www.glagoslav.com

One-Two

by Igor Eliseev

Two conjoined babies are born at the crossroads of two social worldviews. Girls are named Faith and Hope. After spending their childhood in a foster home and obtaining primary education, they understand that they are different from other people in many respects. The problems of their growing up are exacerbated with permanent humiliations from society.

Finally, fortune favors them, slightly opening a door to happiness – separation surgery that theoretically can be performed in the capital. And sisters start their way, full of difficulties and obstacles. Will they be able to overcome a wall of public cynicism together with internal conflicts among themselves? Will they find a justification for their existence and accept it? Searching for the answers to these and many other questions constitutes the essence of this novel...

Glagoslav Publications Catalogue

- *The Time of Women* by Elena Chizhova
- *Andrei Tarkovsky: The Collector of Dreams* by Layla Alexander-Garrett
- *Andrei Tarkovsky - A Life on the Cross* by Lyudmila Boyadzhieva
- *Sin* by Zakhar Prilepin
- *Hardly Ever Otherwise* by Maria Matios
- *Khatyn* by Ales Adamovich
- *The Lost Button* by Irene Rozdobudko
- *Christened with Crosses* by Eduard Kochergin
- *The Vital Needs of the Dead* by Igor Sakhnovsky
- *The Sarabande of Sara's Band* by Larysa Denysenko
- *A Poet and Bin Laden* by Hamid Ismailov
- *Watching The Russians (Dutch Edition)* by Maria Konyukova
- *Kobzar* by Taras Shevchenko
- *The Stone Bridge* by Alexander Terekhov
- *Moryak* by Lee Mandel
- *King Stakh's Wild Hunt* by Uladzimir Karatkevich
- *The Hawks of Peace* by Dmitry Rogozin
- *Harlequin's Costume* by Leonid Yuzefovich
- *Depeche Mode* by Serhii Zhadan
- *The Grand Slam and other stories (Dutch Edition)* by Leonid Andreev
- *METRO 2033 (Dutch Edition)* by Dmitry Glukhovsky
- *METRO 2034 (Dutch Edition)* by Dmitry Glukhovsky
- *A Russian Story* by Eugenia Kononenko
- *Herstories, An Anthology of New Ukrainian Women Prose Writers*
- *The Battle of the Sexes Russian Style* by Nadezhda Ptushkina
- *A Book Without Photographs* by Sergey Shargunov
- *Down Among The Fishes* by Natalka Babina
- *disUNITY* by Anatoly Kudryavitsky
- *Sankya* by Zakhar Prilepin
- *Wolf Messing* by Tatiana Lungin
- *Good Stalin* by Victor Erofeyev
- *Solar Plexus* by Rustam Ibragimbekov
- *Don't Call me a Victim!* by Dina Yafasova

CPSIA information can be obtained
at www.ICGtesting.com
Printed in the USA
BVHW031053100519
547857BV00014B/14/P